W9-AXI-556

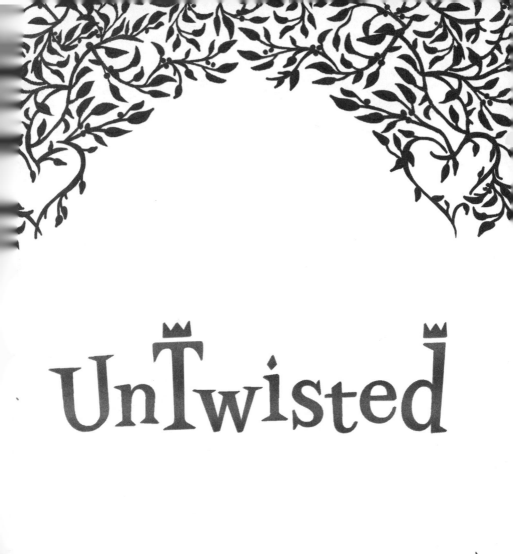

UnTwisted

UnTwisted

A Twinchantment novel

Elise Allen

Disney • Hyperion
Los Angeles   New York

First Edition, April 2020

1 3 5 7 9 10 8 6 4 2

FAC-020093-20052

Printed in the United States of America

This book is set in Century Schoolbook Pro/Monotype

Designed by Jamie Alloy

Library of Congress Control Number: 2019955483
ISBN 978-1-368-00863-1

Reinforced binding

Visit www.DisneyBooks.com

To Maddie, always,
and to the 2018 Broadway revival cast
of *Angels in America*
(if you know Maddie, you know why)

UnTwisted

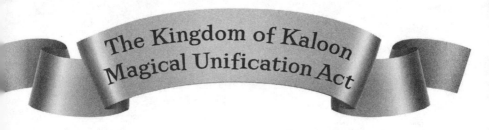

The Kingdom of Kaloon Magical Unification Act

In acknowledgment of the new Era of Equanimity between those with magical powers (Mages) and those in the general populace, the following rules shall now and forever forward be enforced in the kingdom of Kaloon:

1. All Kaloonians shall be treated equally, be they Mages or members of the general populace.

2. Magical Animals shall be full Kaloonian citizens, afforded the same rights as humans.

3. No discrimination shall be tolerated on the basis of a citizen's magical abilities. This applies to the general populace discriminating against those with magic, as well as Mages discriminating against the general populace.

4. No Mage shall use their powers to control or harm another human or Magical Animal, with the exception of clear acts of self-defense.

5. No Mage shall use their powers to gain an advantage against a member of the general populace in a game of chance or sporting event, unless such an event is specifically engineered to include said magic.

6. In an effort to educate Kaloonians on our shared history and integrated future, all human children between the ages of twelve and eighteen, be they Mages or of the general populace, shall attend Maldevon Academy, as shall Magical Animals of the equivalent developmental level.

This act is law, and supersedes all previous acts, most notably the Magic Eradication Act, which is rendered strictly and irrevocably defunct.

Should anyone defy the rules laid out in this act, they are in violation of the law, and shall face sentencing by the General Council of Kaloon.

So it is written and sealed from this day forward.

Prologue

"Do you, Flissa and Sara, swear your eternal loyalty to the kingdom of Kaloon? Do you pledge yourself, heart and soul, to make its best interests your primary concern from this day forward?"

"We do," the princesses said in unison.

The twins glanced at each other as they spoke, each seeing the enormity of the moment in her sister's eyes. It was their Ascension Day, the day they officially took their place in line for the throne of Kaloon, but this wasn't how either of them expected it to go. The ceremony was supposed to occur in the cobblestone courtyard in front of the palace, before the entire kingdom. It was supposed to be a day of triumph, where they stood together and proclaimed their twinhood without fear of repercussion from the Keepers of the Light.

Instead they stood together in dim, flickering sconce-light in the caverns beneath the castle, surrounded only by those palace residents deemed too young, too old, or too frail to fight in the revolution. Katya, Rouen, Primka . . . none of them were here. Even their parents had only come to the caverns to recite the vows for the ceremony and would return to battle the second it ended.

"Do you, Flissa and Sara, swear to the best of your ability to seek justice for your people and render it rightly, impartially, and wisely, in compassion and in truth?"

The king and queen spoke the words in hushed tones as they stood behind Flissa and Sara on the small, cobbled-together dais. The princesses couldn't see their parents in the semidarkness, but they knew each one held a sparkling gem-encrusted tiara, one for each sister.

"We do."

Like their parents, Flissa and Sara kept their voices low. It felt wrong to speak out when they were technically in hiding, and in a place that had once been used by Dark Mages for terrible purposes. When the sisters first saw this enormous room with its impossibly high, rocky ceilings, the dirt floor was dotted with craggy spikes still stained with ancient blood, and the room ended in a wide chasm of Forever Flames. Now Mages had swept through—good Mages, who had been with the Underground. They'd removed the spikes and contained the Forever Flames under an impregnable magical barrier, then filled the pit with layers of earth and stones, and covered it all with a blanket of the softest sand.

Even with those precautions the cavern would have been off-limits. Then the fighting started, and it became a gathering room and play area for those who took refuge under the castle to live in curtained-off rooms among the twisting halls and catacombs. The residents were children mainly, along with the elderly, the ill, and those who didn't believe in battle no matter what. Flissa and Sara respected the conscientious objectors, but they didn't feel the same way. They wished they could fight for Kaloon, but their parents said they were too young, plus they had to stay safe to protect the royal line. Determined to do their part, they spent their days helping others in their dank, dimly lit refuge: comforting children, nursing the sick, and spending time with the old people eager for someone to sit and listen.

"Do you, Flissa and Sara, swear to be honorable rulers, communicating openly and consistently with both your subjects and the lawfully elected General Council of Kaloon, to make sure the laws of the land are just? And should any Kaloonian law be recognized as unjust, do you swear to work together with the Council to change said law, so all Kaloonians can live in righteous harmony?"

"We do," Flissa and Sara said, glancing at one another again. This was a new part of the vow, one that King Edwin had only added after the twins had returned from their journey to the Twists and shared everything they'd discovered about the Keepers of the Light and their tyranny. On that very day, the king and queen secretly sat down with Katya, Rouen, and their other most trusted advisers to write the Magical Unification Act.

Writing the act was simple. Enforcing it would be harder. The king and queen had tried to work with the magical Underground to ambush Grosselor, the leader of the Keepers, and take him down, but Grosselor had found out about the attack. He'd gathered his loyal followers and retreated to the magical prison of the Twists, where he rallied the darkest, most malevolent Mages.

Now the two sides were locked in combat, and the Dark

Mages were winning. Those who visited the caverns said the battle was pushing closer and closer to the palace. If the Dark Mages reached it—if they took over the castle and invaded the caverns—Flissa and Sara knew they would do their best to fight back. They also knew their newly discovered magical skills wouldn't stand a chance. The whole royal family would be wiped out, and the Keepers of the Light would win. The kingdom's only hope was that the Shadows—highly powerful good Mages who had been magically hibernating in the Twists—would rise up and join the fight.

At the moment, there was no sign of that happening. Quite the opposite: Flissa and Sara had both heard whispers in the catacombs that the Shadows had been a myth all along.

"Then by the power vested in us by the royal ancestry of Kaloon," the king and queen continued, "we hereby assert and proclaim your place in the Royal Line of Ascension. May the universe smile upon Princess Flissa and Princess Sara, and may the universe smile upon Kaloon."

The gathered crowd echoed it: "May the universe smile upon Princess Flissa and Princess Sara, and may the universe smile upon Kaloon."

Princess Flissa and Princess Sara.

The words were electrifying, and as King Edwin and Queen Latonya lowered the matching tiaras onto the girls' heads, the motley crowd burst into applause. Both sisters beamed, then reached out and squeezed each other's hands. The kingdom was locked in a magical battle of good versus evil, and these could very well be their family's last days, but after twelve years—their entire lifetime—of living a lie, their subjects had embraced them as two separate people.

Flissa and Sara smiled down at the faces looking up at them in the flickering sconce-light. There was Rodrick, the white-haired, stooped-over gardener who had been tending the palace gardens since King Edwin was a child. He wiped away tears as he applauded Flissa and Sara, and the twins remembered the story about his young wife, whom the Keepers had exiled to the Twists on their wedding day when she made the mistake of raising her *left* hand to swear the oath of marriage. Left-handedness was considered a sign of magic; Rodrick never saw her again. There were also the somber, towheaded five-year-olds with large, moonlike eyes. These identical boys were the sons of Abrel, one of the king's bravest guards. Flissa and Sara had been around Abrel all their lives and felt close to him, but they'd never even known he had children. He and his wife had said their child died at birth. They'd kept the boys hidden so the Keepers wouldn't exile them for their twinhood.

Since they'd been in the catacombs, Flissa and Sara had heard endless stories like these from people who had seemed perfectly happy on the outside but who actually lived in mortal terror of the Keepers of the Light. Every one of them was grateful to the princesses and eager for the chance to take their kingdom back.

As Flissa and Sara rode the continued applause, their eyes locked on those of two more familiar figures in the crowd: a tall boy with dark, stringy hair that fell in his face and a stone-faced girl whose white-blond hair was shaved into intricate patterns, except for a ponytail high on her head.

Galric and Loriah.

The two stood together at the back of the group, separated a bit from the others. Galric's haunted eyes still held the pain of deep loss, and Loriah, whom Flissa and Sara insisted be smuggled out of the Twists before the fighting began, was still on constant alert, her eyes always shifting to catch a sneak attack. Both of them felt more comfortable outside the catacombs, running messages and supplies for the fighters, but neither would have missed the Ascension Ceremony for the world. For the first time since he lost his father, Galric's smile lit his whole face, while Loriah clenched her jaw and clapped with a grim ferocity, as if daring anyone else to be happier for the princesses than her.

King Edwin and Queen Latonya moved next to the girls, taking their hands so the four of them made a chain. They raised their joined hands, the crowd cheered, and for just a moment—despite the raging battle, the underground catacombs, and the constant fear of what might come next—for just a moment it felt like anything was possible.

Six Months Later

Chapter 1
Flissa

Forty-one . . . forty-two . . . forty-three paces. Flissa touched the far wall of the room she and Sara shared. *Now, how many if I walk on my hands?* She tilted into a handstand and started to move. *One . . . two . . .*

"How do I look?"

Flissa vaguely heard her sister's voice from the other end of the room, but she paid it no attention. She needed all her concentration to find decent handholds amidst the piles of Sara's clothes on the floor. Besides, if she *reeeeally* focused on each little task she gave herself, she could forget what they had to do today. *Five . . . six . . .*

"Flissa!"

So much for focus. Flissa flipped back to her feet, expertly avoiding the pointy tip of Sara's favorite calligraphy pen, which was inexplicably embedded in a pile of tights.

"How do I look?" Sara asked again. She struck a dramatic pose, one arm cocked behind her head, the other outstretched. "It's perfect, right? Wait. Don't answer until you check out the twirl."

Sara spun, and the pleated flare skirt of her flaxen-yellow silk dress gave a dazzling swirl, while the lightly ruffled neckline on its close-cut bodice flounced slightly. When she stopped spinning, she reeled like an off-duty royal guard who'd had too much mead. "Bad idea," she said woozily. "Too spinny."

She staggered three steps to Flissa's bed and collapsed facedown on the duvet. Then she turned her head and grinned. "But pretty, right? Perfect for a first-day-of-school grand entrance?"

She said "grand entrance" with the vowels dragged out and fancy. Like they were going someplace fabulous and special and not brutally intimidating at all.

"It's pretty," Flissa said.

Sara narrowed her eyes. "You don't sound sure. Are you sure?" She flopped onto her back. "Aaaargh! I wish Loriah still lived in the palace. She'd tell me exactly what she thought of this dress."

"I can tell you what Loriah would say." Flissa folded her arms and arranged her face in an exact replica of Loriah's low-lidded unimpressed stare. "It doesn't matter what you wear. At all."

Sara snorted appreciatively. "You're right; that's what she'd say. But she'd be wrong. It does matter. And you know it matters because it took you *days* to figure out your outfit."

Weeks, actually. And countless coin flips. Flissa had started fretting about it long before Sara had asked her.

"The dress is beautiful on you," Flissa assured her sister. "In fact, it's so beautiful that it makes me think maybe I should wear a dress too."

She meant to say it lightly, but Sara clearly saw through her.

"No," she said. Then she rolled clumsily off the bed, a thumping tumble of yellow fabric. She took Flissa's hand and led her to the full-length mirror at the end of the room. "That's why you chose your outfit first, remember? You look wonderful. You look like *you*."

Flissa studied their side-by-side reflections, and her heart sank.

It wasn't that she didn't like her outfit. She did. She wore her favorite black velvet jodhpurs, and a cream-colored tunic with sleeves that puffed over her arms but cinched tight at her wrists. Combined with her soft-soled shoes, it was the kind of outfit she loved best—perfect for breaking into a run . . . or turning upside down and walking on her hands to take her mind off the day ahead.

What she didn't like was looking at herself next to Sara.

They had always looked exactly alike; it's how they were able to pass themselves off as one person—Princess Flissara—for so many years. They were the exact same height and had grown the exact same inch over the last six months. Their skin was the exact same shade of brown, and their eyes the exact same violet. Even when they stopped pretending to share an identity, even when they dressed differently and changed their hairstyles, Flissa took comfort in the fact that they still *could* look exactly alike. And at the end of each day, when they changed into their still-matching nightclothes and took down their hair, they always had.

But now Sara had cut her hair and pierced her ears.

She'd gotten their mother to do it last night, right before bed, without even consulting Flissa about it first.

That wasn't just a change, it was a statement.

Now Sara's earlobes glistened with tiny silver-and-crystal studs, and her hair was short in the back and longer on the top, where it curled into springy ringlets. The effect was stunning. She looked beautiful, sophisticated, a little bit older . . . and absolutely nothing like her twin sister.

Flissa ran her hands down the long, thick braid that lay over her right shoulder. "Maybe I should just redo my hair. Put it up, maybe."

"So it looks shorter?" Sara asked knowingly.

Flissa bit her lip and looked down at her feet, but Sara took her hands and ducked to meet her eyes.

"Flissa, you don't have to worry about anything. You should be excited. We're going to *school*. You know what's at school? Books, and studying, and more books. And Athletics—an actual class where we have to run around and get sweaty. It's everything you love rolled up into one. I'm the one who should be dreading it. For you it's a dream come true!"

"You do make it sound fun," Flissa admitted. "But it's not the classes I'm worried about. It's . . ."

Flissa didn't want to say it out loud. She knew how desperately Sara wanted to go out in the world and meet new people, and she had every right to do it. But what sounded so exciting to Sara seemed like torture to Flissa. Flissa had spent her whole life making formal chitchat with dignitaries and visitors at royal balls, but she'd never let anyone get close; Sara was the only real friend she'd ever

14

needed. Now she had Loriah and Galric too, and that was wonderful, but that was enough. She had no desire to go to school and see their perfect foursome overrun by the teeming throngs Sara would bring in to join them.

"Your first day of school!" Primka, the small bird who had once been their tutor, flew in from one of her crevices near the ceiling, crying out as she swooped in happy circles. "I never thought I'd see the day! *Never!* Not that I think you need school for your education, of course. I'm sure I've already taught you far more in twelve and a half years than you could ever learn in—"

Primka looked down at the girls and reeled back, one wing dramatically over her chest.

"Sara!" she gasped. "You're wearing yellow!"

Sara nodded. "It's pretty, right?"

"It's *yellow!*" Primka said again. "I take it back. I've clearly taught you *nothing* because you've obviously lost your *mind!* Yellow!"

"You're wearing yellow," Sara noted.

"I *am* yellow!" Primka huffed. "There's a difference!"

"It's a much lighter shade than the Keepers' yellow," Flissa offered. Sara looked at her gratefully, but Primka wasn't placated. Her feathers fluffed up twice their normal size, and her pink cheek feathers grew red as she flitted madly back and forth between the two princesses.

"'A lighter shade,' she tells me," Primka said to no one at all. "As if that's an excuse for a *princess of Kaloon* to wear a color that reminds the whole kingdom of the worst period in our history. And on your first day of school! What kind of impression do you think you'll make on the other students? What will the Untwisteds think? I'll tell you what they'll think; they'll think you're making some kind of statement, that's what they'll think. And *all* our work, and *all* our sacrifice, and . . ."

Flissa caught Sara's eye and nodded. There was a time when they'd have laughed together at Primka's histrionics and let her drone on while they conspired under her beak. But by now they'd been through too much with the songbird to dismiss her that way.

Besides, Primka had a point. Sara's dress was nothing like the Keepers' canary yellow, but maybe it wasn't the wisest choice.

"It's okay," Sara said. "I can change the color."

"I'll help you," Flissa offered. She held out her hand, but Sara shook her head.

"I've got it."

Sara closed her eyes, then held her hands in front of her face. Wiggling her fingers, she ran them down the front of her body. Tendrils of red mist swirled around her dress, enveloping it.

When the mist cleared, her dress was no longer yellow; it was royal blue.

"Better?" Sara asked. She held out a finger, and Primka perched on it. She looked Sara up and down, then nodded.

"Much," she said, clearly impressed. "And you did it all by yourself."

"I've been practicing," Sara said.

"It shows," Flissa said. "You're really good."

Sara beamed, which was a relief. It meant she hadn't heard the edge in Flissa's voice. Flissa had always been the better student, but when it came to magic, Sara was the one who excelled. Flissa understood why; even though she'd come to terms with the fact that she and Sara were Mages, she was still afraid of magic. She vividly remembered what she'd done to the nose-ringed guard in the Twists—how she'd taken over the girl's body and forced her to turn her own knife against herself. Every time she thought about it, Flissa burned with anger all over again. She could feel the magic surge through her, overwhelming and out of control.

She didn't like that feeling. She knew practicing would help, and she did her best, but she couldn't throw herself into it the way she did with all her other studies. She preferred when she and Sara did magic together, combining their red-and-cream-colored magical signatures to produce charms like the pink glow that had made them invisible on their way back from the Twists, or the pink shield that had saved them from Mitzi's deadly dark curse.

Tap-tap-tap.

Flissa, Sara, and Primka all looked toward the window, where a blue orb the size of an apricot bumped against the glass.

"A bubblegram!" Sara cried.

She ran toward the window, stumbled over a pile of her laundry, then fell forward, smacking her palms against the wall to stop herself from falling over. She yanked open the window and the blue orb floated to Flissa, coming to a stop directly in front of her face. When it popped, Loriah's no-nonsense voice rang out.

"It's a sea of TTs, Fliss. I'm surrounded and I expect backup. Meet me at the ring tree. Hill above the school. Can't miss it."

17

Sara scrunched her face and tilted her head. "TTs? What does she mean?"

Flissa blushed. She'd told Loriah how much she was dreading the "teeming throngs," and Loriah loved the term because she felt the same way. As far as Loriah was concerned, she had one main friend: Flissa. Through Flissa she'd gotten close to Galric and Sara, but she agreed the foursome was plenty. Anyone else was just extra and annoying.

Of course, Loriah wasn't one for tact; it didn't occur to her that tossing around the "TT" might make Sara ask all kinds of questions.

"Not sure," Flissa said unconvincingly. "Here, let me just answer her back."

Flissa reached into her pocket and pulled out a small glass vial filled with message milk. She might have been wary of magic in general, but message milk was one of the best things to come out of Kaloonification. At first only Mages carried the vials, but now they were universal. Flissa and Sara didn't know anyone who didn't tote one with them at all times.

She unscrewed the top, which was connected to a thin wand that ended in a jagged loop. Flissa gently tapped the wand against the side of the vial to get rid of the excess fluid, then held it in front of her. She could see the sheen of message milk inside the loop; it was ready to receive.

"This message is for Loriah," Flissa said.

The wand glowed blue: destination registered.

Flissa moved the loop in front of her mouth and spoke into it. As she did, a blue bubble emerged. It grew with her words.

"*Sara* and I got your message," she said pointedly. She hoped Loriah would understand the implication—that Loriah should be more discreet when sending bubble-grams to the palace—but she doubted it. Discretion wasn't Loriah's forte. "See you at the ring tree. End."

At the word "end," the strawberry-size blue bubble broke off the cone and floated out the window. Flissa knew it wouldn't stop until it had found Loriah and relayed its message.

"Enough dawdling," Primka said. "Now down to breakfast with you. Everyone's waiting to see you off on your first day."

"Everyone?" Sara asked. Her eyes gleamed eagerly.

"Indeed," Primka said. "Your parents, Rouen, Katya, Galric—"

"Yes!" Sara cried. She flung her rucksack over her shoulder, then took Flissa's hand. "Come on!"

Flissa grabbed her own bag midstride as Sara clumsily pulled her out of their room and down the hall to the main door of the Residence, Primka right behind them.

"One second," Flissa said, slipping her hand out of Sara's grip. "I forgot something. Be right back."

Before Sara or Primka could object, Flissa raced back into their room. She ducked behind the opened door and pressed her back against the wall. She closed her eyes and tried to still her thudding heart with long, deep breaths . . . but they came out as wheezes. Finally she gave up and tugged at the chain around her neck to pull out her charm necklace. She opened it to reveal a thin wooden coin, on which a six-year-old Sara had painted portraits of the king and queen. She squeezed the coin tight within her fist.

"King, I go to school. Queen, I refuse," Flissa whispered.

She moved the coin into flipping position on her thumb . . . but she couldn't flick it into the air. She simply stared at it. The image of their mother looked benignly back at her.

After an eternity, she let the coin drop back into her palm.

"No. I have to make the choice myself."

"Flissa?" Sara called from the hall.

Flissa bit her lip and gave the coin another squeeze, then slipped it back into the locket.

"Coming!"

Chapter 2
Sara

"Come *on*!" Sara called back into the Residence.

This was madness. Her head would literally explode if Flissa didn't come out in the next second. Primka had already lost patience and flown downstairs, and Sara was tempted to do the same, but she couldn't. She knew Flissa was nervous, and she'd absolutely stick by her sister's side as much as she could, but she didn't want to be late. This was the biggest day of their entire lives!

Okay, maybe it was a bigger day when Kaloon won the Battle for Unification. And maybe the day they saved their mother's life from a terrible curse was bigger too, but still, today was *huge*, and Flissa knew how much Sara was looking forward to it.

"Finally!" she gushed as Flissa emerged. "Come on, we have to hurry."

She grabbed Flissa's hand and pulled her toward the Grand Staircase, moving so quickly she tripped over a bump in the rug and went flying. Flissa caught her arm before she could tumble down the stairs.

"Thanks," Sara said. She hoisted her skirts in one fist and grabbed the banister with her other hand, then watched her feet as she carefully trotted down the steps. She jumped the last two . . . and promptly fell to her knees. As Flissa helped her up, Sara glanced to her left, down the long marble corridor filled with tapestries and decorative tables. She remembered how she used to run down that hall, bumping her shins every step of the way, desperate to get to the Weekly Address on time. She could practically feel the strain in her legs as she pounded up the hidden back staircase to the balcony.

Now those stairs were gone, and so was the balcony. The long hallway ended in a giant pile of stone and wood debris, a casualty of one of Grosselor's magical blasts.

That wasn't his only casualty either. So much of Kaloon had been shattered in the Battle for Unification. Homes blasted by powerful magic were left in rubble, or worse. Sara remembered when Galric had come back to the catacombs after one of his runs around the kingdom, collecting scrap metal to melt down into sword blades. He'd been ghost pale and breathlessly told them about a blacksmith's shop that had been hit with a magical blast and transformed before his eyes into a giant snake made of rocks, its fangs dripping with purple venom that sizzled against the ground where it fell.

He'd been lucky the beast hadn't reared back to strike. Instead it had swatted him with its tail as it turned to go after Rouen and the rest of the royal forces fighting nearby. The impact had sent Galric flying into a rock pile that sliced open his arm and gouged his face just under his left eye. The pain was terrible, but Galric managed to pull out his vial of message milk and send Rouen a bubble-gram before he passed out. If Rouen hadn't gotten the warning, his entire flank would have been ambushed and slaughtered.

Thinking about Galric made Sara even more eager to see him. She poured on speed and ran down the hall, and Flissa kept up with her step for step. When they turned and ran by the kitchen, she was hit by a blast of tantalizing scents that made her mouth water. Filliam, the new head chef, had grown up in the Twists and knew how to cultivate the most delectable magical plants. He'd turned the kitchen into a fantasyland of flavors that lit up parts of her tongue Sara hadn't even known existed. Filliam was proud of his work and always invited the princesses to come in and taste his new dishes, but Sara couldn't. The kitchen had been Mitzi's domain, and every time Sara even peeked inside, she remembered how the two of them had laughed together, sharing secrets while Mitzi snuck her nibbles of different treats. Sara had thought of Mitzi like a second mother, and even though no one had ever said so, she knew it was her fault that the cook had gotten close enough to her family to nearly destroy them all.

Sara didn't want to think about that. Not today. She grabbed Flissa's hand and ran into the ballroom.

"The schoolchildren are here!" Primka proclaimed as they raced through the door . . . and immediately thumped into a massive wall of flesh.

"There's my girls!" Katya cried.

She wrapped her arms around them for a huge hug. Katya's pillowy girth was full of love and everything good, but it also blocked Sara's view of everything else in the room. And every*one*.

"I need a picture," Katya said. She turned around while keeping Flissa and Sara firmly in her grasp. "Galric, come here. Squish in. I need you in this too."

Now that Katya had turned them around, Sara could see Galric. He looked completely mortified, which was often Katya's effect on him, especially now that she had gone from his secret guardian to his full-time parent. But when he saw Sara, his eyes widened.

"Whoa," he said. "You cut your hair."

Sara nodded as best she could from under Katya's arm. "Uh-huh. You like it?"

"Yeah, you look great!" he said. Then he blushed and added, "I mean . . ."

"Picture!" Katya insisted. "Now."

Chastened, Galric hurried to Katya and stood in front of her, right between Flissa and Sara.

"This'll be a good one," Rouen said, and Sara heard the familiar chinking sound as he walked across the room. Rouen had lost a leg in the Battle for Unification; not even his powers and the strongest magical medicine could save it. His metallic replacement was sleek and strong, made by Kaloon's best blacksmith, and so well crafted that Rouen swore he didn't even miss the original. "What do you think, Vincenzo?"

Vincenzo, the new royal portraitist, had already set up his easel and paints and begun to sketch. He stood on a chair to do his paintings, which would have been unthinkably rude for the previous royal portraitist, but Vincenzo was a sloth and needed the extra height. He was also brilliantly talented, and Sara's own technique had improved immeasurably since she started studying with him.

The sloth put his claws to his lips and kissed them. "The pose is perfection." Then he glared at the princesses and Galric. "But if any of you move, I shall paint the most hideous version of your face you can possibly imagine, then hang the portrait here in the ballroom for all to see."

Galric laughed, but it fizzled quickly under Vincenzo's glare. That almost made Sara giggle, but she bit her cheeks to stop. Vincenzo wasn't joking; she'd seen the horrible paintings he'd made of people who crossed him.

As they all posed for Vincenzo, Sara watched the sloth's eyes so she'd know when he wasn't paying attention to her and she could sneak glances at Galric. It was amazing how much he'd changed since they'd first met. He'd gotten taller, for starters. Or he just *stood* taller. He didn't slouch the way he used to, as if he was worried his presence might bother someone. And, like Sara, he'd cut his hair, only he'd done it months ago, when he, Loriah, and so many other young Kaloonians had jumped in to help the war effort: delivering notes for those without message milk, gathering spare metal to melt down for weapons, running supplies to fighters, and helping to transport the wounded to medical care. He'd said it was too distracting to do all that with his hair flopping down in his face, so he lopped it off and wore it swept back from his forehead. Now when he caught Sara's eye, he wasn't peeking out from behind a curtain. He was really looking at her.

Sara checked to make sure Vincenzo was focused on Flissa. Then she quickly crossed her eyes. Galric laughed.

"That's it!" Vincenzo snapped. "Now you shall get a plobquat for a nose!"

"What?! Wait!" Galric complained.

"You're still moving," Vincenzo said. "Feet for ears."

"He does deserve it," Katya said, "but it would mean a lot to me if you'd just paint him as he really is."

Vincenzo sighed. He didn't like to give in, but it was difficult for anyone to say no to Katya.

"Fine," he said. "Just as he is. Including the large pimple on his nose."

"Aw, come on!" Galric complained, and this time Sara, Flissa, and Katya all laughed out loud. Eventually they pulled themselves together, and Vincenzo finished the portrait in no time. It looked amazing; Sara only hoped that one day she'd paint just as well.

"Those earrings," Galric said. He hadn't even noticed them until he saw them in the portrait.

"Like 'em?" Sara asked.

"Ow. Didn't it hurt?" he asked. "You stabbed yourself through the ear!"

"Technically our mother did the stabbing," Flissa said. "And the polite thing to say isn't 'Ow,' but 'Yes, they're very pretty.' Which they are."

"Thank you, Flissa," Sara said, and she enjoyed the way Galric blushed at the rebuke. "And no, it didn't hurt at all."

"'Course not," Katya said. "And even if it did smart a touch, a little ear-stabbing is nothing compared to this." She grabbed Galric's arm and rolled up his loose-sleeved shirt to reveal the lower part of the pink scar that ran from his wrist to his shoulder. "Got your arm cut clean open, but

26

you kept going on and helping the cause. And you got this one for your trouble too."

Katya pointed to the small scar under Galric's left eye. It was almost invisible now; Sara could only see it when he smiled. Then it folded in like a crescent-shaped dimple.

Galric blushed even redder. "Everyone here knows about the scars, Katya," he said softly. "You don't have to keep pointing them out."

"But I do," Katya said. "You're a hero, and I want everyone to know it."

"That's right, you are," said Rouen. He moved next to Katya and put his arm around her waist. "We're very proud."

Katya and Rouen kissed. Immediately Sara grabbed Flissa's hand and squeezed. Of all the things they'd learned about Katya in the last several months—that she was a powerful Mage, that she was a leader of Kaloon's magical Underground, that she had vouched for Galric when he was little and kept him from the Twists—the strangest by far was that she was married to craggy-faced Rouen.

Sara glanced toward Galric, thinking he'd share the joke, but he just smiled at the couple with love in his eyes. It was sweet, really. Katya had always been like a mother to him. Now, with his real father, Gilward, gone, it looked like he'd welcomed Rouen into the role.

"So you're excited for the first day of school, are you?" Katya asked the girls. "We heard you running down here."

"Of course you did," Primka said, lighting on Katya's shoulders. "Years of etiquette training, and they thump around like elephants."

"Ran, huh?" Galric said. He turned to Flissa and

grinned. "So that means she tripped and you had to catch her . . . ten times?"

"Twenty at least," Flissa said. "Maybe thirty."

"You're both awful and I hate you," Sara said, though of course she didn't mean it. During the Battle for Unification, Flissa, Sara, Galric, and Loriah had spent most of their time together—every minute that Galric and Loriah weren't out helping the fighters, really. They'd gotten so close that they teased each other easily, and none of them took it seriously.

Well, except Loriah. She could tease, but she didn't like getting teased back. Sara and Galric had both made the mistake of trying, and it hadn't gone well.

"Where's Nitpick?" Flissa asked.

"Where do you think?" their dad's voice boomed joyfully. "He followed us into the kitchen to try and steal our meal!"

King Edwin and Queen Latonya beamed as they walked into the ballroom, each with a giant tray of pastries, breads, and savories of all shapes and sizes. Nitpick, the tiny black kitten, trailed at their feet.

"He didn't have to steal anything," Queen Latonya replied. "You kept sneaking him treats."

"Nitpick!" Sara crouched low; the kitten ran across the room and leaped into her arms. She buried her face in his fur. "Mmmm, I love that you're still a kitten."

"Of course he is," Flissa said. "He has magic in him. Remember how young Grosselor looked? And he'd been alive well over a century."

"That's right," Rouen said. "We Mages always look particularly attractive."

Katya giggled—*giggled*—and swatted him. Sara kicked Flissa in the leg—was she seeing this?

"Happy first day of school!" the king said as he and Queen Latonya set the trays down on one of the large round tables that dotted the ballroom.

"Aw, sweet. Thanks!" Galric said. "I love frosted tarts!"

He grabbed one and had it halfway to his mouth before he saw the king's raised eyebrow. Then he froze.

"I mean . . . um . . . thank you, Your Majesties," he said in his most stiltedly polite voice. "It is truly a privilege to dine with you, as always. Thank you for welcoming me, and, um, for your ever-present kindness and munificence, and . . ."

The tips of King Edwin's mustache turned up, like they always did when he was amused. He smirked at Queen Latonya. "Should I let him continue?"

The queen smiled back, but it was Katya who answered.

"Oh, sure. Let him grovel for a while. It's good for him."

"And thank you for your kingliness . . ." Galric continued. "And queenliness . . . and general royalositude . . ."

"He's resorted to making up words," Queen Latonya said. "Now we're just being cruel."

Sara laughed. "Galric, stop. They're just our parents. It's okay."

Galric lowered his voice. "I know, but your dad did that one-eyebrow-up, don't-forget-I-rule-you thing."

He meant it just for Sara, but of course her parents heard too.

"We don't rule anyone," Queen Latonya said lightly. "Not alone anyway. We govern in concert with the General Council." Then she turned to Rouen and Katya. "Speaking of which, after we get the kids off to school . . ."

She let the sentence trail, but her meaning was clear. Rouen and Katya had both been elected to Kaloon's General Council, a new governing body created in the wake of Kaloonification. The General Council was made up equally of Genpos—people without magic, from the general populace—Mages, and Magical Animals from all over Kaloon. If the king and queen needed to discuss something with them away from Flissa, Sara, and Galric, it was probably important.

"Is there a problem?" Rouen asked.

"Nothing serious," King Edwin said. "A little unrest with the academy starting. Unification comes with some growing pains."

"I'm sure it doesn't help that the General Council chose Amala for head of school," the queen said.

"Of course we did," Katya replied. "She's the best person for the job."

"I don't disagree," the queen said, "but I know the perception, especially among Genpos. It's not good."

"What's wrong with Amala?" Galric piped up. "She's a Shadow—the most powerful Shadow. She led the final charge against Grosselor. We'd have lost the Battle for Unification without her."

"Right," Sara said. She was impressed by how confident and knowledgeable Galric sounded, and wanted to show that she knew things about the battle too. "She was the first Shadow to wake up from their magical hibernation. She's the one who rallied all the others."

Galric looked at her and nodded. "Exactly."

"That's true," Flissa said. "But Amala's also extremely old. She was married to Maldevon, and she was one of the reasons people believed Grosselor when he said Maldevon was a Dark Mage."

Galric scrunched his face. Apparently he didn't know this part of the story. "She was? Why?"

It was the queen who answered. "Back in Maldevon's time, Amala adamantly believed that those with magic were superior to those without. She made no secret of the fact that she wanted all people without magic exiled from Kaloon."

"They called her the Cleaner," Rouen added, "because she wanted to 'clean' Kaloon of all non-Mages."

"But she changed," the king said. "Even back then she changed. Maldevon helped her see things differently. We know this; that's why she rose up and helped us."

"*I* know that," the queen said, "but there are Genpos who believe she only fought for personal reasons, as revenge for what happened to her husband. They're afraid that if she's in charge of Maldevon Academy, she'll use that position to pursue an anti-Genpo agenda."

"Ridiculous," Katya snorted.

"Again, I agree," the queen said, "but some people— including some students, we've been told—are very unhappy. It's something we need to watch."

"Indeed," the king said. Then he turned to Sara, Flissa, and Galric. "Will you let us know if you see anything? Anyone making trouble, reacting poorly to Amala?"

Galric stood taller. "Is this a . . . Are you giving us an official royal mission?"

Sara saw her dad's mustache twitch. He wanted to laugh, but instead he put a hand on Galric's shoulder and said, with extreme solemnity, "Yes, son. Yes, I am."

Galric set his jaw. "Then I'll be proud to carry it out."

Sara rolled her eyes. "Okay, you have to stop. Dad, we will absolutely watch for you, but I bet everything'll be great. The only thing that won't be great is us getting there late, so . . ." She nodded her head toward the doorway.

"You're right," the queen said. "You have to get moving. Grab some breakfast; you can take it to go."

Sara, Flissa, and Galric each wrapped some breakfast pastries in napkins and put them in their bags, then the grown-ups all swarmed and hugged them goodbye. Primka wrapped her wings so tightly around Sara's face that she couldn't breathe.

When the bird released her, Sara laughed. "We're just going to school. You weren't this worried when we went to the Twists!"

"I know," Primka sobbed. "It's just that you're so grown-up. All of you."

Primka threw herself across Galric's face. He coughed and spluttered. "Um . . . thanks."

Rouen and Katya each took one of Galric's arms and strode down the hall to the front gates, while the queen linked her arms with Flissa's and Sara's and followed.

"I know I don't have to tell you this," she said, "but please be good to everyone you see at school. You're princesses; you need to show everyone that Kaloonification is a good thing, and sending everyone to school together is the best way to bring all of Kaloon's different subjects together."

"It *is* the best way," Sara said. "Everyone'll see it."

"I'm sure you're right," the queen said. "I'll miss having you around the castle, though."

She wrapped them in another big hug, and Sara tried not to stiffen. She loved their mom, and she loved that Mom cared so much, but honestly, everyone was acting like she, Flissa, and Galric were leaving home and wouldn't come back. They were going to *school*. Yes, it was a huge deal, but not in the way everyone else seemed to think.

Their mother finally pulled away.

"I love you," she said. "Both of you. Now go."

"Bye!" Sara called.

She ran out the door as fast as she could and didn't even dream of looking back.

Chapter 3
Flissa

Flissa watched Sara run out, then threw her arms around her mother again. "I don't want to go," she whispered into her mother's shoulder.

The queen squeezed Flissa tightly, then moved back and gave her a shiny-eyed smile. "Did you say something?"

Flissa made herself smile back and shook her head. "Just that I'm excited."

It hurt to lie, but how could she tell the truth? Her mother had just told her and Sara that Kaloonification's success depended in part on how well they handled school. How could she possibly say she'd rather stay home? Even if she did speak up, what could her mother do? School attendance was a rule. It was in the Magical Unification Act. How would it look if a princess of Kaloon asked for a special exclusion?

Awful. That's how it would look. Absolutely awful.

"Flissa, come here!" Sara called from outside. "You won't believe it!"

Flissa's jaw tightened. She knew she shouldn't be mad at her sister. It was wonderful that Sara was excited about school. Of course she was. She loved making new friends and meeting new people. It made Sara happy, and Flissa wanted her sister to be happy. She really did.

"*Flissa!*" Sara called again.

"Coming!"

Flissa ran out the door and instantly felt herself relax. Her favorite horse, Balustrade, stood majestically waiting for her, and the sight of him melted her heart. She ran up and hugged him tightly around his neck.

"Good morning, Balustrade," Flissa said, pressing her nose to his. "I'm glad you're coming with me."

"And you're not glad about us?" groused a familiar voice. "What are we, chopped liver?"

Flissa's heart jumped. She wheeled around and saw two horses, one gray and the other black. Sara and Galric stood grinning between them.

"Gus?!" Flissa cried. "Klarney?!"

"At your service," Klarney said, bending a foreleg and bowing low.

"Told ya you wouldn't believe it," Sara said.

Gus and Klarney had been instrumental in helping Flissa and Sara get through the Twists and save their mother's life, but neither sister had seen them since, and they'd often wondered if the horses had made it through the Battle for Unification alive.

Flissa hugged them both. "We missed you so much! How are you?"

"Absolutely delightful," Klarney said. "We found ourselves a lovely little field off in the outskirts of the kingdom. About ten horse families, lots of space . . ."

"Yeah," Gus said. "Klarney here planted us our own

grove of blarnage trees. All the blarnages we can eat."

"Your favorite," Galric said. "I'm surprised you'd ever leave."

"Me too," Gus said pointedly. "But *someone* insisted we clomp all the way across creation just to—"

Klarney stamped a hoof, and Gus rolled his eyes.

"I mean, I *wanted* to clomp all the way across creation and offer my services for your first day of school."

"And we are most appreciative," Flissa said. She reached into her pocket and pulled out some of the sugar cubes she always kept handy for Balustrade. She held several on her palm and enjoyed the velvety brush of Gus's lips as he licked them up.

Behind her, Balustrade whinnied.

"Patience, my love," Flissa said. "You'll get yours."

She gave a handful of sugar cubes to Klarney, then rewarded Balustrade with the biggest share of anyone. As he ate, she scratched his nose and whispered gently, "Don't be jealous. You know I'll always love you best."

"As well you should," Klarney said, and Flissa blushed because she'd forgotten how well he could hear. "I know horses, and that one is most definitely a keeper."

"We should go," Sara said. "We don't want to be late." She reached up, grabbed Gus's mane, and tried to pull herself onto his back. She tried three useless hops, then gave up and pointed at the ground. A puff of scarlet mist appeared. When it cleared, a three-step staircase made of what looked like white marble stood in its place. "Much better," Sara said. She climbed the stairs and easily swung herself into place.

"Pretty cool," Galric said from his position astride Klarney. "Kinda cheating, though."

Flissa agreed; any good rider should know how to climb onto a horse, but of course she'd take Sara's side.

"She's just playing to her strengths," she said as she swung onto Balustrade.

"Exactly," Sara said. She pointed at the stairs and made them disappear in another cloud of red mist. "And it's not like we're in a contest or anything, so it's fine."

"We *could* be in a contest," Galric said with a grin. "Let's do it, Klarney! Last one to school's a rotten plobquat!"

"Onward!" Klarney cried. He took off at a full canter, and Sara squealed as Gus ran after him.

Flissa had no desire to race to school; she'd actually been excited about a long, leisurely ride on Balustrade, but there was no way she'd let Gus and Klarney outshine her glorious stallion. "Git on, mighty Balustrade!" she shouted.

A little nudge from her heels and he was off. It took him exactly three seconds to catch up to Gus and Klarney.

"Well played, Balustrade!" Klarney called as Flissa and Balustrade zoomed past him. "Excellent stride!"

After that, Flissa blocked out everything else, especially their destination. She pretended they were just out for a ride. For forty minutes they raced over fields and past villages, and Flissa marveled at all of Kaloon's changes. There were so many somber reminders of the battle, like the charred swaths of land, and the construction from all the rebuilding.

Then the wind changed direction, and Flissa caught the overpowering scent of roses. She used to like the smell.

Now it made her stomach churn because she knew the cause: it was the remnants of the Twists.

The Twists had always existed in its own magical realm; only its entrance, the Brambled Gates, had appeared in Kaloon properly. Flissa had seen it firsthand. The gates appeared out of nowhere as a tiny dot in the air, then grew into a thick, thorny, living forest. If you walked into the forest, you entered the gateway to the Twists; if you walked around it, you'd see it was thin as a piece of parchment. That's why at the end of the Battle for Unification, after everyone had been evacuated and only the darkest of Dark Mages like Grosselor and his closest followers were forced to remain inside, all the Shadows and all the strongest Mages were able to surround the Brambled Gates. Then, as the Gates closed and shrunk down into that tiny floating spot that contained the entire Twists, the Shadows and Mages hit it with all their combined magic.

"Did you destroy it?"

That's what Loriah had asked when Katya told them the story. They were all in Katya's cottage at the time—Flissa, Sara, Loriah, and Galric—and Flissa remembered the look on Loriah's face. Her jaw was set, but there was something soft in her eyes. Flissa had wondered if Loriah might feel a little sad about losing the Twists forever. It had been terrible, of course, but all the free-flowing magic had also made it oddly beautiful, and for so many years it was the only home Loriah knew.

"We did not," Katya had said. "We banished it to the magical plane. The dragons, the man-eating holes in the ground, the tar pits, the fire-spitting cobra trees, and of course the darkest Mages . . . they still exist, but they can't get through to Kaloon anymore."

"Huh," Loriah had said, folding her arms and leaning back into Katya's couch. "You should've destroyed it."

Flissa didn't feel the same way. Condemning the Dark Mages to a lifetime in the Twists with no hope of escape seemed like a much more fitting punishment. Galric had agreed with Loriah; he thought the Dark Mages would *enjoy* a lifetime in the Twists, and it wasn't fair that they got to be happy after ruining so many other lives. Flissa saw his point, but she didn't particularly care whether the Dark Mages were happy or not. As long as they were far away from Kaloon and couldn't hurt anyone but each other, she was fine with their fate.

Flissa's only complaint was that the Twists didn't disappear without a trace. They left a scar—a thorny rosebush on the far outskirts of Kaloon. It floated in midair, just like that dot of the Brambled Gates had when the Shadows and Mages blasted it with their magic. The rosebush was brown and withered, with jet-black roses whose rotten petals curled in on themselves, but it was very much alive, and its scent was so strong that when the wind blew in the right direction, it perfumed the entire kingdom.

Flissa didn't like it. To her the scent was a taunt, a warning that dark magic never really went away. Not entirely. She had shared her fears with Katya, who assured her that the floating rosebush was harmless. It was a shell of old magic. It didn't radiate power, and it couldn't cast enchantments. She said the only fallout from the Twists happened in the moment of its destruction, when shock waves of magic radiated through Kaloon. This Flissa already knew; the evidence grew every day, and she saw constant reminders on her ride to the academy. She galloped Balustrade over fields of orange grass, just like the kind that had grown in the Twists. They passed trees that grew in topiary shapes—giant, leafy rabbits and elephants and bears. They rode past a field of pink, spherical gourds as large as a grown man's chest.

Then Flissa heard chimes.

The ring tree.

She slowed Balustrade to a walk as she approached. The tree was massive, with a trunk so wide that Balustrade could stand sideways and hide completely behind it. The trunk rose to twice Flissa's height, then split into two halves that curved around to form a perfect circle. Countless leafy limbs branched off from the top of the circle, bearing not fruit, but tiny organic bells that tinkled in the breeze.

Loriah sat in the middle of the circle, her back against one side, one leg dangling free and the other bent in front of her. She still wore her white-blond hair in a high ponytail, but the rest of her head was no longer close-cropped with markings shaved into it. Instead she'd grown it out into a sleek cap with bangs, and she'd traded in her rough-hewn leather clothes for leggings, a simple cotton shirt, and soft-soled shoes like Flissa's. If someone wasn't close enough to see the fine scars that crisscrossed her skin, they'd never imagine she'd spent her life in the Twists.

"Took you long enough," she said. "I thought you ditched me."

Flissa had already dismounted Balustrade and was scrambling up the ring tree's trunk to join her. "No you didn't."

"Nah, I didn't," Loriah admitted. "You wouldn't."

Flissa settled herself on the other side of the tree trunk's wide circle, mirroring Loriah's position. From this height she could see Sara and Galric approaching on Gus and Klarney, but they were still far away. She lowered her voice all the same. "Are the teeming throngs all terrible?"

Loriah shrugged. "Beats me. I stick to my dorm and do my own thing. I don't know why your folks made me leave the palace in the first place."

"Because students without immediate family members are supposed to live in the dorm," Flissa explained for the zillionth time.

"Uh-huh. But I'm friends with the royal family. Isn't that supposed to make me special?"

"You *are* special," Flissa said. "But you can't get special treatment *because* you're our friend. It sets a bad example."

Loriah rolled her eyes. "Whatever. You haven't seen the place since they finished it, have you? Check it out."

Loriah jerked her head over her shoulder, and Flissa leaned forward to look. The school had been one of the first priorities after Kaloonification, but it was still a massive undertaking that required the cooperation of Mages, Genpos, and Magical Animals. When Flissa and Sara had left for their most recent trip outside the kingdom, it was still unfinished, and she hadn't had a chance to see it since they'd returned.

Staring at it from up above, Flissa found it hard to believe it was finished even now.

In order to save time, Maldevon Academy wasn't built from scratch. It was fashioned from the remains of Grosselor's compound—a magically hidden enclave of large, luxurious homes reserved for the most elite members of the Keepers of the Light. The magical shield that had rendered the compound invisible to anyone uninvited was gone, but the buildings still sat deep inside a valley so you couldn't see them until you were at the very top of the surrounding hills . . . or perched in the center of the ring tree.

Flissa wasn't sure how the buildings had been arranged originally, but now, from high above, Flissa could see they made the shape of a K, for Kaloon. The original buildings had all been different bright colors—mint green, teal blue, coral pink, and of course Keeper yellow—but when they were moved and magicked into one school, all the colors ran together, making the Academy a pastel patchwork, like when Sara spread paints on her palette and ran through them with a toothpick to see what kind of design she'd make. While it was hard to tell the buildings' size from up above, they definitely looked tall but oddly . . . gloppy.

"It's like they're made from candle wax," Flissa said.

"They're not," Loriah said. "But yeah, they look it. Something about all the magic it took to shove 'em together. Wait till you see it from down there."

"What's it like inside?"

Loriah shrugged. "Don't know. They haven't let us in yet."

Flissa kept staring down at the academy. From where they sat in the tree, the bottom of the K faced them, and the ground there was groomed into a large garden. The left side was laid out in the shape of Kaloon's royal seal. The right was laid out in the shape of a rigdilly, a beautiful three-petaled flower that once grew only in the Twists, and which for many imprisoned there became a sign of hope. The two gardens were separated by the academy's

42

walkway but linked by four natural leafy arches, a symbol of Kaloonification.

The top part of the K opened out to sports fields. Flissa thought she could make out a hoodle field and jousting fields, then three more pastel buildings in the far distance.

"Those are the dorms," Loriah said when Flissa asked. "Boys' and girls'. And the third one's the orphanage. For kids who lost their families, but are too young to go to school. And all that space off to the side, where the K opens up, I heard that's outdoor classrooms. Some of the larger Magical Animals aren't into the inside thing."

Flissa nodded. She'd heard about all of it from her parents, but it was amazing to see it for herself.

"It's so colorful!" Sara cried.

Flissa hadn't even realized her sister and Galric had arrived, but now they were just beyond the ring tree, and sat on Gus and Klarney at the edge of the steep hill that rose above the academy.

"Hold up," Galric said. "Is the building . . . stretching?"

Flissa looked down. Sure enough, it looked like all four ends of the K were slowly growing longer.

"Yeah," Loriah said, "it does that. The mixed-magic thing turned everything weird. Sometimes the buildings like to stretch. They get taller too. It all goes back eventually."

"I remember hearing about that now," Flissa said, recalling snippets of conversation between Katya, Rouen, and her parents. "It's not just the mixed magic, it's also that it's all fairly new. Apparently the stretching and moving isn't dangerous and it'll settle over time."

"I hope it doesn't; I love it," Sara said with a grin. "Should we go down and meet everybody?"

"I guess," Galric said.

He looked uneasy. Flissa was glad she wasn't the only one.

"We can go," Loriah said, "but I've met everyone I want to meet."

She and Flissa clambered down from the tree, then they both hopped onto Balustrade. Flissa looked at her sister's face, gleaming with excitement as she gazed down at their future.

Flissa sighed. There was no point putting it off any longer.

"Onward, Balustrade," she said. "Let's go to school."

Chapter 4
Sara

"Hurry, Gus! Hurry!" Sara cried as they jounced down
the hill. Both Klarney and Balustrade were far ahead, and
Sara didn't want to miss out on a second.

"Hold your horses," Gus said. "Ugh, I hate that saying."

He took his time, but Gus finally met up with Klarney
and Galric at the bottom of the hill. Up ahead, Sara saw
a pebbled path at the bottom of the K. The path went
through the two gardens Sara had seen from up above, and
a stream of kids her age and older piled out of carriages and
disappeared down its length. The sound of buzzing voices
electrified Sara; it was like walking into a royal reception,
except better because she didn't know what to expect.

Sara was so excited, she forgot to magic herself up
another set of steps. She swung her legs to one side of
Gus and plopped clumsily down to the grass, then quickly
hopped up and turned in circles, trying to see her backside.

"Tell me I don't have grass stains on my dress," she said.

"Okay," Loriah said as she got off Balustrade's back.
"You don't have grass stains on your dress."

Sara looked at her face. She had no idea if Loriah

was telling the truth. "For real? Or I *do* have grass stains and you're just saying I don't because that's what I told you to say?"

Loriah smirked and shrugged.

"You're good," Galric said. "No stains. Just . . ." He awkwardly swiped at the back of her skirt. "There. All clean."

"Thanks."

Despite having seen it a million times, Sara was still amazed by how easily Flissa dismounted Balustrade—like water slipping off a duck. Once she was off, she pressed her forehead against his nose. "See you when it's time to go home."

Balustrade nodded nobly, as if in answer, then turned and galloped away.

"Later, Blusters!" Galric called after the horse.

Balustrade whinnied back, and Flissa gave him a glare so withering they all laughed. No matter how much she liked Galric, Flissa would never get over the fact that he'd bonded with *her* horse.

"We'll be on our way as well," Klarney said. "But do visit. And never hesitate to reach out if you need us. We'll come in a jiffy."

"Exactly," Gus said, "Or, you know, we'll come whenever we're actually free. See ya!"

Klarney reared back majestically. By the time he planted his front hooves back down, Gus was already out of sight. "No sense of drama, that one," Klarney muttered, then took off after his friend.

"Come on!" Sara cried. She ran to the pebbled walkway and darted in before any of the others. "Hi!" she called to everyone she passed. "Hey! Hi there! Hello!"

Most people said hi back. Some of them gave her that look—that eyes-wide, *oh my gracious it's the princess* look. She'd seen it a million times before, but this time everything was different.

"Sara, wait!"

She heard Flissa behind her, but she pretended she didn't. It was terrible, she knew, it was just . . . for the first time ever, she wasn't half of Princess Flissara, she wasn't out performing royal duties, and she wasn't hanging out with friends who knew her and Flissa as a pair. She was just herself. Sara. Starting fresh in a brandnew place.

She wasn't sure whom to approach first, so she just stood tall, held her head high, and kept saying hello to everyone. Lots of people seemed to already know each other. They stood in groups, both along the path and scattered around in the gardens, talking and laughing together. She noticed that a lot of the groups seemed to dress alike. There were girls in dresses like hers, and boys in velvet breeches and doublets. Others wore simpler frocks, or rough-hewn fabrics with frayed edges, and several clusters of people wore mostly leather, with their hair in the unusual cuts and styles that Sara had seen in the Twists. Magical Animals seemed to group together too, and she was delighted when she saw an adorable Pomeranian dog standing on the back of a bushy-bristled hog.

"Oh!" she gasped. "You're giving her a real piggyback ride!"

They stared daggers at her.

"First of all," the Pomeranian growled gruffly, "I'm a dude. Second of all, my friend here's a boar. Not a 'piggy,' a boar."

"'Piggy' is an offensive term," the boar said. Her voice was high-pitched with an upper-crust accent. "It's species-ist. I would expect more from a princess, *Princess*."

She said the title like it was a horrible insult. Sara considered telling the boar *she* was being royal-ist, but instead she just apologized and waited for Loriah, Galric, and Flissa to catch up with her. She was still eager to be her own person, but a little backup might be nice too.

As she waited, she checked out everyone who walked by and always smiled and said hi. There were a lot of twins, which Sara now expected, even though she'd found it truly bizarre when Kaloonification began. Until the Keepers of the Light fell, she and Flissa had been the only twins she knew, but it turned out they weren't even the only ones sharing an identity to survive. Now Sara saw several pairs of identical-looking siblings, a few of whom still dressed exactly alike. Sara wondered if that was by choice, or just a habit they couldn't let go.

"Hey," Galric said as he, Loriah, and Flissa caught up to her. "You disappeared."

"Sorry," Sara said. "I got excited and walked faster than I thought. So . . . is there such a thing as species-ist?"

"What'd you do?" Loriah asked.

"Nothing! Nothing on purpose. I just . . . I called a boar a piggy."

Loriah, Galric, and Flissa all groaned.

Sara gaped at her sister. "Oh, come on! How would you know that's bad? You've met exactly the same Magical Animals I have!"

"Yes," Flissa said, "but I also listen when Primka tells

us things. The Magical Animal community has been very specific about their designations."

Sara was about to object that it was impossible to keep track of every single thing Primka told them when she always chirped a mile a minute, but a loud female voice cut her off. *"No way!"* the voice screamed. "It's you!"

Clearly someone had recognized Flissa and Sara, so Sara put on her biggest smile and turned to see five kids her age, maybe a little older. Three girls and two boys. All of them wore rough-hewn pants and tunics, and their hair hung in asymmetrical lines. One had several piercings in her ear and a small tattoo on the back of her hand, another wore thick-soled boots.

Sara knew that look. They were Untwisteds—people like Loriah, who'd spent their lives in the Twists but had been freed to live in Kaloon.

The girl with the multiple piercings left the group and ran up to them. Her frizzly black hair bounced with every step.

"Hi!" Sara said. "It's great to meet—"

"Galric, right?" the girl asked. She zoomed right past Sara and straight to him. "You're Galric!"

Galric frowned, confused. "Um . . . yeah, but—"

"I knew it!" the girl shouted. She turned back to her friends, and Sara noticed her curls weren't spread all over; one side was shaved from the top of her ear down, so the curls there made a little awning over that part of her head. "I *told you* it was Galric."

She turned back to him and held her hands up, palms touching. To Sara's surprise, Galric mimicked the gesture exactly. The two slapped their hands together one way, then the other, then clapped and crossed their arms, slapping their hands on their shoulders.

When it was over, Galric's smile was genuine. "Hi."

"Hey," the girl said.

She moved a lot when she spoke, Sara noticed. Like she was bobbing and weaving in a boxing match. "I'm Krystal. I've heard *tons* about you." Then she looked at his face and gasped. "No way! That's the scar you got from Grosselor, right? And I heard there's one on your arm too. Can I see?"

To Sara's dismay, the girl grabbed Galric's sleeve and pulled it up to reveal the thick pink rope of seared flesh. "Whoa," she said. "That. Is. So. Cool."

"It's a scar," Loriah said drily. "It's not cool, it just is."

"And I didn't get it from Grosselor," Galric said, clearly embarrassed. "A giant magic snake smacked me into a rock pile. That's all."

"A giant magic snake enchanted by . . . ?" Krystal asked, though she obviously knew the answer.

"Okay, Grosselor," Galric admitted. "But still, it wasn't like I was fighting or anything. I mean, I passed out at the sight of my own blood."

"*After* you sent the warning that saved our fighters," Krystal said. "Pretty heroic if you ask me."

Krystal leaned forward a little and swayed back and forth on her toes as she smiled at Galric.

"How do you know all this?" Sara asked. "Were you there?"

Sara didn't mean to sound confrontational, but once again she'd managed to offend someone. Krystal stepped back and raised an eyebrow.

"You don't have to be a *princess* to hear things," she said. "Word gets around."

As Krystal looked at her friends and exchanged annoyed eye-rolls, Sara leaned closer to Flissa and Loriah. "Why does everyone here say 'princess' like it's a bad word?"

"Oh!" Krystal suddenly squealed. "You just got here, right? You haven't seen it yet. Come on!"

Krystal grabbed Galric's hand and ran with him down the path. He stumbled after her, casting a helpless glance back at Flissa, Sara, and Loriah as he went.

"I know where she's taking him," Loriah said.

Flissa smiled. "I have a feeling I do too."

Sara couldn't believe it. "How am I the only one who doesn't know anything? And don't tell me it's because I don't listen to Primka," she added when Flissa opened her mouth to answer.

"I was actually going to say it's because you don't listen to Mother and Father when they talk about General Council business, but I won't if you don't want me to."

"Just . . . show me where they're going," Sara said.

"This way," Loriah said.

She led them down the path between the gardens. Sara still called out hellos to people as she passed, but she was more focused on craning her neck and rising onto her tiptoes to try to see Galric. He was tall enough that she caught glimpses of him above the crowd, but looking for him meant she couldn't watch where she was going.

"Oh, hey! Sorry . . . Hi! Sorry . . . Really sorry—and hi!" she said as she bumped into who knew how many people and stepped on way too many toes.

Then she followed Loriah out of the tree-lined walkway

and into the main courtyard, right at the center of the K. Her jaw dropped.

Next to her, Flissa smiled. "It's perfect."

"It" was a giant bronze sculpture of Gilward. When Sara knew him, he was old beyond his years: gaunt, wrinkled, and hunched over. In the sculpture he was young, and he stood tall and proud. He posed majestically on a high dais, legs apart, hands outstretched. In one palm he held a perfect rigdilly flower. In the other he held an exact replica of the amulet he'd left for Galric—the amulet they'd used to find him in the Twists.

It left Sara breathless and sad. She could only imagine how it made Galric feel. "Wow," she said.

"Mother and Father commissioned it in honor of all the Kaloonians wrongly imprisoned in the Twists," Flissa said reverently. "It's made from the armor of soldiers who fell in the Battle for Unification. The metal was melted down and recast to make the statue."

"It's beautiful," Sara said.

Her skin prickled with pins and needles. She had to find Galric. She rose back on tiptoe and scanned the courtyard. Most people weren't even looking at the statue; for them it was just part of the scenery.

Then she saw him. He stood with Krystal and her friends, but he wasn't paying attention to them. He just stared up at his father's face.

Sara pushed through the crowd to get to him. His head was craned back, and Sara saw the tears in his eyes. She slipped her hand in his and squeezed.

"You really do look like him," Sara said.

Galric didn't answer, but he squeezed her hand back.

Then a bell rang, and Sara looked around. For the first time, she took in the vast expanse of her new school. It had seemed big enough from up above, but now it was truly immense . . . though maybe it had just stretched taller, like Loriah had said it would. Standing in the middle of the K as they were, the pastel-swirled walls rose high in front of them and to either side, and Sara could now see where the smaller buildings had been magically squished together, because doors and windows sat in odd locations, and the entire structure seemed to droop in places, as if it were made of ice cream that had sat too long in the sun.

"Look!" Flissa said, pointing up to the sky.

Sara thought Flissa would be pointing out the bell; it was so loud it had to be enormous and very close . . . but Sara didn't see it at all. She still heard its peals, and with every chime, something else erupted into the sky: rainbow fireworks, a loud drumroll, a fuchsia flame. . . .

"It's the magical signatures of every Mage who helped build the school," Flissa said.

The last chime was accompanied by the loud caw of an eagle. When their echoes faded, everyone in the courtyard cheered.

Then a female voice rang out, as loud as the bell chimes had been, but again, even though Sara looked everywhere, she couldn't find the source.

"It is my honor to welcome you all to Maldevon Academy," the voice said. "I am Amala, your head of school."

A murmur rippled through the crowd. Most people sounded impressed, but after the conversation about her this morning, Sara listened closely and could hear several disapproving clucks, groans, and even a couple boos.

"Mom and Dad were right," Sara whispered to Flissa. "Not everyone's happy about her."

"If we see anyone specific, we should probably find out their names so we can let them know," Flissa whispered back.

Sara understood that was what their parents had asked, but she didn't want to spend her first day of school ratting people out. Besides, groaning and booing weren't the same thing as actually causing trouble. "Do you know where she is?" Sara whispered, changing the subject.

Flissa shook her head. "Wherever she is, she's projecting her voice with magic. Smell."

Sara took a deep breath. "Oranges."

"But no orange trees around," Flissa noted. "It has to be her magical signature."

"Some of you may know me," Amala said. "Some lent your assistance in the Battle for Unification."

Raucous hoots and hollers rose up from the crowd. A knot of boys reached out to Galric and thumped him joyfully on the back. He was surprised but grinned and bumped fists with them. Across the courtyard, a young elephant raised its trunk and trumpeted. Boys and girls all through the crowd threw their fists in the air and whooped, and several people turned to one another and did the same handshake Krystal had done with Galric. Sara watched the pair closest to her, trying to memorize how it went.

"Today, however, is a new day," Amala's voice continued. "Today we are the same. We are not simply Untwisteds and lifelong Kaloonians, not Mages and Genpos. We are . . . one Kaloon!"

Sara heard a single, clear chime, followed almost immediately by a *BOOM* so loud it made everyone jump. Sara looked up to the sky; she thought it was more fireworks, but she saw nothing.

Then the stench hit her. A blinding mix of sulfur, manure, and vomit. Her eyes watered, and her stomach lurched.

"Ugh!" Loriah winced and squeezed her nose shut, then quickly removed her hand. "Argh, that's even worse! I can *taste* it!"

Flissa bent over double. "I can't breathe . . . It's horrible."

Sara herself held a hand to her throat and tried to keep from retching.

All around them, everyone in the courtyard was groaning, coughing, or crying out.

Everyone except Galric, who had spent years working in the royal manure pits. He looked down at Flissa, Sara, and Loriah like they were nuts.

"Oh, come on. I mean, it's bad, but it's not *that* bad."

"A stink spell," Amala's voice rang out, more matter-of-fact than annoyed. "It'll take more than that to disrupt opening day."

For a second the smell of oranges intensified, mixing with the vomit/manure/sulfur in a stench so hideous Sara thought she might pass out, but immediately after that a beautiful breeze washed through the courtyard, whisking away the horrible odor and replacing it with the clean, fresh smell of the ocean on a summer day. As everyone took deep, grateful breaths, Amala's voice chuckled.

"You might not see me, but trust that I can see you."

She waited a moment to let that sink in, then raised her voice in celebration once again. "As I was saying, we *are* one Kaloon, and together we celebrate this first day of classes!"

One person cheered, and in an instant it rippled through the crowd until they were all whooping out loud. Sara hooted and hollered, completely swept up in the crowd's delight. She loved it; it made her feel connected to everyone there, like they were all part of something bigger than any one of them.

When the noise died down, Amala spoke again. "You will now get your schedules, and soon after that the bell will ring. When you hear this sound"—the bell rang out a high, chirping peal—"you'll have five minutes to get to class. When it rings like this"—a low, resounding bass *BONG* echoed through the courtyard—"then classes begin."

Sara heard loud flapping, and the largest flock of birds she had ever seen soared up from the other side of the building and blanketed the sky.

"May Maldevon smile on us all!" Amala's voice cried.

The birds swooped down toward the courtyard, and as they got closer Sara realized they weren't birds at all. "They're scrolls," she said. "With wings."

One of them dove right down to Sara, then flitted impatiently in front of her face.

"Gotta be our schedules, right?" Galric asked, wincing away from a scroll flapping in front of him.

Loriah snatched the one nearest to her. "Cool," she said. "Let's see what we've got."

Sara pulled her scroll from the air. The second she touched it, the wings disappeared. Sara ripped off the scroll's wax seal and rolled it open. "Sara" was written at the top in delicate calligraphy. She thrilled at the sight.

"So?" Galric said. "Are we in the same classes?"

They huddled together and compared.

"This is dumb," Loriah said. "We barely have anything together."

It was true. All four of them were never in the same class, and Sara only had two classes in common with Galric, none with Loriah, and one with Flissa.

"Maybe it's a mistake," Flissa said. "The school can't possibly expect everyone to be with entirely new people. Maybe if we say something, or talk to Amala . . ."

"Then we'd be setting a bad example, right?" Sara said. "And it's probably *not* a mistake. Remember the stink spell? It's like Mom and Dad said, not everyone's happy about the whole everyone-going-to-school-together thing. So maybe it's good that we're all mixed up. Maybe everyone's all mixed up, and if we complain about it, we're part of the problem."

It was a noble argument, and it was absolutely true, but Sara was also excited to tackle the school day on her own. Sure, she'd messed up a couple of times already, but those were little mistakes. The rest of the day she'd be flawless.

Krystal bounded over. "What've you got?" she asked Galric.

She put her hands on his arm so she could lean over and look at his scroll. Sara felt her shoulders tighten.

"Second block together. And third . . . and fourth . . . and seventh!" Krystal cried. "Cool!"

"Yeah, it is," Galric said. "Oh, I don't think I introduced you to my friends. This is Loriah, Flissa, and Sara."

Sara chose to ignore the fact that she and Krystal hadn't exactly hit it off in their first conversation. Instead she smiled. "Really great to officially meet you, Krystal," she said.

And just to show that there were no hard feelings, she held out her hands, pressed together like she was ready to do the same handshake she'd seen Krystal, Galric, and the other boys do.

"Uh-oh," Loriah said, rolling her eyes. Galric blanched a little, and Krystal looked at Sara's hands like they were dead fish.

"What are you doing?" Krystal asked.

"What do you mean?" Sara said. "It's the handshake thing. I was watching, and I think I've got it."

Loriah gently pushed Sara's hands down. "Just stop. You're embarrassing yourself."

"What?" Sara asked. "What am I doing wrong? I saw it; this is how it starts."

"It's just . . ." Galric said, "that was the signal we used in the battle. When we were running messages and things. So we knew who was on our side."

"Okay, well . . . I was on your side," Sara said.

"Right," Krystal said. "But you weren't *out there*. You and your sister stayed in the palace. Protected."

Flissa stepped up next to Sara. "Because that's what was required of us," she said icily. "And if you'd like to talk about being *out there*, perhaps Sara and I could tell you about our time battling carnivorous plants and dragons and Dark Mages in the Twists."

"Ooooh, nice one," Loriah said. Then she looked at Krystal. "What do you say to that?"

Sara was mortified. She knew Flissa was standing up for her, but that was the last thing she wanted. She wanted to handle this on her own and make it better, not offend Krystal more than she already was.

"Flissa, it's fine," she said. "I'm sure Krystal knows all about the Twists. It's obvious she's from there."

Galric winced and Krystal's jaw dropped open.

"Ouch," Loriah said.

Sara looked at all of them in disbelief. "What?! What now?"

"It's *obvious* I'm from the Twists?" Krystal said. "Really? What makes it so obvious?"

Sara blushed. She didn't want to say it, but now she felt like she had no choice. "I don't know . . . your hair," she said miserably. "And you have that tattoo on your hand. And all the piercings."

"Your ears are pierced," Krystal shot back.

Sara desperately wished some Twist magic would open a carnivorous hole in the ground and swallow her. She didn't think it was possible to blush harder, but she did. "Yes, but just once in each ear. You . . ." She shook her head and tried to start again. "Look, I'm sorry, obviously I'm wrong, it's just . . . your look is like what we saw in the Twists, and not like what we saw when we went around Kaloon."

Sara was dying. Everything she said only made it worse, and Krystal wouldn't stop glaring at her. It was like she was daring Sara to keep talking.

"Maybe you were seeing the wrong people when you went around Kaloon," Krystal finally said. Then she turned to Galric. "I'll see you in class."

Krystal disappeared into the crowd just as the bell rang its high-pitched peal. Loriah gave Sara a friendly nudge as the two of them, Galric, and Flissa joined the flow of students moving into the building.

"You weren't wrong," Loriah said. "She's totally a Wisher."

"A Wisher?"

"Someone from Kaloon who wishes they'd lived in the Twists, so they dress up like they had," Loriah said. "They think Untwisteds are cool and badass. Which, I mean, *yeah,* we are, but you'd have to be an idiot to want that."

"I don't understand," Flissa said. "If she *wants* people to think she's from the Twists, why did she get so upset with Sara?"

"'Cause Sara's a princess," Galric said. "It's different."

"But that's hardly fair," Flissa said. "It was a simple misunderstanding. It isn't right to—"

"Forget it," Sara said sharply. "Let's just get to class. I don't want to be late."

Quickening her gait, she trotted up the steps to the main entrance of the school, right at the center of the K. Sara took a big breath of still-orange-tinged air and tried desperately to recapture her earlier feeling of elation.

It didn't work. Her stomach had a strange knot in it that hadn't been there before, and it wouldn't smooth out.

That was okay, though; the day had just started. There was lots of time to make everything better. Apparently there were new rules since Kaloonification, and Sara just had to be a little more careful while she learned them, that's all. It wouldn't take her long. In the meantime, she'd make sure she looked exactly how she'd felt this morning: excited and ready for anything.

She took one last deep breath, then she painted on a smile and pushed through the doors of Maldevon Academy.

Chapter 5
Flissa

Flissa was angry. As worried as she'd been about Sara finding new friends and leaving her behind, it was even worse to see her so completely deflated when all she'd tried to do was be nice.

She tried to catch up with her sister, but Sara had disappeared into the crowd.

"Sara?" she called as she ran up the main stairs and into the building. "Sara?"

"She probably went to class," Loriah said. She'd kept pace with Flissa and was right next to her.

"Hey!" Galric said as he jogged to catch up to them. He'd lagged behind because students kept stopping him to shout hello and exchange fist bumps and special handshakes. Krystal apparently wasn't the only person who thought he was a war hero. "Is Sara okay?" he asked. "I thought Krystal was kind of hard on her."

"She'll be fine," Loriah said. "Sara's a big girl. Have you checked out this place, though? It's wild."

Flissa had been so busy scanning the crowd of people and animals for Sara, she hadn't even looked around. Now she did. They were in a massive spherical atrium—the center of the K. The same chaotic pastels that swirled through the outside of the building decorated the inside as well. A large fountain teeming with koi fish sat in the center of the room, with water bubbling out of a rigdilly statue in its middle. There were six arched passageways out of the room. Two of them led to the wings making up the backbone of the K, one to each leg, and two other archways led outside: one to the fields behind the building, and the other to the outdoor classrooms in the mouth of the K.

The strange part was that none of the archways were regular curves. They were warped and wavy, and Flissa felt like she was looking at the whole room from underwater.

"How do we know where to go?" Galric asked. Then he wheeled to the sound of his name and raised a hand to yet another person who called out to him as she passed. "Oh, hey!"

Flissa ignored the Galric fan club and instead noticed several students staring down at their opened scrolls and flipping them over. She was sure the back of her scroll had been blank, but when she unrolled it and turned it over, a map to her first class appeared. She quickly held it out to Galric and Loriah.

"Look—maps in magical ink," Flissa said. "Sara must have found hers and left."

"Got it," Loriah said, pointing to her map. "So you and I have History of Kaloon, right here."

"I'm at the fields for Athletics," Galric said. "Catch up with you later!"

Galric took off, then Flissa and Loriah walked through the fun-house archway that led to the top of the K's stalk.

Unlike the main atrium, this wasn't a dome exactly, but nothing was square. There were no right angles anywhere. The marbled floor rose and fell in waves, and part of the ceiling must have been repurposed from another home's facade because there was a front door, complete with a round, dangling knocker right in the middle.

"So when did your folks say the magic's supposed to settle?" Loriah asked as they trudged up a steep hill in the floor.

"It shouldn't take too long," said Flissa. "Maybe by the first holiday break?"

The girls heard shouts and cheers behind them and turned to see a group of six older kids—boys and girls dressed in leggings and tunics—whiz down the rolling hall at breakneck speed. They all wore boots with wheels magicked onto them, and zoomed over the hills on their way to class. All the other students in the hall watched, most of them clapping and cheering, though Flissa noticed some people stood with their arms folded and rolled their eyes or sneered as the roller-booters sped by.

Loriah grinned. "We should try it."

Flissa was nervous but excited. "With your magic or mine?"

"Seriously? Unless you're making the wheels to save your sister, my magic'll be way stronger."

Flissa blushed. Sometimes Loriah knew her far too well.

Loriah concentrated and pointed down at their feet. Flissa smelled the strong odor of lavender, then she rolled out of control down their hill and straight toward a clutch of well-dressed girls her own age.

"Sorry! Coming through! Can't stop!" she shouted. The girls jumped apart, all staring at her with either disdain, shock, or a mix of both. "Loriah!"

An instant later, Loriah grabbed her hand and zipped her down the hall, curving around several other groups of students.

"You get used to it quick!" Loriah shouted over the rush of air in their faces. "Come on, last door on the left!"

She released Flissa's hand and poured on speed, pumping her arms. Flissa followed. She had no idea what she was doing—she'd never been a vehicle before—but she forced herself not to think about it so her body could do what felt right. She thrust out her legs one at a time, pumped her arms, and in no time she was racing down the hall, easily shifting her weight to avoid every obstacle. She was so focused on Loriah, she didn't look at anyone else, and only barely heard the voices that asked, "Princess Flissa?" with varying degrees of admiration or horror.

Loriah hooted when Flissa finally overtook her. "Speed demon!"

Flissa didn't let up until she reached her classroom. Then she grabbed the doorjamb with her left hand, swung easily inside . . . and realized she had no idea how to stop. And unlike the halls, this classroom was cluttered with individual tables and desks, with only the smallest aisles between them—aisles already cluttered with people's satchels and stacks of books.

"Oh no . . ." she said, desperately shifting her weight to avoid a large leather bag. "I'm sorry, I—*aaargh!*"

The scream came as she thwacked into a desk and bent over double, sprawling out over books and papers.

"So you're Sara," the girl seated there said. "The clumsy one."

"No, I'm Flissa," she admitted. "The exceptionally embarrassed one."

"Nice to know the princess of Kaloon takes school so seriously," sniped a harsh male voice from the front of the room.

Flissa forced herself upright and turned to look at the man. He was younger than Flissa's parents, with rumpled dark hair, dark eyes, and cheeks whose slight sunkenness was somewhat hidden by a scruff of a beard. He wore his brown teacher's robe open, and Flissa saw the black leather pants and wrinkled white shirt beneath it. He was clearly agitated. His jaw worked, and his neck twitched to the side a bit when he spoke. "Good to know that integrating with Untwisteds like myself is so important to you."

"It *is* important to us," Flissa said, her face burning with shame. "To me. I wasn't trying to be disrespectful, I just—"

"I did it to her," Loriah said as she walked in the door— *without* wheels on her feet, Flissa noticed. "Pranked her." Loriah held up her right hand with the middle three fingers raised, a signal that represented the three-petaled rigdilly, and one Flissa had learned the Untwisteds would give each other to signal solidarity. "My bad."

Loriah tilted her fingers to point at Flissa. The scent of lavender filled the room and Flissa felt the wheels disappear from her feet. The teacher gave Loriah a smirk.

"No harm, then," he said. "Find a seat, both of you. The bell will ring in a minute."

As he turned his back, occupying himself at the

chalkboard in front of the class, the girl on whose desk Flissa had sprawled spoke up. "Shame," she said. "I thought you'd made the wheels yourself. I heard you're a Mage."

Flissa turned to look at her. Even though the girl was sitting, Flissa could tell she was tall, with long, wavy brown hair that hung over her shoulders. Her eyes were startlingly emerald green. She wore a cropped leather jerkin over a cotton blouse with leather leggings and had the hardened look of a lifetime in the Twists . . . but Flissa didn't want to make Sara's mistake and assume anything.

"I *am* a Mage," Flissa said, though the words felt strange in her throat. She wasn't ashamed of her powers, but the idea that they were hers was still so new, it felt like a lie to claim them as her own.

"Good for us all, then," she said. "We should have a little magic in the palace."

Flissa considered educating her on the fact that magic had been in the palace forever—that she had in fact been raised by Katya, a Mage so powerful and trusted that she was the first elected to the General Council, and Primka, a Magical Animal. She wanted to speak loudly enough that the teacher would hear, and tell this girl that the royal family—at least *her* royal family—had always been on the side of what was right, they'd just been raised with the wrong facts. She wanted to tell her all of this and convince her . . . but her mother had expressly told her and Sara to be nice to everyone, and she didn't want to seem like she was starting an argument.

"I'm sorry I fell onto your desk," she said instead.

The girl shrugged. "I've dealt with worse. I'm Zinka. Untwisted, if you're wondering."

"I'm not," Flissa said quickly.

"'Course you were. Everyone does. About everybody." Zinka darted her eyes to the back of the room. "Your friend's waiting for you. You should probably head back to her before Teacher Eldridge catches her saving you a seat and realizes she didn't actually prank you."

Flissa followed her gaze. Loriah had found a desk in the back. She sat sideways in it, her legs extended so they rested on the chair next to her. Her eyes bored holes in Flissa, and when Flissa met them, Loriah raised her eyebrows and cocked her head, nostrils flared. She wanted Flissa to get over there *now*.

"Thanks," Flissa said, though something about Zinka made her uneasy. She wasn't sure if the girl approved of her or not, and for some reason—maybe because Zinka was the first new person Flissa had met at Maldevon Academy—she cared. "I'm Flissa, by the way. I mean, I kind of already said that, but not officially, and—"

"Go," Zinka said, nodding toward Loriah.

Right, Flissa thought. *Doesn't approve.*

Flissa scrambled back to the seat Loriah had saved for her. "Thanks for covering for me," she said.

Loriah nodded, then stared straight ahead and pretended no one else existed, which was her go-to state with everyone except Flissa, Sara, and Galric. Apparently that was how they were going to play things around Teacher Eldridge as well. At least for now. Flissa took the time to scan the room as the last students trickled in. Maldevon Academy was required for all human Kaloonians ages twelve through eighteen, plus all Magical Animals at the same developmental level. That was a wide age span, so the school was divided by year: first-years through completion-years. First-, second-, and third-years took classes together, as did fourth through completion. This worked out well for Flissa. While she and Sara were first-years, Galric and Loriah were seconds, but they still all had the chance to see each other in class.

Gazing at the other seventeen students in the room, Flissa couldn't really distinguish between firsts, seconds, and thirds, nor could she absolutely tell forever-Kaloonians from Untwisteds, or where in Kaloon anyone came from, but there were some hints. She saw a couple of girls she was sure she recognized from royal balls, though back then they didn't have sour looks on their faces, nor did they sit slumped in their seats with their arms crossed angrily over their chests. When one of them caught Flissa looking, she nudged the other and pointed. They both quickly smiled and waved, sitting up a bit straighter. Flissa smiled back.

Flissa also noticed a boy with spiky purple hair and round glasses who might have been one of Krystal's friends, but she wasn't sure. Like many of the other students, he looked happy to be in class and chatted with people he knew while he waited for the lesson to begin. Aside from Loriah and now Zinka, everyone else was new to Flissa, including an owl and a large raccoon, and Flissa wondered if her mother would think it was her job to get to know them all. Just the idea exhausted her.

Then a loud *BONG* rang through the room. Immediately their teacher turned away from the blackboard and grinned.

"I'm Teacher Eldridge," he said. "Welcome to History

of Kaloon, where you'll learn the *real* story about how this glorious land we call home actually came to be." His neck twitched slightly to the side and back again. "Our first lesson takes us back to the very beginning of Grosselor's rise, when he fooled King Lamar into basically turning Kaloon over to the Keepers of the Light, and introduces the question we'll ponder all year long: The royal family—brilliant coconspirators, or painfully ignorant dupes?"

He grinned and looked right at Flissa as he said it. She turned red but resisted the urge to sink down in her seat. Instead she raised her hand.

"Yes, we have a question from Princess Flissa."

"Are those truly the only two options?" Flissa asked.

Teacher Eldridge's head twitched to the side. His grin grew tighter, but it didn't fade. "Yup, just those two."

"With all due respect, that seems like you're limiting our ability to think creatively, and form and express our own opinions based on what we learn," Flissa said. "Isn't that what school is all about?"

Teacher Eldridge looked thoughtfully up at the ceiling before looking back at Flissa. "Tell you what," he said. "If you can write a . . . let's say . . . ten-page essay by the end of the week convincing me, I'll believe there are other options. How's that?"

Next to her, Flissa heard Loriah snort. Flissa smiled. "Challenge accepted."

The rest of Teacher Eldridge's lecture wasn't inaccurate, but it was definitely the version of history least flattering to the royal family. Flissa didn't interrupt once. She even took copious notes. When the bell rang to end class, she played into Loriah's earlier lie and rose without even looking at her friend. She was several steps down the hall before Loriah's pounding feet caught up with her.

"You're psyched, right?" Loriah asked. "Eldridge totally thought he was blasting you, and you're loving it."

"Ten pages in a week?" Flissa said. "I could write ten pages *tonight*. I could've written ten pages *in class*. I want to start it right now. I can't wait for him to read what I've got to say."

They laughed together, then a dry voice cut them off. "Hey, besties, wait up."

They turned and saw Zinka striding their way. She was even taller than Flissa had imagined, easily half a head taller than Galric. She could pass for a fourth- or fifth-year, though she couldn't be more than a third to be in their class.

Loriah scowled. "We're not your besties."

Zinka rolled her eyes. "I know *that*; I meant with each other." She flashed Loriah the three-fingered Untwisted sign, then turned to Flissa. "Nice work standing up to Eldridge," she said. "Where're you headed?"

Flissa took out her schedule scroll and looked at it. "Magic Lab," she said. "Lower leg of the K."

"Me too," Zinka said. "I'll walk with you."

"I've got Literature," Loriah said, making a face. "Lower K-stem." She peeked at Flissa's schedule to compare. "Looks like I'll see you at lunch."

Flissa was suddenly terrified that once she and Loriah were out of each other's sight, they wouldn't connect again all day. "I'll look for you," she said. "Save me a seat."

"Sure," Loriah said noncommittally, then she continued down the hall while Flissa and Zinka branched off through the main atrium.

"Guess you've gotten a lot of that," Zinka said. "People like Eldridge."

"Actually, no," Flissa admitted. "After Kaloonification, Sara and I traveled all over with our parents, and everyone seemed very happy."

"'Cause your folks shielded you, I bet. Didn't want to subject the precious princesses to anything they wouldn't like. No offense," she added before Flissa could object. "I'm not saying it came from you. Just the people around you. Maybe the people around your parents too, I don't know. They didn't do you any favors, though. People want things to be all hearts and rainbows with Kaloonification, but they're just not."

"Why?" Flissa asked. "This is the way things used to be before Grosselor. The way they should have been all along. Everyone should be happy."

"Really? Everyone?" Zinka asked. "Did you see those girls in class? The ones with the fancy dresses, like they're going to a palace ball instead of school? The ones who kept looking around and whispering? Bet you anything they've got titles. Duchesses, countesses, viscountesses . . . am I right?"

"Countesses, I believe," Flissa admitted. "I've met them once or twice."

"Of course you have. Their lives were good. They were rich, they were powerful, and as long as the Keepers of the Light kept everyone with magic locked up in the Twists or hidden away, they'd *stay* rich and powerful. You think they're happy with Kaloonification?"

"They should be," Flissa said. "Just because a person or animal has magic and it's legal now, that doesn't mean they're going to take anyone's money and power."

"Sure it does," Zinka said. "It already started with the General Council. Your parents used to be in charge of everything—at least they thought they were. Now they're sharing their power with a General Council filled with Mages and Magical Animals."

"And Genpos," Flissa noted. "Everyone's included."

"And that's the problem," Zinka said. "Not for me, but for the ballgown girls. If you wanted power before, you made nice with the royal family and you kissed up to the Keepers of the Light. That's all people had to do, and they had it made. Now there's a General Council, and the Genpos on it aren't even the ones who had power before. I'm up on things. I know. There's a couple Untwisteds on there, some Kaloonians from the poorer villages . . . you mixed things up."

"Yes!" Flissa said. She was frustrated that Zinka knew so much but still didn't seem to understand. "My parents want *everyone* represented. That's the point."

"Right!" Zinka said. "But not everybody wants things mixed up. If you were on top before Kaloonificaiton, mixing things up can only bring you down. People don't like that. Maybe your parents don't care, but they're not exactly normal Kaloonian royals. Their kids are Mages. You think they would have been so excited about changing Kaloon if there really had been just one, non-magical Princess Flissara?"

Flissa opened her mouth to answer, but then she closed it again. *Would* they have wanted to do the right thing and revolt against the Keepers if Flissa and Sara hadn't been twins?

It was impossible to answer, really. If they hadn't been twins . . . well, they wouldn't have survived Mitzi's curse, for starters. But if there had been no Mitzi, then Queen Latonya never would have been cursed, and the royal family never would have learned the truth about Grosselor, so Zinka's whole question was moot.

But if someone *had* told them the truth . . . if someone had come to the king and queen and their non-magical Princess Flissara and explained what Grosselor was really doing, would any of them have believed it?

Flissa didn't know. She liked to think they would, if the evidence was there, but she honestly wasn't sure.

Instead of answering Zinka, she asked another question. "Okay, so maybe some rich and powerful people aren't happy with Kaloonification—*yet*," she said. "What about all the Untwisteds? What about everyone who has magic or signs of magic and doesn't have to live in fear anymore? Shouldn't they all be happy?"

"Kinda," Zinka said.

"Kinda?!"

"Hey, look, I'm thrilled to be out of the Twists," Zinka said. "I was born there. My parents died when I was little and I was *alone* there. It was bad. But now I'm out . . . and it's like that's it. There's no consequences for anyone. All the people who sent my parents away . . . yeah, Grosselor and his followers are gone, but what about everyone else? What about the people who ratted out Mages? Or all the people who didn't say anything, but looked the other way, even if they knew the Keepers were wrong? They just get to go on, with their families and their homes and their roots, while people like me have to start all over again. Here's our class."

Flissa had been so stunned by Zinka's words she'd

74

actually forgotten they were walking to class. Now Zinka gestured to a melted-wax archway on their right, but Flissa wasn't ready to walk in. Not yet. She touched Zinka's arm so the girl would stop walking.

"You're right," she said. "What you're saying . . . it's obvious, and it makes perfect sense, and I'm embarrassed I never saw it that way. I'm sorry."

Zinka smiled a real smile that warmed her emerald eyes. "I'm glad," she said. "That means a lot."

She nodded toward the classroom, and Flissa walked in with her, side by side. Even though their conversation had been heavy, she felt buoyant.

Maybe Sara wouldn't be the only one to find new friends at school.

Maybe Flissa had just found one too.

Chapter 6
Sara

Sara was already in the Magic Lab classroom when Flissa walked in. She hadn't had a long walk to get there; her first class was Ethics, held in an outdoor classroom. Two ponies were in the class, and Sara had tried to make conversation by telling them she had friends who were magical horses and asking if they knew Gus and Klarney.

The ponies had given her a withering look that Sara was starting to understand all too well. She'd said something wrong.

"No," said the chestnut pony with the long black mane, "not all magical ponies and horses know each other."

"We shouldn't be surprised," the gray-and-white pony said to her friend. "Anastasia said she's species-ist."

Sara felt like she'd been smacked. "What? No! Who said that? Who's Anastasia?" Then she realized. "Is that the pig?"

"Boar!" the two ponies spat in unison. Then they turned their backs on Sara and flicked their tails at her as she protested.

"Boar! Yes! I meant boar! That was just a mistake!"

The ponies wouldn't turn around, and once Sara realized the entire class was watching her have a conversation with two pony butts, she moved to one of the tree stumps that doubled as seating for the human students—*not* the kind of place she'd planned to sit when she put on her beautiful gown this morning—and did her best to be inconspicuous for the rest of the class. When it was over she was the first to leave and quickly made her way to Magic Lab.

The classroom was at the very end of the K's lower leg, and it was enormous. Like everything at Maldevon Academy, the tall, domed room had no regular shape—it was circular but dripped and drooped in odd spots, and the six misshapen arcs of stained-glass windows had bled together to make each one a twisted, dreamlike version of what was pictured—like the image of Maldevon that had become a vibrantly colorful grotesque, with a giant toothy mouth stretching vertically across the window and a single giant blue eye on top. The room itself, created by magic and used to practice magic, seemed alive. Its walls expanded and contracted at regular intervals, like it was breathing. There was no furniture, just a large circular patch of well-manicured soft orange grass that grew impossibly out of the varnished wood floor.

Sara didn't make eye contact with anyone else in the room. She was still eager to meet new people and make a name for herself, but so far everything she'd tried had been a complete disaster. Better to wait for Flissa and tackle this class as a unified front. Maybe they could even go to Amala and ask for more classes together, like Flissa had suggested. It wouldn't set *that* bad an example.

Then Flissa walked in with a tall girl with wavy brown hair down past her shoulders, bright green eyes, and a simple leather jerkin that somehow looked more elegant on her than any ball gown had ever looked on anyone. Every student in the room looked up at her and stared, but the girl didn't seem to notice. She said something to Flissa that Sara couldn't hear, and they laughed together.

"Flissa?" Sara said.

Only then did Flissa see her. She looked surprised, like she'd forgotten they even had a class together.

"Sara, hi!" She turned immediately to include the tall girl. "I want you to meet my friend Zinka."

"Hey," Zinka replied, but before she could say anything more, the whole room echoed with the same voice they'd heard outside in the courtyard this morning.

"Welcome!"

A red satin pillow lowered from a spot so high on the ceiling, Sara hadn't even seen it the entire time she'd waited in the room. Everyone looked up, amazed, as it floated down and came to a stop, hovering just above head-height over the patch of orange grass. Without being told, every student in the room moved into an awed circle and stared at the woman who sat cross-legged on the pillow, which turned slowly in midair.

"Amala," Flissa said softly.

Sara knew Amala was ancient, but she looked young enough to be in her completion year. Her skin was ash-gray from the generations spent in magical hibernation, but it was smooth and without a single blemish. Similarly, her hair was snowy white, but it was thick and luxurious, flowing like a waterfall until it pooled beautifully around her knees. She wore a simple white shift, with her green head-of-school robe over it.

"This is Magic Lab," she said, her voice as smooth as silk, "a class for Mages only. You heard me say this morning that we are all one Kaloon, both Genpo and Mage. That is true, but the fact remains that as Mages, you are special. You have unique skills, unlike any other creatures, and right here is where you'll learn to understand your powers . . . and your potential."

Sara flicked her eyes to Flissa. Was she hearing the same thing Sara was? Because it certainly sounded to Sara like Amala hadn't left her Genpos-are-inferior ideas behind.

If Flissa had noticed, she didn't show it. She stared at Amala, bright-eyed.

Maybe Sara was overreacting.

"When I was young," Amala continued, "magic was a skill in which we took great pride. Mages were respected for their powers and trained from an early age. At last, the time has come again for Mages to take their rightful places of honor in Kaloon, but first you must learn the depths of your magic and how to control it. We'll start with a question: What does everyone know about magic? Please raise your hands."

Flissa raised her hand high.

"Princess Flissa," Amala said. "What can you tell us?"

Flissa stood taller. "Every Mage has their own distinct magical signature, as unique to that Mage as a fingerprint."

"That is correct," Amala said. "You'll note that as I float above you, the room smells like oranges, yes?"

Everyone took deep breaths and murmured their agreement.

"That orange scent is my unique magical signature, but magical signatures aren't limited to scents. Some are visual, like colored lights or mists or shapes; while others are sounds, like a gong or a chirp. And while some magical signatures can be similar, it's true that no two are exactly alike. Now who else can tell me something about magic?"

Sara raised her hand high, but Amala called on a girl across the circle from her. The girl's dark hair hung in endless plaits. She wore a simple dove-gray dress and had deep brown eyes, and as she gestured Sara saw she had a sixth finger on her right hand.

"Mages can combine magic to make their powers stronger," the girl said. "Right?"

"I was gonna say that," Sara whispered to Flissa. Zinka, on Flissa's other side, gave her a raised-eyebrow glare, like Sara had committed a sin by whispering during Amala's class. Sara blushed and turned back to the teacher.

"Correct, Harper," Amala said. "And when magic combines, magical signatures combine. At least where they can. My orange scent can't exactly mesh with a trumpet blast, but one Mage's red signature and another Mage's white signature would combine to make a much more powerful pink."

She rotated toward Sara and Flissa as she said this and gave them a knowing nod. Sara couldn't help but smile; it felt good to know this powerful Shadow was singling out Flissa and Sara, and using their combined magic as an example.

"One more before we start working," Amala said. "Anyone else have a fact about magic?"

"I do," Zinka said without raising her hand.

Amala didn't seem to mind. "Yes?"

"There were gems in the Twists," Zinka said. "Blinzer stones. They were magical. Mages back there would've done anything—to anyone—to get them."

Her voice was dull, and Sara didn't dare wonder what had been done to her in the name of getting the magical stones.

"I mined for them," said a short girl with bright red hair cut into a bob. She wore torn black leggings and a red doublet that poufed like a tutu at the bottom. When she spoke, the silver stud in her tongue clanked against her teeth. "Not my choice, but . . . you know. I never found them, though."

"That's not surprising," Amala said. "For those who don't know," she added as she turned slowly to address the whole room, "blinzer stones have the power to magnify magic, and even radiate a charm or a curse across otherwise impossible distances. They were an unintentional byproduct of the magic used to form the Twists, which is the only place they were ever found."

"*If* they were ever found," muttered a boy with ice-blue eyes and a scar down one cheek. "I heard they aren't even real."

"Oh, they're real," Amala said. "Just very rare. I myself have only seen one, but that was a long time ago, shortly after the Twists were first created . . . not long after I was imprisoned there."

Everyone went silent. Nobody talked about what it was

like in the early days of the Twists. Nobody was alive from that time except for Amala and the other Shadows. They had experienced the terrible moments that had changed Kaloon's history forever, but Sara knew from her parents that none of them liked to talk about it. Sara could feel the anticipation in the room as the whole class waited for Amala to continue.

When she didn't, Zinka spoke up, her voice soft and solemn. "Did you use it?"

"The blinzer stone?" Amala asked. "I considered it. I thought it might have given us a chance to stop Grosselor— maybe escape the Twists and fight back. The problem with blinzer stones is they're not precise instruments. You can't control how little or how much the stones will magnify your powers. Even a Mage with good intentions could accidentally do more harm than good. So I chose not to use it. And when we tried to escape and fight back, we failed. Maybe if I'd used the stone things would have been different . . . or maybe I'd have destroyed us all. Impossible to say."

Amala's eyes drifted to the warped stained-glass image of her husband, Maldevon, but Sara didn't think that's what she saw at all. She seemed far away, and suddenly looked almost as old as her years.

No one said anything for a long time, then Sara gently cleared her throat. She didn't want to upset Amala by asking a question, but she was too curious to swallow it.

Amala snapped back to life and turned in her direction. She looked like herself again, and to Sara's relief she didn't seem angry. "Yes, Sara?"

"The blinzer stone," Sara asked, "if you didn't use it, what *did* you do with it?"

"I tried to destroy it," Amala said, "but blinzer stones are almost impossible to destroy. I encased it in magic instead and buried it deep underground—even deeper than we Shadows when we went into hibernation. Unless someone discovered it, and we have no reason to believe anyone did, it's now sealed away on another plane, along with all the other blinzer stones and the rest of the Twists."

"Excuse me," Flissa said, raising her hand as she spoke, "but *would* all the blinzer stones be sealed away with the Twists? Because other things from the Twists escaped— like orange grass, and things like the ring tree. Couldn't blinzer stones be in Kaloon now too?"

"That's an excellent point, Flissa," Amala said, "and it's something we Shadows have been investigating, since you can imagine how dangerous the stones would be if they fell into the wrong hands. It does seem unlikely, given how rare they were in the Twists, but it's far from impossible. Magic is unpredictable, and large bursts of combined powerful magic even more so. There could be blinzer stones in Kaloon; they could be out in the open, high in a tree, or deep underground. Or they could all remain in the Twists. Only time will tell."

Sara jumped as Amala smacked her palms down on her thighs. "Enough about magical *theory*," the Shadow said. "Now I want to see where you are with your *skills*." She waved a hand and the orange scent in the room intensified. A moment later, a small, round platform with a gray square of clay at its center appeared in front of each student.

"Yes!" Sara exclaimed delightedly. "I love sculpting!"

She knelt down to grab the clay, but her face bonked into a dome that appeared over it with a fresh blast of orange scent. Everyone in the room laughed.

"Any Genpo can mold clay with her hands, Princess Sara," Amala said as Sara stood back up, rubbing her throbbing nose. "I want you to sculpt with magic."

The dome over Sara's clay disappeared, and Amala turned to include the rest of the class. "Anything will do. There is no wrong way to approach the assignment. If you can only make a dent, make a dent. If you can make a ball, make a ball. If you can build a scale model of Maldevon Academy complete with every unique bend and arc . . . well, then you should be up here teaching and not me."

Amala kept rotating in the air, watching the students as they all concentrated on their clay slabs. A cacophony rose up from those with aural magical signatures, an array of lights, mists, and sparkles danced over some clay blocks, and Sara's nose was bombarded by different aromas, all of which thankfully blended together in a non-retchworthy way.

Sara knew this would be a simple assignment. She'd recolored her dress and created stairs out of thin air this morning; she could certainly create something out of clay. The question was *what* to create. She wanted something that would impress Amala and let her know that Sara would clearly be the top student in her class. The scale model of Maldevon Academy would have been amazing, but she certainly didn't have the skills to pull it off, and a bad attempt would be worse than nothing at all.

Sara noticed Amala had rotated away from her, so she looked around the room to see what everyone else was doing. Flissa's mouth was screwed tight, and sweat beaded her upper lip as cream-colored mist danced over her clay block. Sara could see it slowly folding in on itself, molding into the clumsy rectangles of an uneven, lopsided staircase. Across the room, the girl with the red bob faced the clay like it was a foe in a standoff, her legs wide, hands twitching at her sides. She squinted as the top of the slab melted into a gloopy, candlewaxy mess. As for Harper, she held her tiny finger to her mouth as she concentrated. Mist that looked like rainbow confetti covered her clay slab, and as Sara watched, the back of the slab started to mold itself into plaits that resembled the girl's own. The rest of the slab was still featureless, but Sara thought the braids were impressive. The boy with ice-blue eyes seemed to be melting his clay inward so it looked like a volcano, while strobing lights danced around the clay of a girl with stringy black hair as it rolled itself out into a long worm. A stocky boy with his tongue between his teeth made his clay mold itself into a blarnage fruit that looked good enough for Gus to gobble down.

A single, clear chime suddenly echoed through the room, and it made Sara stand taller. She recognized it right away—she'd heard it right before the stink spell went off in the courtyard this morning. She turned and heard it again . . . just as Zinka's clay morphed and molded. Sara watched, stunned, as Zinka concentrated on the clay, and that same chime went off each time the slab made a drastic change.

She grabbed her sister's arm and pulled her close.

"Flissa," she whispered in her ear. "It was Zinka. The stink spell; I heard her magical signature before it started."

"What?" Flissa's eyes were unfocused. It was the same look she got when Sara pulled her away from a book she'd been reading. "What do you mean? There *was* no magical signature before it started. I didn't hear a thing."

"I did, though! And it was that same—"

"Aaaaand, time!" Amala said from her perch in the air. Everyone in the room relaxed and all the dings, buzzes, chimes, and other magical signature sounds gave way to relieved sighs. Sara vaguely heard Flissa complain under her breath, "Sara! You didn't let me finish!" but she was far too horrified by her own clay to pay her sister any attention.

It was untouched. She'd been so busy checking out everyone else's work that she hadn't even started.

Amala must have known. She specifically turned until she was inspecting the sculpture directly to Sara's right, then rotated away from Sara, just so Sara would have plenty of time to sweat before Amala got to hers.

"Oh no," Flissa whispered.

Sara was sure Flissa's eyes would be filled with sympathy, but she didn't want to look. She had to think of a way to fix this. She could magically sculpt her clay now, while Amala was facing the other way, but she was standing in a circle with all the other students. Everyone would see, and someone would tell Amala, assuming the Shadow didn't sense it on her own. Sara didn't think getting caught cheating was what her parents had in mind when they asked her to set a good example at school.

All she could do was wait and listen to her heart thump until Amala got to her.

"Very good work indeed . . ." she said as she rotated past Harper. Her clay slab had rounded out into a head shape since the last time Sara looked. The braids were incredible, though the face was completely featureless.

Amala kept rotating. "Good start . . . Yes, very nice . . . I like that detail, good . . . Excellent effort . . ."

She stopped when she reached Zinka's piece. "Now *that* is impressive. Very nice work, Zinka. Everyone, I want you to look at Zinka's sculpture."

Sara obeyed. Zinka had turned the slab of clay into an incredibly lifelike sculpture of a cat. It was midstride, its long tail curved up with a slight bend at the tip. The detail was impeccable. Sara could see the nap of its fur, the individual toes and claws . . . Zinka had even made long, thin whiskers—so long and thin that the clay shouldn't have been able to stay upright until it was fired in a kiln, but Zinka's magic was strong enough to make them defy gravity. Sara wasn't sure what impressed her more: Zinka's skill as a Mage or as an artist. Yet even as she admired the sculpture, she couldn't get that magical signature out of her head. It was absolutely the one she'd heard before the stink spell went off. Zinka had to be the one who'd cast it.

Amala finally moved on from Zinka's cat sculpture to Flissa's stairs. "Not bad," she said. "Not terribly imaginative, perhaps, and a little rough around the edges, but not bad at all."

Then she turned to Sara's clay and frowned.

"Interesting," she said, staring at Sara's untouched slab of clay. "And here I'd been told you were a Mage. Perhaps you belong in a Genpo class instead."

Sara knew "Genpo" wasn't an insult, but Amala made it sound like one. "I'm not a Genpo," she said tightly. "I was watching everyone else and I got distracted. I'm sorry."

"I see," Amala said. "Then let's give you a chance to show what you can do. Distraction-free. Unless you'd rather that slab stand as your assignment."

"No," Sara said quickly. "I'll do it."

This was the best outcome ever. She knew she could mold clay, and now she got to do it in front of everyone. She could make something seriously impressive while Amala and the whole room watched.

She looked down at her slab and was about to begin . . . when an image of the boar sneering at her flashed in front of her eyes—the one who said "princess" like it was a curse. She saw the ponies from class who turned their backs on her, and Krystal's disgusted face when Sara said she was from the Twists, and the looks her own sister and her friends gave her when she'd tried to do that handshake. She heard the laughter all over again from when she reached for the clay and bapped her nose, and her own voice singsonged in her ears: *You're gonna fail again . . . you're gonna fail again . . .*

Sara shook her head. This was stupid; she was getting in her own way. She needed to relax and let her magic flow. She took a deep breath . . . then she balled up her hands and scrunched her face.

You're gonna fail again . . .

Someone across the room snorted and said, "Grunt." Several other students giggled.

"Grunt" was what some Mages called Genpos, because

Genpos had to struggle and sweat to do what Mages could do with ease.

It wasn't a nice term.

Sweat dripped down the back of Sara's neck.

"I see," said Amala.

"No!" Sara blurted. "You don't. I'm good at this. I am. Wait."

She bent her knees a little and balled her hands at her side. She squeezed every muscle in her body.

Now the red mist appeared. Only wisps, but they floated around the block of clay and smoothed its corners.

"I think that's enough," Amala said.

Why was this happening? "It's *not*," Sara said. She heard the tears in her voice and hated them. "I can do more."

But she couldn't. Not now. It wasn't working. When she needed it most, her magic wasn't working. It was trapped behind all her bad thoughts and she couldn't clear them away. Why was this happening to her?

Then Flissa grabbed her hand. Instantly, electric heat coursed through Sara. It hummed between her ears, blasting everything else away. She was clear now; she could feel the magic coursing through her body and streaming out to the clay, which was quickly coated in a bright pink mist. It was her own and Flissa's magic combined, but Sara felt in control, as if for once she was the athlete and Flissa was bolstering her and cheering her on. Without even thinking about it, Sara magically folded and molded the clay into a round head with two perfectly chiseled faces: Sara's on one side, Flissa's on the other.

Two sisters, back-to-back, with only the hair over their foreheads to tell them apart.

Sara vaguely heard all the other students gasp and mutter, but nothing was as powerful as the flow between herself and Flissa. Sara was captain of the boat and their combined power was the wind in its sails, bearing them along so fast she could only steer as it whisked them along faster and faster. She carved more detail into the double sculpture as it grew bigger and bigger, impossibly filling up the center of the grass circle and knocking over the other, punier clay sculptures until it rose as high as Amala. Then the two mouths on either side of the clay opened in unison and sang out a single, beautiful note . . .

Which cut off when the faces exploded into a massive spatter of wet-clay shrapnel.

Everyone screamed, and Sara instantly snapped back to herself. The clay was everywhere, splashed across people's faces and over their clothes. Sara felt it weighing down her curls, and when she looked down at her blue dress it was spattered all over in gray.

"I'm sorry," Flissa said. She looked dazed and even more clay-spattered than Sara. "I didn't think it would get so . . ."

"*Now* I see," Amala said.

She turned away, and Sara's cheeks burned because Amala *didn't* see. She didn't see at all. Sara was good at magic, good on her own, just like she'd always been good at meeting people on her own, except now that she had the chance to *really* be on her own, nothing was working at all.

When the bell rang, Sara strode out of the room as

fast as she could. She ignored Flissa calling her name behind her.

She'd started the class thinking Flissa might save her, but now she knew the truth. With or without her sister at her side, Maldevon Academy was a complete disaster.

Chapter 7
Flissa

"I wish Amala hadn't put Sara on the spot like that," Flissa said. She and Zinka had their next class, Athletics, together, so they walked side by side down the hall. Flissa kept an eye out for her sister, but Sara had run out of Magic Lab and slipped into the crowd so quickly, Flissa had lost sight of her right away.

"What else was Amala gonna do?" Zinka asked. "Sara flaked on the assignment."

"She didn't flake exactly," Flissa said. "It's like she said. She just got distracted." Flissa remembered *what* had distracted Sara too—her feeling that Zinka was the one who set off the stink spell that morning—but she wasn't going to share that with Zinka. "I just think Amala set Sara up for everyone to gang up on her. It's not right. The whole point of Maldevon Academy is unity."

"I don't know," Zinka said with a snort. "Everyone seemed pretty united when they were screaming at your exploding giant clay heads."

Flissa stared at her, openmouthed and apparently with more disdain than she realized because when Zinka turned her way, she laughed and held her hands up in surrender. "Whoa! Not an insult. It's a compliment. Don't send me to the royal dungeons."

"We don't have royal dungeons," Flissa said. "And how exactly is that a compliment?"

"Are you kidding?" Zinka asked. "Did you see my little clay cat? I mean, it was good—"

"Best in the class," Flissa noted.

Without breaking stride, Zinka did a flourish with her hand and bowed. "Yes. Thank you. But it didn't grow into a lion and roar. You and your sister have skills. I wouldn't want to go against you in a fight—at least not when you're together."

"We're always together," Flissa said automatically. Then she blushed as she realized how ridiculous that sounded when Sara was nowhere in sight.

She and Zinka had reached the main atrium. The melted-arched doors to the back fields had stretched wider since this morning, which meant the staircase leading down from them now tapered drastically. The fresh air felt glorious on Flissa's face, and she tipped her head back to bask in the sun. It energized her, and she was glad she had Athletics next; every muscle in her body came to life in the crisp fall air, and all she wanted to do was run.

"Race you to class," Zinka said.

Flissa smiled. It was like Zinka had read her mind. "I would, but I'd have to look at the map. I don't know where we're going."

"I do," Zinka said. "And you won't beat me, so you may as well follow."

Zinka sprinted off, lightning-fast. Flissa gave chase,

her braid bouncing up and down as she followed Zinka over the mottled pattern of green-and-orange grass, around a topiary garden whose naturally growing elephants raised their leafy trunks and trumpeted as they ran by, and past the jousting fields, where a bunch of older kids roughhoused with a pack of young cheetahs and tigers. Zinka was taller than Flissa and had a longer stride, but Flissa pumped her arms to stay just behind her—only far enough back for Zinka to navigate the way. As they ran, Flissa and Zinka blew past several other students who seemed to be heading in the same direction, and Flissa knew they'd nearly reached their destination when she saw a group of ten students up ahead. They were gathered in loose bunches around a short man with a bald head and orange mustache and beard. He wore teachers' robes.

"Zinka!" Flissa panted.

Without breaking stride, Zinka turned.

Flissa grinned. "See you in class."

Flissa bore down with everything she had and tore past Zinka. The taller girl tried to put on a burst of speed of her own, but Flissa had surprised her and it was too late. A nanosecond before Zinka, Flissa thumped a foot down next to the teacher, then tumbled to the grass. "I win!" she crowed between panting breaths.

Next to her, Zinka rested her hands on her bent legs and gulped in air. "Only because you cheated," she said. "I thought you were running as fast as you could go."

She held a hand out to Flissa, who grabbed it.

"That's not me cheating, that's you underestimating me," Flissa noted as Zinka helped her to her feet. "You shouldn't do that. Next time I might throw you in the royal dungeons."

"See, and you always told me there *were* no royal dungeons," said another girl as she linked her arm through Flissa's. The girl was petite, with hair curled into perfect long ringlets. The waist of her dress was cinched in a style Flissa had always found completely impractical and absurd, and the dress itself was the exact same shade of sunshine yellow as the Keepers' robes. Clearly she didn't have a Primka to tell her this was in poor form.

"Jentrie," Flissa blurted as the girl's name popped into her head. She'd seen her at the palace many times, but she didn't think they were exactly on arm-linking terms. Maybe she'd been closer with Sara's half of Princess Flissara.

"Yes, it's so good to see you!" Jentrie squeezed Flissa's arm within hers, then walked a few steps with her, steering her away from Zinka. Flissa turned back to try to include her, but Zinka had her arms folded and was shaking her head.

Jentrie bent her head close to Flissa's. "Are you as miserable here as I am?"

Flissa didn't know how to answer. Was Jentrie nervous about meeting new people too?

Then the bell to start class rang, and the teacher clapped his hands. "Well," he said, "that's the bell, and it looks like we're all here . . . so how about we start class, huh?"

He looked at the students expectantly, as if waiting for an answer. The man seemed like an odd choice for an Athletics instructor, in that he didn't look terribly athletic. He had a bit of a potbelly that pooched out the front of his robes, and even though the temperature was mild and he wasn't running around, sweat ringed his bald head. Flissa supposed that could be from nerves rather than exertion, but was he really that intimidated by a small group of first-, second-, and third-years?

He still hadn't continued his thought. He looked from student to student, waiting for someone to answer his not-really-a-question.

"Yes," Flissa said. "Starting class would be wonderful."

He gave her a grateful smile. "Thank you, Your Highness." He placed his palms together and gave a slight bow in her direction, which was completely unnecessary and made Jentrie roll her eyes.

The teacher clapped again. "I'm Teacher Lazando, and this is Athletics. We have Athletics here at Maldevon Academy because it puts the 'cool' in 'school.'"

He smiled and nodded, clearly proud of his joke and eager for someone to appreciate it. He looked from student to student, waiting for someone to laugh.

No one did.

"'Cool' in 'school,'" Flissa finally said, forcing an appreciative chuckle. "That's funny."

Jentrie bumped Flissa with her hip and shot her a *what are you doing?* look, while Lazando gave another one of his mini bows with his hands pressed together. People whispered and giggled.

Jentrie was probably right; she should have kept her mouth shut.

"Now let's get those muscles moving and play Dodge 'Em!" Teacher Lazando said.

Most of the class groaned, but Flissa smiled. She'd

never played Dodge 'Em, but getting her muscles moving sounded like heaven.

"Actually, Teacher Lazando," Jentrie said, "I won't be playing. My parents are Duke Renmar and Duchess Eliza, who honestly didn't want me coming here in the first place and definitely wouldn't approve of me running around on a field *dodging* things, especially in this dress. So I'll be sitting out. I'm sure the princess feels the same way."

Flissa was stunned, and even more so when Jentrie gave Flissa a knowing look and squeezed her arm tighter. Flissa shook her head and removed herself from Jentrie's grasp.

"Actually, no," she said. "I'm happy to play. It sounds like fun."

Groans rose up from the group. Apparently it didn't sound fun to anyone but Flissa. Jentrie's jaw tightened and she glared, but what was Flissa supposed to do? Did Jentrie really think she'd take her side and sit out class?

"You can wait on the bleachers, Jentrie," Teacher Lazando said. "Just know this is a class, so if you don't participate, I'll need you to spend the block writing me an essay about why you made that choice. If you opt out of *that*, I'll have to give you detention. So you decide on that, and meanwhile . . . we'll start picking teams!"

He said it with a rousing fist pump, like he expected everyone to cheer. No one did.

"Okay, team captains," he continued. "Skeed and Your Royal Highness Princess Flissa, step right up."

Teacher Lazando gave a bow as Flissa and the other captain, Skeed, the boy with glasses and spiky purple hair from her History of Kaloon class, stepped forward. Sara would have had no problem standing in front of everyone, but Flissa felt exposed. She wanted to stare at the ground, but she knew her mother wouldn't approve of that. Flissa was supposed to set an example and be welcoming, so she forced herself to look at all the other students and try to catch their eyes. Most of them just looked away.

Skeed had first pick and chose Zinka, while Flissa picked Jentrie. She thought that might make things better between them and that getting picked first might make Jentrie excited about playing the game.

"Thank you, Princess Flissa, for your faith in me," Jentrie said coolly, "but like I said, I'm sitting out."

Flissa blushed and moved on to her next choice. She felt bad that she didn't know anyone's name. She knew some faces—either from the palace or royal events or her trips around the kingdom—but without the names all she could do was point and say "You" each time she picked someone. Each time she did it, she felt like she was letting the person down, and they were insulted their princess had no idea who they were.

Finally everyone was divvied up between the two teams. Then Teacher Lazando waved an arm, and Flissa heard a swarm of bees buzzing. When the sound faded, she and the rest of her team wore thin-knit forest-green vests over their clothes, while the other team wore similar vests in blue—the colors of Maldevon Academy, and a way to tell the two teams apart.

"Here we go!" Teacher Lazando shouted.

He threw his arms in the air. More buzzing, then six round balls appeared and bounced onto the field. The game was on, and all Flissa's worries melted away. She was on a field, ready to play; that meant she was home. As she raced to grab a ball she listened to Teacher Lazando shout out the rules: hit someone from the other team with a ball and they're out, last person standing wins for their team. No hitting in the head, catch a ball before it bounces and you get the thrower out, deflect a ball with another ball and you're safe.

Flissa was the first to snatch a ball, and instantly hurled it at Skeed, thwacking him in the leg. The second she looked up, she spotted another ball zooming toward one of her teammates, who wasn't paying attention. "Look out!" Flissa cried. She sprinted across the field, but Zinka got there first. She lifted Flissa's shocked teammate off her feet so that the ball hit the girl's backside.

Flissa smiled. "Nice move."

"Thanks."

"Okay, that's legal this time and Larissa's out," Teacher Lazando shouted from the sidelines, "but from now on no picking people up and smacking them into the ball. Didn't really think I'd have to say that explicitly, but lesson learned. Play on!"

Flissa saw a ball on the ground and raced for it. A second before she arrived, Zinka somersaulted in front of her. She grabbed the ball midroll, then grinned wickedly at Flissa.

"Better run, Princess."

Flissa did. She serpentined between members of Zinka's team so Zinka couldn't hurl her ball at Flissa without risking someone on her own side.

Zinka wasn't the only one after Flissa. Balls zoomed around in every direction, and it seemed like everyone's first priority was knocking the princess out of the game. That was okay; Flissa loved the challenge. She did a handspring over one ball and a diving tumble under another. She saw a blue-vested boy throw a lobbing arc and raced top speed, then jumped as high as she could to snatch it in midair.

"Out!" Teacher Lazando pointed to the boy who threw the ball, but Flissa had already wheeled to face her next threat. She wielded the ball in her hands like a shield, deflecting one, two, three other balls before they could hit her, knocking them down by her feet. She grinned down at the balls. "Thanks for the ammunition, blue team!"

The blue team ran, but Flissa's aim was excellent. *Wham-wham-wham-wham!* Every ball hit its mark.

While Flissa decimated the blue team, Zinka did the same to the green. Before long, only the two of them were left on the field. They each had a ball, with two others at their feet. They stood facing one another, Zinka towering over Flissa.

"This is where you go down, Princess."

"*That* is where you're mistaken, Zinka."

Flissa was patient. She wouldn't move until the time was right. They stood for what felt like an eternity, staring into each other's eyes, both swaying to stay light on their feet. Then Zinka faked a throw, palmed the ball, and instantly threw it to where Flissa would have lunged to get away, but Flissa hadn't taken the bait. While Zinka was hurling all her weight into a bullet-throw doomed to miss, Flissa gently lobbed her own ball . . . which hit Zinka in the hip.

"WINNER!" cried Teacher Lazando, throwing his arms in the air. "Princess Flissa!"

The bell in the main building chimed. The period was over; they had five minutes before their next class.

"Thank you, everyone!" Teacher Lazando called out as they streamed away from the field. "Great class today, right? And, Jentrie, since you didn't write your essay, expect a scroll—I look forward to seeing you in after-school detention."

Flissa looked for Skeed, her opposing team captain, to tell him good game, but he was already long gone. She saw him running toward the main building, clearly eager to get to his next class on time.

Jentrie bobbed up to Flissa with a huge smile on her face and pulled Flissa close, then she hissed in her ear. "You shouldn't hang out with the Untwisteds. They might act like your friends, but they hate everyone who got to live in Kaloon, even Mages like you."

When Jentrie pulled away, her smile was big as ever, and she even waggled her fingers at Zinka as they passed.

"She's weird," Zinka said when Jentrie walked off, then she clapped a hand on Flissa's shoulder. "Cool game, though. You should try out for hoodle with me after school today."

Before Flissa could respond, Teacher Lazando was at her elbow, his hands already pressed together for that little bow he couldn't stop doing around her. "Princess Flissa," he said, "Your Highness . . . may I have a word?"

"Find me at lunch," Zinka said. "Or I'll find you."

She loped off, leaving Flissa with Teacher Lazando, who rolled forward expectantly on his toes and tapped his still-tented fingers together. "I won't lie," he said. "It's a real honor meeting you."

101

Flissa blushed. Again. "Honestly . . . I'm just another student. I'm really not looking for any kind of special treatment."

"Have you had Ethics class yet?" Teacher Lazando asked.

Flissa furrowed her brow. Did he think she was being unethical? "Um . . . no. No, I have that next."

"Ah. Well, when you do, you'll meet my brother. He's *also* named Lazando, because my parents weren't as clever as yours and didn't give us two names we could push together."

Teacher Lazando grinned as if he'd just told Flissa a big secret, but if he had, Flissa didn't get it . . . until suddenly it clicked and she understood. "Ohhh," she said. "You and your brother are identical twins. And you . . . you pretended to be the same person?"

"Our entire lives," he said. He had stopped bouncing on his toes. His voice was somber now, and in it Flissa felt the weight of every one of those years. "It's how we were raised. It was the only way my parents knew to keep us and our family out of the Twists. Not just them; we didn't have a better answer either. We stayed one Lazando even after our parents passed away. Only one of us could go to their funerals, of course."

His voice cracked. He ran his hand over his bald head and let his breath out in a whoosh.

"Sorry," he said. "I just want to say that I know where you've been. We weren't royalty, of course, but still . . . I know. And I know how hard and scary it must have been for you to take the stand you did and tell the truth. People like my brother and me . . . we owe you a lot. *That's* why it's an honor to meet you. Not because of your title. That."

Flissa's chest swelled as she suddenly understood why she was here—why it was so important she and Sara had come to Maldevon Academy, and why they needed to stay, no matter how confusing or difficult things got.

"Thank you," she said. "It's an honor to meet you too. Truly."

It didn't seem like enough, but Flissa had no good words to express how she felt. If Lazando wasn't her teacher, she would have hugged him.

For a second Teacher Lazando looked like he might cry, but then he cleared his throat. "The bell will ring soon," he said. "I'm sure I've made you late for your next class. Good thing it's with my brother; I'll send a bubblegram to let him know you have an excuse. That way you won't get detention."

"Thank you," Flissa said. "And thank you for the class— it was wonderful!"

"The royal seal of approval!" she heard him crow as she raced away. "Thank you, Your Highness!"

This time Flissa didn't blush; she smiled.

Chapter 8
Sara

Sara had finished her third-block class and was walking through the crowded main atrium to get to her fourth when she heard it: a rumbling sound so low and loud that it shook the floor.

The screams came next.

Everyone in the atrium froze and looked at one another, searching for answers in each other's faces. Was it the building? Had the mixed magic caused some kind of horrible disaster?

"It's in the courtyard!" someone shouted, then someone else pushed open the thick, misshapen front doors, and Sara was borne along with the crowd and rushed outside.

What she saw there made her stomach turn inside out.

It was the bronze statue of Gilward, the one in the middle of the courtyard. He was still there, still standing majestically with his legs apart and his hands outstretched, but now his lips were moving and he bellowed out the words, "GENPOS BEGONE!"

He said them over and over again, in a booming deep voice that sounded nothing like his own. A crowd of students had gathered to watch, and from her spot atop the front stairs Sara could see them all. Most watched in mute horror as the statue spoke, though Sara saw a group of girls she recognized from the palace who were screaming with their hands clamped over their ears. Sara saw other faces in the crowd twisted in anger, and fists balled up at people's sides. And though they tried to hide it, Sara also saw people smirking, or giggling behind their hands.

To Sara they were all just background. She was looking for only one person, though she fervently hoped he had a class out of earshot on the back fields or the outdoor classroom and didn't even know what was happening.

Her heart sank when she saw him. Galric was diagonally below her, at the bottom of the stairs, and he looked furious. His lips pressed together in a thin line, his nostrils flared, and every time the statue started another round of "Genpos begone," his jaw clenched tighter.

Sara pushed through the crowd to get to him. "Sorry . . . 'scuse me . . . sorry . . ."

"Ow! Hey—stop!" snapped Krystal. She was right next to Galric, and she wasn't budging to make room for Sara. Fine. Sara moved to Galric's other side and stood at the edge of the stair just above his, making them the exact same height. Galric didn't look at her, but he clearly knew she was there.

"He wouldn't say that," Galric said tightly. "He would *never* say that."

"Never," Sara said. "I know."

Gilward was a Mage, but Galric was a Genpo, and Gilward loved him more than anything. Never in a million years would he say anything like what his statue was bellowing now.

Krystal reached out and gripped Galric's upper arm. "I see the magical signature. Look at the corners of his mouth."

The statue stood tall on its dais; there was a long distance between it and their spot on the stairs. Sara had to squint to see what Krystal meant, but finally she did—a faint purple mist wisping from the sides of Gilward's mouth.

"Purple mist," Sara said. She was excited; now they could do something instead of just standing here. "I see it. We just need to find out who has that signature, and—"

"I *know* who has that signature," Krystal said. "It's Skeed."

"Seriously?" Sara said. "Great! I mean, not great that he's doing it, but great that we know. We can go tell Amala. Come on!"

"No!" Krystal snapped. "I'm not telling *Amala* anything. She's probably loving this. She'd shout the same thing if she wouldn't get in trouble. And I'm not busting Skeed. He's my friend."

Sara's jaw dropped. "Your *friend*? Your *friend* is doing this? And you're okay with that?"

"No, *Princess,* I'm not okay with it, but I'm not running to Amala either."

"Just stop," Galric said. "Nobody has to tell Amala. She'll see the signature and figure it out."

A blast of orange scent whooshed through the courtyard, so strong it made Sara's eyes water. The statue stopped speaking and froze in its regular pose. As a rule, magic could only be removed by the Mage who cast it, but there were exceptions. A very strong Mage could undo someone else's magic—especially magic from a weaker

Mage. Skeed may have been strong enough to move a statue's lips and make it speak, but there was no way his skills came even close to Amala's.

As it had this morning, Amala's voice boomed over the courtyard.

"The bell has sounded and fourth block has begun," she said. "If you leave right now, your tardiness will be excused. Any student who does not leave immediately will receive detention."

"That's it?" Sara said, stunned. "That's all she's gonna say? 'Go back to class'?"

"Told you," Krystal said. "She hates Genpos."

Half the crowd dispersed, but a lot of people didn't move, and Sara could tell they were as upset as she and Krystal. Then the orange scent wafted up again. "As I assured everyone this morning," Amala said, "even when you can't see me, I see you. This insult will not go without consequence, but I will also not allow it to get in the way of your school day. Leave now and be excused; stay and get detention."

That seemed to help. Everyone slowly trudged out of the courtyard. Only Galric didn't move, not even to answer the steady stream of people who acknowledged him, or clapped him on the shoulder as they walked past.

"Not cool, man."

"I'm so sorry."

"I can't believe someone would do that."

When only the three of them were left, Krystal put her hand on Galric's arm again. It was like she couldn't talk to him without touching him. "Come on," she said. "We should get to class."

"You go," Sara said. "I'll stay with him if he wants to stay."

She wasn't saying it to get rid of Krystal—at least, she wasn't saying it *entirely* to get rid of Krystal—she was genuinely trying to be helpful.

Krystal didn't take it that way. "Big sacrifice," she snorted. "Like they'd give detention to you, *Princess*."

Sara's chest tightened. "Stop calling me 'Princess.'"

"Why?" Krystal asked, tossing her dark curls. "You're the princess. I'm supposed to call you that. Would you rather 'Your Most Royal Highness Majesty'?"

She extended a leg in front of her and gave a deep bow with an ornate arm flourish.

"No! And *stop*! I've been nothing but nice to you."

Krystal was still bent low, but she picked up her head and looked at Sara with wide, sympathetic eyes and her lips in a pout. "You're right," she said. "The Princess of Kaloon deigns to be nice to me, and I don't fall to the ground and kiss her feet? What am I thinking?"

Sara's blood boiled. Her magic bubbled inside her, and she raised her hands to lash out and hit Krystal with a blast of who-knew-what . . . but the second she realized what she was doing, she gasped and wrapped her arms tightly around herself. She took deep breaths, terrified about what she'd almost done. She'd never reacted to anyone like that, but no one had ever frustrated her like this. No matter what Sara said, Krystal found a way to twist it into something she didn't mean.

Suddenly Sara heard flapping, and she looked up to see three winged scrolls, just like the kind they'd received that morning with their schedules. When they flew close, Sara and Krystal both grabbed theirs, while Galric's scroll had to flap into his cheek several times before he finally turned away from the statue of Gilward to snatch it.

"Detention," Sara said, reading the scroll she'd unrolled. "Today after school."

"Huh," Krystal said. "Who knew? I guess princesses *can* get detention."

Sara gritted her teeth. In her head she was still playing out what would have happened if she'd unleashed her magic on Krystal. She imagined the girl in the infirmary, cursed and withered like her mom after Mitzi's curse. Amala would be able to remove it, but how would Sara live with herself if she'd attacked someone like that? How could she face her parents and Flissa?

She had to keep better control of her emotions. There was no other choice.

Galric looked down at his detention scroll, then up at the statue of his father. He ran his hand over his forehead, as if pushing back the lock of hair that used to hang over his eyes. "We should go to class," he said. Then he turned to Sara. "Krystal and I have Magical Botanicals. You?"

"Same. Guess we'll all be together," Sara said as her stomach twisted into a knot. "Fun."

* * *

Magical Botanicals was exactly zero fun.

The teacher, Dame Yentley, was a short, round dumpling of a woman whom Sara knew because she hung around the palace. Literally "hung around the palace," because the woman's face was in many of the ballroom's portraits—not because she was so close with the royal family, but because every time she was at a banquet and saw a portrait being painted, she'd jump in and pose with the subject. Sara was positive Dame Yentley had never asked her, Flissa, or her parents a single question and knew nothing about them at all, but she loved to tell people they were "like family" to her and would cite all the portraits to prove it.

"Princess Sara!" Dame Yentley had gushed when Sara walked in. "I'm so thrilled you're in my class! You should know," she added, turning to the room, "that I'm practically an aunt to Princess Sara. I've spent so much time at the palace, my face is practically their wallpaper!"

She laughed far too loudly. No one joined in.

"I'm sorry we're late," Sara began, but the woman waved off her apology.

"Nonsense! No excuses among family. We've already picked lab partners, so why don't your two friends work together, and you can work with me! Won't that be scrumptious?"

Sara bit her cheeks to stop from grinning. Flissa's biggest pet peeve about Dame Yentley wasn't her social climbing, it was how she always used terms like "scrumptious," "delicious," and "yummy" to describe things that weren't food or drinks. It made Flissa crazy.

"Delectable," Sara replied, catching Galric's eye. She knew he'd get it, and she smiled as he bent his head and covered his laughing fit with a cough.

That part was fun, but then Sara spent the period stuck with Dame Yentley at the front of the room while Krystal and Galric huddled together at a lab table in the back, chatting and laughing the whole time. Now it was lunch, and as the three of them walked to the dining grounds, Galric and Krystal were still laughing about something having to do with a toadstool and a slimy bug that didn't seem funny to Sara at all. She considered walking ahead of them and just going to find Flissa—she couldn't wait to tell her about yummy Dame Yentley— but she knew Galric would want to sit with Flissa and Loriah too, so she figured she'd grit her teeth and wait out the walk.

Finally they made it to the plains between the athletic fields, the dorms, and the orphanage, where a multitude of picnic tables, troughs, bird feeders, and slop bins had been magically arranged—it had to be magically; there was no other way for everything to appear so quickly. Since they'd come all the way from the greenhouse, Sara, Galric, and Krystal were among the last to arrive, and Sara was amazed by the sheer number of people and animals. The crowd was at least three times the size of the ones at Weekly Addresses, and the noise of everyone chatting and eating was almost deafening.

Sara craned her neck. "Do you see Flissa anywhere?" she asked Galric. "Or Loriah?"

"No," Galric said. He and Krystal were scanning the crowd too, then Krystal jumped up, waving her arms.

"I see a table!" she said. "Come on!"

She grabbed Galric by the wrist and pulled him after her. Galric looked helplessly over his shoulder at Sara. "I guess we're going this way," he said.

Sara considered not following, but what if she couldn't find Flissa and Loriah? Then she'd just be wandering all by herself and friendless for the entire lunch period. Just thinking about it made her stomach clench so hard she lost her appetite. Better to stick with Galric and Krystal; at least one of them wanted her around. She followed them to a picnic table set for six, but only three people were sitting there, two guys and a girl. Krystal pulled Galric to the side with two free spots, leaving Sara to take the remaining seat on the other side of the table. It placed her directly across from Galric, which made the whole thing a little less awful.

"Hey, look!" Krystal bubbled to her friends. "I brought Galric!"

The people on Sara's side of the bench perked up at the sound of his name and greeted them. The boy next to Krystal said hi too, but he looked more like he was talking to his plate. He had long blond hair and wore as much kohl around his eyes as Sara's friend Princess Blakeley of Winterglen, who could go through a full stick in a week.

The table was filled with big dishes of stew, potatoes, vegetables, and biscuits, and Krystal was already loading up her plate when the boy next to Sara said, "Krystal, rude much? Weren't you gonna mention you brought the princess too?"

"What?" Krystal acted surprised, like she genuinely hadn't realized the omission. "Oh. Yeah. Princess Sara."

Krystal went right back to the stew, while Sara turned gratefully to the boy. He had round black glasses, spiky purple hair, and a very slight slouch that reminded her of the way Galric used to carry himself. "Hi," she said. "Nice to meet you."

"You too," he said. "Your sister was in two of my classes already. She's pretty fierce at Dodge 'Em."

"She's pretty fierce at everything. Good luck taking her on in a joust."

The boy laughed. "Not so much the jousting type. I'm more of an art guy. Skeed."

Sara froze. She recognized the name immediately. Apparently Galric did too.

"Skeed," he said. His eyes were dark and cold. "The one with the purple mist. You're the one who cursed my dad."

The kohl-eyed boy lifted his head. "That was you? Not okay, dude."

The girl on Skeed's other side leaned forward, equally scandalized. She had a ring through her nose and a bowl cut that sat so high on her head, it looked more like a hat than her hair. "How could you do that to Galric? He's, like, a hero."

Skeed held up his hands. "Seriously? I didn't do any-thing to Galric. Or to his dad. The statue's not *actually* Gilward. I just wanted to make a point."

Krystal threw a biscuit at him. "It's a bad point," she said. "Everyone here except the Princess is a Genpo—you want us all to 'begone'?"

"I do if you keep throwing food at me," Skeed said. He ripped open the biscuit and slathered it with butter. "But no, you're not the specific Genpos I want to begone."

Galric caught Sara's eye. "We should go. We'll find Flissa and Loriah."

"Great," Sara said, but Krystal quickly jumped in.

"Wait," she said. "Don't go."

"Yeah, for real," Skeed said to Galric. "I have no beef with you, and I'm sorry about your dad. I wasn't thinking about you when I did the charm."

"So what *were* you thinking about?" Sara asked.

"You really want to know? Okay." He gestured to Krystal

and her friends. "I've known these guys since birth, right? None of them knew I was a Mage until Kaloonification. I couldn't tell them. Stay in the closet, or end up in the Twists like Drew's brother or Galric's dad. You think I wanted that? I was scared out of my mind every day."

Drew, the boy with the eyeliner, sank closer to his plate, and Sara had the horrible feeling that his brother hadn't come back to the family after Kaloonification. She didn't dare ask; maybe she'd ask her parents and see if they knew. Instead she turned back to Skeed. "But that's over now," she said. "The Twists are gone. Your friends all know you're a Mage."

"Yeah, and they're cool with it, but that doesn't mean everyone is. I hear what people say. I see the looks some Genpos give me when I do magic. The Twists are gone, but lots of people wish they weren't. They still hate me, they just know it's not cool anymore to say it out loud. So yeah, I did some magic to mess with the Genpos. *Those* Genpos. I didn't hurt anybody, I just wanted to scare them a little like they scared me." He looked across the table at Galric. "You get it, right? We okay?"

Galric's jaw was still working, but the fire had drained from his eyes. He ran his fingers through that missing lock of hair and sighed. "Yeah," he said. "You're not wrong. It's all pretty messed up. Just . . . from now on leave my dad out of it, okay?"

"Deal." Skeed pressed his hands together like he was going to start that battlefield handshake. Galric did the same, and Sara thought they were about to get up and lean over the table to do it, but instead they just nodded and lowered their hands again. Sara supposed this was the long-distance version of the handshake and made a mental note to avoid pressing her hands together like that in front of anyone ever.

Then Sara heard something—voices, speaking in a low chant, but she couldn't make out the words. "Does anybody else hear that?" she asked.

On the other side of the table, Drew's kohl-lined eyes went wide. "No. Way."

Whatever he saw, Galric and Krystal must have seen it too. Galric's jaw dropped, and Krystal froze with a spoonful of stew halfway to her mouth.

Sara wheeled around, but there were too many people and she couldn't see over their heads. Then she stood on her picnic bench and saw it.

Nine Keepers of the Light marched toward the lunch area.

Not real Keepers. They couldn't be. Those were all gone. But she saw nine people in bright yellow Keepers robes, each with a matching hood that covered their head, except for two small eye-slits for eyes. They chanted together as they marched, and Sara heard a mix of male and female voices, all calling out as they pumped their fists in the air.

"MAGES BELONG IN CA-GES! MAGES BELONG IN CA-GES!"

Chapter 9
Flissa

Flissa had already started eating when she heard the chant. She was at a table with Loriah, Zinka, and three other Untwisteds. She'd tried to find Sara, but the dining area was too crowded, and Loriah reminded her that Sara was *Sara*—she'd have no trouble finding new friends to eat with.

There were so many people and animals around and everything was so noisy, at first the voices blended into the background. Flissa vaguely registered them at the back of her mind, a new, rhythmic cadence that had joined the din.

Then she saw them. Nine yellow frocks in a clump. *That's so strange*, she thought. *It's odd enough that Jentrie wore a Keeper-yellow dress, but* nine *people? Apparently the whole kingdom needs Primkas.*

But Zinka was next to her, and when she saw the group, she grabbed the picnic table like she could dig her fingers into the wood.

"Oh no," Zinka said. "No. Inexcusable."

That's when Flissa realized the people weren't in

dresses at all. They were in actual Keepers robes, with hoods over their faces. And their voices were a blend of male and female.

"MAGES BELONG IN CA-GES!" they chanted. "MAGES BELONG IN CA-GES!"

As they marched closer to the picnic tables, Flissa realized everyone had gone silent. Zinka jounced her knee up and down.

"Let's get 'em," she said. "Right now. Before they get any closer. Let's do it."

"No," Flissa said. "We don't want to start a riot."

"*They're* starting the riot," said Dallie. She was a friend of Zinka's who was built like a battering ram, with a headful of bright blue curls and a silver ring through one of her eyebrows. "We'll just finish it."

Flissa's heart thudded as she realized she was at a table full of time bombs. Every girl there bristled and looked poised to strike.

Every girl except Loriah, who busily sopped up the last of her stew with a biscuit. "The biscuits are really good. 'Specially with the gravy. Ring-brow, can you pass some more stew?"

Dallie looked at her, incredulous. "How can you eat right now?"

"Same as any other time. I put the food in my mouth, chew, and swallow. You think I care what the Genpos are saying? Let 'em come at me. I can take 'em."

"Nobody's 'taking' anybody," Flissa said. "Other people will get hurt."

"Not if we take 'em down fast enough," Zinka said.

"MAGES BELONG IN CA-GES! MAGES BELONG IN CA-GES!"

Flissa could feel the tension radiating from every table. She wished she could pull out her message milk and call her parents, but she was afraid if she looked away for even a second, Zinka and her friends would start fighting. She didn't blame them; she wanted to stop the chanters too. But a battle between Mages and Genpos would be death for Kaloonification. It was her parents' worst fear.

"Let's just wait and see what Amala does," Flissa said. "She won't let this go."

"She'd better not," Zinka said.

Flissa's picnic table was right next to the faculty tables. She could see Amala eye the marchers as they stomped between her table and Flissa's . . . but the Shadow didn't do anything. It was Teacher Lazando who jumped to his feet and ran into the marchers' path. "You *cannot* come here dressed like that!" he yelled, his voice quavering. "And you can't say what you're saying! That is definitely against school rules."

The first Keeper in line strode past him without even slowing. "MAGES BELONG IN CA-GES!"

Flissa's spine tingled. She knew that voice. And when she looked closer, she could see strands of blond hair peeking out from under the hood.

Jentrie.

Teacher Lazando looked pleadingly to Amala, but she only met his eyes and shook her head the littlest bit.

"MAGES BELONG IN CA-GES! MAGES BELONG IN CA-GES!"

"You're not making sense, you know that?!" Teacher Lazando shouted after the marchers. "You say you're against Mages but you're dressed in Keepers robes! Keepers were Mages! This is only a win for irony!"

Teacher Lazando may not have convinced Amala to act, but his shouting opened the floodgates for everyone else. As the group marched into the center of the dining area, every picnic table and animal feeder erupted into shouts and screams. People stood on tables. They threw food. They howled.

And some, Flissa realized, took up the marchers' chant.

Zinka looked at Amala, who was still stone-faced.

"I waited," Zinka told Flissa. "She's doing nothing. It's on."

She pushed her plates aside, then climbed onto the picnic table and raised a fist in the air. "GET THE GRUNTS!" she screamed.

"Zinka, wait!" Flissa said, but it was too late. Zinka's battle cry carried over the din, and within seconds the dining area was filled with magical signatures: sounds and flashes and mists and scents . . . too many to possibly distinguish.

With all that magic mixing together, this wouldn't just be a riot, it would be a massacre.

Yet even though magical signatures flew everywhere, none of them hit their targets. The marchers stood tall as every mist, sparkle, and glow hurled at them burst apart on what seemed like a tall invisible dome, then harmlessly dissipated away.

"They have a shield," Flissa said, "but they're not Mages. So how . . . ?"

Only then did she realize the dining area smelled like an orange grove. She looked at Amala. The woman sat straight and tall on her picnic bench, her waterfall of snowy-white hair draped over her shoulders and down her back. Her eyes were closed, her face calm and expressionless. She was the one shielding the marchers.

"ENOUGH!"

Amala hadn't moved; Flissa was staring right at her. But her voice thundered through the dining area, brash and full of fury.

"NO MORE CURSES!"

"That's a big head," Loriah said, which made absolutely no sense to Flissa until she turned away from Amala and saw the Shadow had somehow projected a mountainous version of her head into the air above the marchers, her face twisted in absolute fury.

"What is the fourth rule of the Magical Unification Act?" the head boomed.

No one answered. The dining area was utterly silent, though Flissa saw that the marchers' mouths were moving and they looked agitated. The shield Amala put over them must be soundproof.

"I will wait," Amala's head said. It set its enormous jaw, and Flissa had a feeling it would wait a very long time. Reluctantly Flissa moved her plates and stepped up next to Zinka on the table.

"No Mage shall use their powers to control or harm another human or Magical Animal," Flissa recited.

Across the dining area a boy also stood on a table, placing him high enough that Flissa could see his purple hair and glasses. It was Skeed, from her Athletics class. "With the exception of clear acts of self-defense!" he shouted, finishing the act. "That's what we're doing; we're defending ourselves!"

The massive nostrils on Amala's projected face flared. "No, you are not. The people below me said loathsome things, and there will be consequences, but their words cannot physically harm you. The combined magic hurled at them was far more dangerous."

"Debatable," Flissa heard Teacher Lazando mutter. Flissa agreed. Words had power too, sometimes more than magic.

"From the very beginning of the day," Amala's projection said, "students from all sects of Kaloon have tried to sabotage this school and what we stand for. I won't allow it, and you will not win. Maldevon Academy—and Kaloonification—will succeed. We *will* stand together."

"Says the Cleaner," Zinka snorted under her breath. "Pretty sure she'd be okay if only *some* of us stood together."

Flissa didn't believe that. If Amala really wanted to get rid of Genpos, she could have let the riot go on. Whoever she'd been before, Flissa was confident she'd changed and truly wanted to bring Kaloon together.

"I'm canceling classes for the rest of the day," Amala's projection said. "Boarders, return to your dorms. Day students, report to the front of the building; we're already calling carriages to pick you up. All after-school detentions and sports tryouts will be moved to tomorrow. And there *will* be a tomorrow, have no doubt. This is not a win for those trying to stop Kaloonification. This is a moment to regroup, replan . . . and consider repercussions."

She cast her eyes down to the marchers. "As for the

nine of you, you're right now in the middle of what could become a very angry mob. I suggest you take this moment to go far away, and get rid of those disgusting robes and hoods. And please know—and this goes for *all* of you"— Amala looked out over the crowd to include everyone—"I see you. Even when you don't see me, *I. See. You.*"

She stopped speaking and waited. The hooded marchers looked at one another, then ran. Amala gave them time to disappear behind the building, then addressed the crowd again. "Don't look for them. You won't succeed. Please simply proceed in an orderly fashion to your dorm or the carriage area. Thank you for a highly informative first day of school, and I look forward to seeing every single one of you tomorrow."

The apparition of her face dissolved into wisps of smoke, and Flissa watched as the actual Amala blinked her eyes open, then quickly rose from her picnic table and strode toward the main building. The other faculty members got up and roamed through the crowd, shouting instructions.

"You heard Amala!"

"Boarders to the dorms, day students to the carriages!"

"Move it! Let's get going!"

Zinka rolled her eyes as she stepped down from the picnic table. "Amala should have let the spells go. It'd serve 'em right."

Loriah snorted, and Zinka frowned at her. "What, you don't agree?"

"No, I don't," Loriah said. "'Get the Grunts'? What's wrong with you?"

"If you don't want to stick up for us, then something's wrong with *you*," Zinka said.

"We're not an 'us,'" Loriah said. "I stick up for *me*, and I don't do it by proving the ignorant Grunts right and acting like an out-of-control monster that belongs in the Twists."

"You think I belong in the Twists?" Zinka said.

"I think you're acting like it, yeah," Loriah shot back.

The two were toe to toe, and even though Zinka was taller and stronger, Loriah looked just as fierce. Their eyes burned with fire, and Flissa knew if one of them threw a punch, the battle wouldn't end until they were both destroyed.

"Hey, hi, hello," said Teacher Lazando as he pushed his way between Loriah and Zinka. "Couldn't help but notice things were getting a little heated here, so, Loriah, why don't you head back to the dorms, and, Zinka, you take a couple minutes to cool off here before you go back too, okay?"

Loriah shrugged like she'd never been upset at all. "Sure." She grabbed the basket of biscuits and dumped them into a napkin. "But I'm taking these to go."

"*All* of them?" Dallie asked.

Loriah raised an eyebrow. "You really want one?"

She tossed a biscuit at Dallie. It smacked her right on her eyebrow ring before it ricocheted into her hands.

"There you go," Loriah said. "Bye, Fliss. Bubblegram you later."

She walked off, then Teacher Lazando moved closer to Flissa and spoke to her gently. "We really do want to get everyone out of here quickly, so I hate to rush you away from your friends, but . . ."

He rolled onto his tiptoes; he clearly didn't want to give Flissa a direct order. She smiled. "It's okay. I'll go."

"Thanks," he said. "And don't worry. This is a blip. A growing pain. Everything you did, everything people fought for, we'll get there for sure."

He disappeared back into the crowd, ordering students to disperse, while Flissa said goodbye to Zinka and her friends, then walked quickly back toward the main building. She had already reached the top of the stairs when she heard, "Flissa! *Flissa!*"

She turned. For the briefest of seconds, the girl with the puffy curls and the earrings was unfamiliar, then she remembered her twin didn't look exactly like her anymore. Sara waved her arm wildly at the bottom of the stairs and stumbled because she wasn't looking where she was going. Galric was right next to her and caught her, then she said something to him, and he looked up and waved too. Flissa saw they were with Krystal—the girl from this morning— plus Skeed and a couple of other people Flissa didn't know.

"Hey!" Sara cried. She threw her arms around Flissa when she reached her, and Flissa almost cried. She'd done well enough on her own, she supposed, and she'd only been away from Sara for a couple of class periods—they'd spent far more hours apart when they were Princess Flissara— but it was such a relief to be back together that Flissa had no idea how she'd managed without her.

"Crazy day, huh?" Galric said as they started the walk through the main building and down to the line of waiting carriages.

"'Crazy'?" Krystal echoed incredulously. "Somebody could have died."

Skeed rolled his eyes. "No one died."

"I didn't say they did, I said they *could have*," Krystal retorted.

"I wonder if they'll shut down the school," Galric said.

"Maybe," Sara said, at the exact same time as Flissa said, "*No.*"

Flissa frowned as she looked at her sister. "You really think Mother and Father will give up that easily? You think the General Council will give up? And Amala?"

Sara shrugged. "Maybe it's not about giving up. Maybe everyone just needs more time to get used to Kaloonification. *Then* we could all go to school together."

Flissa was surprised. For the last six months, Sara had urged their parents to open the school even sooner. "You really think that?"

Sara blushed, like Flissa had caught her in a lie. "I dunno, maybe. I mean, even if you forget all the fighting, the school's dangerous. The walls stretch and move around. What if they break?"

Flissa noticed her sister wasn't meeting her eyes. "I thought you liked the way everything moved around."

"I'm just saying, the school isn't really what anyone expected," Sara said, her words tumbling faster. "So who knows what anyone will do?"

Sara, Flissa, and Galric had reached the front of the carriage line. They said their goodbyes to Krystal and Skeed and piled in, then Sara immediately rested her head against the carriage wall and closed her eyes.

Flissa understood. It had only been half a day, but she

125

was tired too. She mirrored Sara's position and let the carriage rock her to sleep. As she started to doze, she thought about how strange it was. This morning Flissa would have done anything to see Maldevon Academy disappear, but after just half a day she was willing to fight for it to stay.

Chapter 10
Sara

"How did you not hear about this?" Sara railed. "Are you sure you were at the same school as me today?"

Sara, Flissa, and Galric were in the ballroom, sitting at one of the big, round tables with the king and queen, Katya, and Rouen. Nitpick was in Galric's lap, helping himself to the tuna sandwich on Galric's plate. Filliam had provided an excellent afternoon tea complete with scones, finger sandwiches, and delicate pastries, but none of them were in the mood to eat.

"It's not like I heard *nothing*. I heard whispers and things, but nobody told me the whole story. What happened?"

Sara couldn't believe it. A statue of Gilward came to life and shouted "Genpos begone" and Flissa didn't know? Even Katya had heard the story by bubblegram, and she now explained it to Flissa, who sat back from the table, stunned. "When did this happen?" she asked.

"After third block," Galric said. He'd spent the entire story focusing on Nitpick, feeding him tiny bits of sandwich from his finger. "That's why Sara and I have detention. We were late for fourth block."

"Really, Sara?" Queen Latonya sounded disappointed. "Detention? On your first day?"

King Edwin's mustache drooped, and he shook his head.

"Because I was supporting my friend!" Sara retorted.

"To be fair," Rouen said, "we have bigger things to worry about than a detention. Now tell us everything that happened. You don't have to give names if you don't want to; Amala will know, and she can tell us when we see her."

They went through all of it. They started with the stink spell, which Sara very much wanted to say came from Zinka, but she knew Flissa would deny it like she had in Magic Lab. It was fine, though; Rouen was right. Sara didn't have to say anything, because Amala would know the truth. Same with Skeed and Gilward's statue; if Krystal saw his magical signature, Amala must have too. As for the people in the Keepers robes, Sara had no idea who any of them were; she couldn't have named them even if she'd wanted to.

"There was also that thing with the Magical Animals," Galric said.

This was news to Sara. "The Magical Animals?" Sara asked, leaning forward in her seat. "I didn't hear anything about them."

"I didn't either," Flissa said. "What happened?"

"It was in Chemistry class," Galric said. "You probably didn't hear about it because only Genpos take it. And Magical Animals, since they can't cast spells."

"*Mostly* can't cast spells," Flissa said, and Sara knew she was thinking about Raya, the lion who'd captured them in the Twists. She cast incredibly powerful spells, so powerful they'd barely escaped with their lives.

"Right," Galric said. "Mostly. So they take Chemistry with us; you have Magic Lab instead. I didn't have it today, but Krystal did. It's in an outdoor classroom and a bunch of animals had spelled out 'Animal Independence' on the floor in, um . . . well, in . . ."

He was blushing and pained as he looked at the king and queen, like he couldn't bear to say the word in front of them.

"Poop!" Katya cried. "You mean poop, am I right? Just say poop! You worked the manure pits, for the universe's sake, it's poop!"

Galric turned even redder. "Yeah. Poop."

"'Animal Independence,'" Flissa mused. "That's a lot of poop."

"How did Krystal know it was a bunch of animals, and not just one?" Sara asked. Then Galric raised an eyebrow and she realized. "Oh, right. Different poop."

The king let out a deep sigh and pushed back from the table. "So no one's happy, then. Not the Mages, not the Genpos, not the Magical Animals . . ."

Sara sat up taller. Just this morning, she'd been aching to go to school, but the entire day had been a disaster. She'd said all the wrong things to all the wrong people, she'd landed in trouble, and she'd completely tanked her magic class. It wasn't like her. She was always great in new situations. So maybe school just wasn't her place. It didn't make her a failure; it just meant she'd learned her lesson and she should stick to what worked for her.

"Dad, maybe it's not that everyone's unhappy," she suggested. "Maybe they're just not happy with *school*. Maybe it's too soon. I bet if you shut it down and started it back up again in a year or two . . ." Sara quickly tallied up how many more years before she wouldn't have to go, then added, "Or seven, everything would be a lot better."

Flissa fixed her with a penetrating stare. "You said that before, that maybe it's too soon. But I don't think that's right. If we give up on Maldevon Academy, we may as well give up on Kaloonification. It's like Amala said—we can't let the dissenters win."

Sara stared at her sister, openmouthed. She knew Flissa hadn't wanted to go to school in the first place. Not at all. Why was she defending it now?

"You're exactly right, Flissa," Queen Latonya said, and Sara's stomach sank. Their mom rose to her feet and all the other adults—plus Galric, who took a little extra time to first settle Nitpick in his arms—did the same. "We're all heading to the academy to talk to Amala. Sit, Galric. Enjoy the tea. Then if you have any homework to do, get to it because there *will* be class tomorrow."

They all said their goodbyes, Sara's parents kissing her and Flissa on the tops of their heads on the way out. Katya gathered hugs from all three of them before she left, and Rouen clasped the girls on the shoulder, then tousled Galric's hair.

"Looks like it'll all be okay," Flissa said. She had a weird, giddy smile on her face that Sara didn't understand at all. "I'm going to head upstairs and start my homework. I've got a ten-page paper due at the end of the week!"

She scampered out of the room. Galric stared after her in disbelief. "Is it just me," he asked, "or did she say 'ten-page paper' like a normal person would say 'It's my birthday'?"

"Not just you," Sara assured him.

"I guess we should do homework too," Galric said. "Maybe we could work together on the Magical Botanicals paragraph?"

Sara considered it—homework would be a lot less miserable if she was doing it with Galric—but what she really needed was a break from all things Maldevon Academy.

"How about a walk instead?" she asked.

If Sara could have asked for one thing to make her day better, the smile Galric gave her would have been it.

"Yeah," he said. "I'd love that."

They didn't go anywhere special, just grabbed the remaining scones and walked the grounds and chatted about nothing and everything. He told her all about his day—all the things that happened when they weren't together—and seeing the school through his eyes made it seem less awful. She even laughed out loud at some of the stories he told about Krystal. He made her sound funny and goofy and exactly the kind of girl Sara would want to hang out with.

Maybe she'd just had a bad start. Maybe tomorrow would be better. Maybe she'd end up like Galric and Flissa and probably every other person and animal at the school who wasn't actively protesting, and she'd love it.

"Thanks," Sara said.

Galric looked confused. He gave a half smile that showed the new dimple under his eye. "For what?"

"Nothing," she said. "I mean, you know, just . . . everything. For being my friend, I guess."

He gave her a goofy look. "Okay. I mean . . . yeah, of course."

The "duh" was implied, and it made Sara smile.

"Hey, guess where we are," she said.

She expected him to say, "The stables," or "The field," or some other answer that would be correct, but not what she was going for. Instead he looked right into her eyes and said, "Easy. It's the spot where we met."

Sara's heart fluttered. She expected that even less than she expected him to get the "right" answer.

"Yeah," she said, suddenly breathless. "The exact spot."

She met his eyes, and she couldn't explain it, but for the first time she felt like she was looking *inside* him, not just *at* him, and she couldn't look away. She didn't want to. And it seemed like he didn't either.

The fluttering moved to her stomach, and her ears felt hot.

She turned away and nudged a dandelion with her foot, purposely breaking the spell. "I mean, maybe not the *exact* spot," she said. "It's not like I put up a plaque."

"Right," Galric agreed, and started ambling back in the direction of the palace. Sara fell into step next to him. "I mean, you *commissioned* the plaque; you just haven't put it up yet."

"Well, yeah," she said, "of course I commissioned it."

She looked away so he wouldn't see how wide she was smiling.

* * *

"Students of Maldevon Academy," Amala's disembodied voice rang out over the courtyard.

It was the next day, and Sara felt newly abuzz as she stood with Loriah, Flissa, and Galric. Like the day before, Amala had them all gather together before she opened the doors and magically addressed them from wherever she actually was.

"Welcome back. Yesterday was less than ideal. Today is a fresh start, but with this warning: Maldevon Academy has a zero-tolerance policy when it comes to discrimination. Violators won't be expelled; you won't get off that easily. Instead violators will spend even more time in the academic buildings, working closely with myself and the faculty to spearhead our Kaloonification programs."

People and animals in the crowd murmured to one another. Everyone sounded dubious, but Sara saw the poetry in it. The people under the Keepers robes yesterday would probably love to be expelled, and working on some kind of program to strengthen Kaloonification was a perfect punishment for them. She wasn't sure how it would work on someone like Skeed, who had real issues with some of the Genpos, but maybe if he and some of the marchers from yesterday had to work together, it would make a difference to them both.

"To that end, I'm announcing an event: a ball, right here in our fields. The king and queen will be here, the General Council, and of course all of your parents. The ball will occur in four weeks, to celebrate both the end of the first month of school, and the true Kaloonification of our sects: Mages and Genpos who always lived in Kaloon, Mages and Genpos who lived in the Twists, and Magical Animals. The planning committee, who will report directly to me, will consist of representatives from each of these groups. Will the following students please stand at the top of the stairs by the main doors so everyone can see you?"

Sara thought she knew what was coming, and when she met Galric's and Flissa's eyes she saw that they did too. Loriah looked disinterested, but since she generally had resting over-it face, Sara wasn't sure it really meant anything.

"Skeed! Jentrie! Zinka! Nikkolas! Anastasia!"

The crowd murmured and shifted to let the five students through. Three of them were no surprise—Flissa had told Sara late last night about Jentrie, and she'd told Flissa about Skeed. Of the other two, one was a tall boy who looked old enough to be in his completion year. His thick dark hair hung perfectly straight, he wore round glasses with thin wire frames, and he even had a light goatee. Given that the fifth one up there was Anastasia the boar—the same boar Sara had inadvertently insulted yesterday—the boy had to be Nikkolas. He was the only one who looked happy to be up there, smiling and nodding to friends in the crowd. Skeed, meanwhile, slouched and examined his fingernails, while Zinka stood with her hands defiantly on her hips, and Jentrie crossed her arms over her chest and seethed. Anastasia . . . well, to Sara she still just looked the way big bristly boars look.

Galric leaned close to Sara and murmured, "Guess we know who was behind the poop-fest in the Chemistry room."

"I know," she whispered back. "So not cool of Nikkolas."

They both pursed their lips together so they wouldn't laugh. Sara was sure Amala would know if they did.

"So, everyone," Amala's voice rang out, "give a warm

Maldevon Academy welcome to our first . . . Ambassadors of Kaloonification!"

Sara looked at Flissa, and Galric—should they applaud? The rest of the crowd seemed to wonder the same thing . . . maybe because Jentrie, Zinka, and Skeed all scowled like they dared anyone to do it. Then Loriah hooted at the top of her lungs. "WOOO-HOOO!!! Kaloonification! Zinkaaa!" She clapped loudly enough for the sound to echo through the courtyard, which made other students join in. As they did, Loriah grinned and leaned closer to Sara. "I hate that girl," she said.

Sara laughed and joined the applause.

"Listen to that," Amala said. "Already bringing everyone together. Well done. Look for scrolls so you'll know when to meet me, Ambassadors. Until then . . ."

The bell rang and everyone piled into the main building. Sara left her sister and her friends with a huge smile, positive that today would be a perfect day.

She was wrong.

It wasn't the *worst* day, she just wasn't herself. She didn't want to mess up, so she sat in the back of all her classes, kept her head down, and didn't talk to anyone. She didn't even talk to Flissa in Magic Lab because Flissa was deep into some kind of Zinka drama—something about her first Ambassadors of Kaloonificaion meeting getting in the way of hoodle tryouts. Sara couldn't even enjoy seeing Galric at Magical Botanicals since she had to hang out with Dame Yentley, and lunch was a bust because Skeed was convinced the king and queen gave Amala the Ambassadors of Kaloonification idea, and he blamed Sara for it. She had no energy to convince him he was wrong, so she left the table to roam the topiary garden. She thought maybe she'd at least enjoy the solitude, but even that backfired when she got lost and wound up late for Athletics. Teacher Lazando didn't give her a detention, but she fell during Dodge 'Em and spent the rest of the day with a giant grass stain on her butt that wouldn't come out, no matter how much she tried to magically erase it. Even her Art class, which was taught by her friend Dorinda the glassblower, was a disaster because when she went up to hug Dorinda, the whole room laughed at her grassy rear end.

When the final bell rang, Sara nearly cheered out loud.

She'd been wrong to give school a second chance. It wasn't for her, and she had to find a way out of it . . . but first she had to go home and sleep for as long as humanly possible.

Maybe the next seven years.

Instead, the second she stepped out of Art class, a flying scroll smacked into her face. Confused, she opened it.

Detention. The one she'd received yesterday. She'd totally forgotten. Her heart sank when she realized she'd have to stay in this building for at least another hour.

Second floor, the scroll said. That's where she had to go.

Sara didn't know the school *had* a second floor.

Then she saw ink bleeding through from the scroll's back side, where she found a map. She followed it over undulating hills in the floor to a spot in the middle of a hall.

There were no steps in the middle of the hall.

How was she supposed to get to the second floor?

"Look up."

Sara turned and saw Zinka, Flissa's friend.

Flissa's friend. It was a weird thing to think.

She and Flissa had always had the same friends. Maybe Loriah was a little closer to Flissa than to her, but she was definitely friends with them both. If anything, Sara had always been the one to have friends outside their twosome, even if she was living a bit of a lie with them as Princess Flissara.

Zinka, however, was definitely Flissa's friend . . . so it was weird she seemed to know where Sara was going.

"How do you know?" Sara asked.

"You're trying to go upstairs, right?" Zinka asked. "Me too. For this stupid Ambassadors thing. Look up."

Sara did. There was a door right in the middle of the ceiling, complete with a round, dangling knocker.

"Yo," Zinka called. "Open up."

The door swung open and a rope ladder dropped down. Zinka jumped onto it. "See ya," she said, then scrambled up the rope and disappeared.

Climbing. Climbing was not Sara's friend. She closed her eyes, tilted back her head, and moaned, which was of course the exact moment when a pack of older boys walked down the hall and laughed together about the "crazy princess."

Perfect.

Sara sighed and grabbed hold of a high ladder rung, put her feet on a lower rung . . . and immediately the ladder started swinging back and forth.

"Oh no . . ." she said under her breath. "Oh no . . ."

She could barely keep her balance and struggled to put each hand and foot higher than the other. She remembered climbing up the long stone wall beneath the palace, that night she and Flissa slipped away with Galric, and she thought about his advice: Don't look down.

She didn't. She kept her eyes focused on the doorway, even when she heard snickering voices below.

"Is that the *princess*?"

"What is she doing?"

"Check out her butt—that's a *huge* grass stain!"

Soon she was covered in sweat and it felt like she'd been climbing forever, but the ceiling was no closer. How was that even possible?

Knowing it was a bad idea, she looked down.

The students below were ants.

That's how it was possible—the building had stretched while she was climbing. She forced herself to speed up and try to outpace the magically growing academy. By the time she smacked her hands onto the second level and rolled onto the floor, she was soaked, panting for breath, and every muscle ached.

"I hate this school," she said out loud. "I hate it so much."

Still lying on her back, she unfurled her detention scroll again. Sure enough, a new map had appeared, one detailing the second floor. Sara struggled to her feet and followed it.

The upstairs halls weren't like the ones below. Whatever mansion the builders of Maldevon Academy had smacked down on top of the others to make this level had stayed relatively intact . . . just upside down. The furniture had been rearranged so it was now right-side up, but Sara had to watch her step as she walked because the floor was clearly once a coffered ceiling, with protruding beams and wooden carvings.

Sara followed the map to her detention room. The door began above her knee level, and was flush with the ceiling instead of the floor, so she clumsily climbed in. The room was filled with student desks and a larger desk for a teacher, where a pelican sat reading a book. Without looking up from it, he pointed to the blackboard behind him, which read *Detention: No Talking and Do Work Until Dismissed.*

Krystal and Galric were already at two adjacent desks. Sara collapsed into the seat on Galric's other side and leaned back, gulping for air.

She heard a light tap on her desk, then looked down and saw a folded piece of parchment had landed there. Next to her, Galric checked to make sure the pelican wasn't looking, then raised his eyebrows as if to say *Open it.*

Sara did. *U ok?* it said. *U look terrible.*

Sara turned his parchment over, pulled a pen from her bag, and wrote back, *Rope ladder up here the worst. How u and K get here so fast?* She folded and tossed him the note. He frowned as he read it, then wrote back his response. *What rope ladder? We took moving stairs outside lower rotunda.*

Sara let her head flop down onto her desk and didn't move again until the pelican shook her shoulder.

"You fell asleep," he said. "Detention's over. I already sent the others away."

Sara hadn't even realized she'd been napping. She felt

thick and disoriented . . . and she really had to use the bathroom. She got directions from the pelican, but once she clambered over the high threshold of the doorway, she had no idea where she was. She wandered the bizarrely upside-down halls, looking for someone she could ask. Then she heard a familiar voice.

"What you have to understand is that Mages are naturally superior to Genpos."

It was Amala.

"Look how helpless they are. They're no match for you at all."

Sara's skin prickled. The voice was coming from a room just ahead and to the left. She sidled closer and peeked around the doorjamb.

Inside was what must have been a formal ballroom in Grosselor's days. The once-ceiling-now-floor was beamed with gold and covered in intricate oil paintings, while the once-floor-now-ceiling was covered in diamonds of silver, gold, and white marble. Amala stood in the center of the room, with Zinka, Anastasia, and Skeed in front of her, their faces rapt.

Floating in the air were Jentrie and Nikkolas. Both were on their backs, completely prone, mouths open and eyes closed. They were unconscious.

"With a thought, I could take over their bodies and have them do my bidding. I could turn them into trees. I could whisk them far away from Kaloon, so far they could never come back," Amala said. "You could have that kind of power too. Even you, Anastasia, with the right training. There's a reason I chose the three of you. I'm counting on you. I need you to work with me and hone your skills. I

140

need you to spread the word to the right people and animals. If we work together, we can change everything. We can make the world we want."

Sara's heart thudded.

She had just stumbled into the real truth behind Amala: The Shadow hadn't changed at all. She was still the Cleaner. She still planned to get rid of all the Genpos.

And she was going to use Zinka, Anastasia, and Skeed to do it.

Chapter 11
Flissa

Flissa stood on the hoodle field, knees bent and ready to run. She was already panting and sore, but she felt energized, not tired. She was glad Zinka had urged her to try out for the team. Flissa loved sports, and Maldevon Academy offered several—some separated by gender, some by age, some that required magic or were for animals only. In theory Flissa could have taken her pick, but she never would have had the courage to try out at all if it weren't for Zinka.

Hoodle at Maldevon had four different teams, two for girls and two for boys, both separated by age. Flissa was going out for the Girls' Firsts-through-Fourths (FTF) Team, and while she'd never even played hoodle before today, she picked it up easily. She'd played hoodle*hoop*, of course, but that was very different—a child's way to have fun with the same equipment their parents and older siblings used.

A hoodle field was about the length of a jousting field, with a goal at each end. Yet unlike a jousting field, which was perfectly flat, a hoodle field had natural obstacles built in—different ones at every field. They could include hills, boulders, mud pits . . . One person in the group said she'd played on a field in Winterglen that had a stream running right through the middle. All these obstacles were part of the game, and using them was part of the strategy.

A game started when two centers faced off, and a referee threw a hoodlehoop between them. Once a center caught the hoodlehoop on her hoodlehook—a long stick with a crooked end—the game was on.

The rules were simple: Players had to stay inbounds, they couldn't touch the hoodlehoop with their hands, and they had to keep the hoodlehoop spinning on their hoodlehook. To get the hoodlehoop, players could hook the hoop off someone else's hook, intercept a passed hoodlehoop, or slam someone else's hook with theirs so the hoop fell off and the slammer could take it. The aim was to get the hoodlehoop around the opponents' goalpost. The team with the most hoops on the other team's goalpost at the end of the game was the winner.

Flissa twirled her hoodlehook in her hand and waited for Coach Rian to start the game, but the ostrich was in no hurry. She wandered the field, examining the players, checking to see if she'd made the right choices for this final scrimmage.

Twenty girls had come to try out—twenty-one counting Zinka, who had a bubblegram excuse from Amala and joined in late. Twelve were on the field now, six per side. Only nine would make the team.

Flissa was slotted at right forward. Next to her, Loriah stood poised to strike at left forward. She'd sworn she wouldn't go out for the team, but Flissa had promised her a basket of Filliam's blarnage muffins if she agreed. Loriah might have joined in reluctantly, but once she was on the field, she was too competitive to do anything but fight.

Zinka stood in front of them, their center. She'd been acting tense and snappy all day. Flissa had noticed at Magic Lab that a few of her nails were broken down to the quick, and she had dark circles under her eyes. During class, Flissa had assumed Zinka's stress was because she was worried about juggling her Ambassadors meeting and hoodle tryouts, but that wasn't an issue anymore. She was here on the field, but she was still rubbing her eyes and shaking her head like she had to snap herself back to reality.

"Zinka . . . you okay?" Flissa whispered.

"I'm fine!" Zinka hissed. "Now get ready to play. I don't want to get cut 'cause we're not paying attention."

Flissa set her jaw and moved back into her stance.

"Here we go," Coach Rian declared. "Game on!"

She picked up a hoodlehoop and twirled it on her wing, then tossed it in the air between Zinka and the opposing center. The other girl caught it easily . . . until Zinka slammed her hook with her own and jarred the hoop loose. It rolled on the ground, and Zinka scooped it onto her hook and spun it down the field. Flissa and Loriah both ran full speed, each eager to get open in case Zinka needed to pass. Beverly-Ann, a chimpanzee, was all over Flissa, but Flissa feinted left, then ran to the right, losing Beverly-Ann just as Zinka hurled the hoop her way. Flissa jumped up and snagged it out of the air. When Beverly-Ann barreled after her, Flissa raced up the nearest boulder, leaped over Dallie, who was playing blocker on the other team, and hurled the hoop to Loriah, who was wide open near the goalpost. Loriah flung the hoop with the perfect touch—it didn't even tap the post as it soared down over it and smacked to the ground.

"YES!" Zinka roared. She ran to Flissa and high-fived her, then did a double fist pound with Loriah, who cried out, "Killin' it, sister!"

"'Sister'?" Flissa asked under her breath as she and Loriah trotted back into position for the next toss.

"What?" Loriah said. "It's a battle. We're winning. Doesn't mean I like her."

Whether they all liked each other or not, Loriah, Zinka, and Flissa made a formidable offensive trio. By the time Coach Rian rang the finishing gong, their side had clobbered the other team, twelve to two.

"Good game, everyone," Coach Rian said. "Time to line up."

The players all stood in a line as the ostrich paced, looking them up and down. Flissa's heart thumped. She wanted this. Badly.

"You all played well," Coach Rian said, "but you can't all make the cut. Here's who I want. Center, Zinka."

Zinka smiled and nodded, like she knew it was coming and wouldn't have accepted anything less.

"Right blocker, Beverly-Ann."

"Yes!" the chimp pumped her fist.

"Left blocker, Trinni."

Trinni hollered as she fell to her knees and gave a fist pump. Flissa didn't know Trinni well, but she was fearless on the hoodle field. She had long dark hair pulled back in a ponytail and possibly the loudest voice Flissa had ever heard.

145

"Goalie, Dallie."

"Yeah-yeah-yeah!" Dallie ran at Zinka, leaped into the air, and chest-bumped her.

"Left and right forward, Flissa and Loriah."

"We did it!" Flissa cried, grabbing Loriah's arm. "We did it, we did it, we did it!"

"Uh-huh," Loriah said. "And now you're squeezing my arm, which I need to play the game, so . . ."

Flissa let go. "You're happy, though. I can see it. You're smiling."

"Am not," Loriah said, smiling wider.

"Three alternates, Nichelle, Odelia, and Rosalie. And yes, I'm well aware Rosalie is my daughter, but she's also exceptionally good, so I don't want to hear it. Everyone else, better luck next time. Those of you who made it, first practice after school tomorrow." As the girls who were cut walked off, Flissa saw Coach Rian smile for the very first time that day. "Congratulations, team," she said. "Rosalie, come on. We're going home."

"Congratulations, everyone!" Rosalie cried as she ran off with the coach.

Everyone called out their goodbyes to Rosalie, then hugged or high-fived or fist-bumped one another, introducing themselves to anyone they didn't already know. They started heading out after that. Dallie and Odelia walked back to the dorm; Beverly-Ann, Nichelle, and Trinni made their way to the front entrance to catch carriages. Flissa was about to say goodbye to Loriah and join them when Zinka approached.

"Hey," she said to Loriah. "I know we had some issues yesterday—"

"You had issues," Loriah clarified, setting her jaw. "I was *right*."

Flissa was pre-exhausted just thinking about helping these two have a conversation. "Maybe let her finish first," she suggested. "It sounds like she's trying to apologize."

"Wrong. I've got nothing to apologize for." Zinka glared at Flissa long enough to let that sink in, then she turned back to Loriah. "But since we're on the same team now, it's fight together or die."

"Fight together or die," Loriah agreed.

They looked brutally serious and wouldn't break from each other's gaze.

"*Metaphorically* die," Flissa noted. "And metaphorically fight, if we're being honest. I'm quite positive the rules of hoodle don't actually let us—"

As if answering to a signal only they heard, Loriah and Zinka suddenly reached out and hugged each other.

"Wow," Flissa said, stunned. "Okay. That's . . . that's great. You're friends now."

"Comrades," Loriah corrected her.

Zinka nodded. "Sisters-in-arms. Come hang in my room. Both of you. We'll celebrate."

Flissa wasn't sure if they were celebrating making the team or Zinka and Loriah's newfound sisterhood. Either way was fine, but she had no idea how long carriages stayed outside the school to take people home. "I'd like to," she said, "but I don't know if I can."

"Sure you can," Zinka said. "Bubblegram your parents and tell them you made the team, so you'll be a little late. Or better—tell them you made the team, but you'll be late because you're 'interfacing' with an Ambassador of Kaloon-ification."

"That's good," Loriah said. "And you should definitely do it, because even though Zinka and I are blood now, I still don't like her that much, so it's better if you're with us."

Zinka nodded like this wasn't insulting at all, and Flissa once again marveled at how time in the Twists turned all social norms on their head.

"Okay," Flissa agreed. She pulled out her vial of message milk and sent the bubblegram to her parents, letting them know where she'd be. She did toss in the part about the Ambassador of Kaloonification, though she didn't say "interfacing," and she left out the part about making sure Loriah and Zinka didn't kill each other. She was going to add that she'd send a bubblegram to the stables when she wanted to come home, so whoever was on duty could send a carriage, but Zinka and Loriah told her there was a carriage depot on campus. All she had to do was send a bubblegram there and a carriage would take her home.

With that done, the three of them walked across the fields to the girls' dorm. As Flissa had noted yesterday when she saw Maldevon Academy from above, there were three buildings at the far end of the school's dell. All of them had been stand-alone mansions when Grosselor was in power. A mint-green building off to their right housed the orphanage. It looked bright and cheery, with a sweet picket fence around a newly mowed lawn, a sandbox, a swingset, and a jungle gym. Several little kids ran around the yard, giggling and squealing as they played and chased one another. Two of the kids—little girls who had to be around seven years old—saw them walking and ran up to the fence to watch. One of the girls was blond and the other had reddish-brown hair. Their fists were filled with dandelions gone to seed.

Flissa broke out in chills. She whipped around to see if Loriah saw the same thing she did, and knew instantly the answer was yes. Loriah stared right at them, wide-eyed and unblinking.

The girls looked just like Loriah at that age, and her childhood friend Anna. The way they were the day Loriah lost control of her magic and accidentally hurt Anna. The day Flissa saw it all and inadvertently sent Loriah to the Twists.

"Hi!" the girls shouted. They waved, but the reddish-brown-haired girl accidentally waved the hand with all the dandelions, and its seeds flew everywhere. That made the other girl squeal with delight, and she shook her flowers too so they could both dance in the seed-storm.

"Hey!" Zinka waved back to them. Flissa waved too, but she didn't trust her voice not to break. She reached out and squeezed Loriah's hand—the one with the sickle-shaped scar on the back—and Loriah squeezed back before quickly pulling away.

"Gimme a sec," Loriah said.

She loped to the orphanage and plucked all the dandelions outside the fence, where they girls couldn't reach them. "Every one's a wish," she said as she handed the massive fistfuls to the beaming girls. "Just close your eyes and blow. And make sure you share."

"Thank you!" the girls chorused.

"I didn't know she was such a softie," Zinka said as Loriah walked slowly back.

"Only sometimes," Flissa said.

They continued to the girls' dorm, a pastel-blue mansion with stairs leading up to a wide wraparound porch. The porch held a few tables and chairs, two hammocks, built-in benches, and a porch swing. Several girls sat out there chatting, playing games, or doing their homework, and Flissa thought there was something lovely about all of them just casually being in one another's space. It gave her an odd pang for Sara.

Several of the girls looked up to say hello as Flissa, Loriah, and Zinka passed, and while Loriah of course didn't reciprocate, Zinka and Flissa did.

The front door of the dorm was painted bright red, in quirky contrast to the pastel-blue exterior, and Zinka flung it open and walked inside. Flissa, then Loriah, followed, and from the main foyer Flissa caught only a quick glimpse of a hallway branching off to a kitchen and several other rooms before Zinka led them all up a staircase. It went up half a flight, then reached a landing and changed direction before heading the rest of the way up.

It was on the landing that Flissa slammed into something hard.

"Ow!"

Loriah laughed.

"Stop laughing—that hurt!" Flissa said. She looked in front of her. There was absolutely nothing at all there, but her nose stung.

"Well, yeah," Loriah said. "You just walked into a magic wall."

"A magic wall?" Flissa sniffed the air, looking for traces of lavender, Loriah's magical signature. "Is this a joke?"

"Not a joke," Zinka said. "You're not allowed above the first floor unless you live here. You have to get permission first. Otherwise the wall stops you. Sorry—forgot about that."

"And you didn't feel the need to warn me?" Flissa aked Loriah.

"I kinda wanted to see what would happen." Loriah turned her palms up.

As Zinka pulled out her vial of message milk and sent a message to the Dorm Fairy on Duty, Flissa poked her finger at the empty space in front of her and it made a clonking sound.

"It doesn't like you," Loriah said. "But me? I can go in . . ." She reached right through the empty space. "And I can go out." She pulled her arm back, then stuck it through a few more times. "In . . . and out. In . . . and out. It's so fun! Wanna try?"

She smirked wickedly at Flissa, who rolled her eyes back. "No. I don't."

A bright pink fairy zipped downstairs, a pink contrail in her wake. Flissa had heard that several fairies from the Twists had found employment at Maldevon Academy, and only now she realized this was the first she'd seen. Apparently they worked at the dorms as opposed to the actual school. She wondered if they worked at the orphanage too.

This particular fairy looked irritated, and Flissa had a feeling that even though she was the Dorm Fairy on Duty, she hadn't thought she'd have to do anything for a while. She wore a bathrobe, her hair was in tiny curlers, and she flitted in the air with one hand on her hip.

"Sorry to bug you," Zinka said, "but Flissa's my guest. She's allowed up, and she can come into my room."

"Same for me," Loriah said. "She's my guest too. Room thing too. Standing invitation. She can come anytime."

"Seriously? Is this a contest?" Flissa asked.

"If it is, I'm not losing," Zinka said. Then she turned back to the fairy. "Standing for me too. Room and all. Anytime."

Zinka gave a *so there* look to Loriah as both the fairy and Flissa rolled their eyes. Then the fairy flew in front of the three girls and stared at them. She looked them carefully up and down, then nodded and zipped away, leaving another trail of pink.

"That's it?" Flissa asked.

"She just wanted to get a good look at you," Zinka said. "Now you're in their system."

Flissa believed her, but she didn't want to slam her nose again. She held out her arms first, but even after they went through the no-longer-solid invisible wall, she moved slowly and winced against the potential impact.

"You look ridiculous," Loriah said. "There's nothing there anymore."

"I know," Flissa said. "I just don't . . . you know . . . *know*."

She didn't fully relax until she'd made it up the second half of the stair flight. After that she had no problem racing up two more levels with Loriah and Zinka to the third floor, where they stepped into a long, wide hall that branched off to the left and right. Square windows with a view of the academy lined one side of the hall. The other side was lined with identical bluish-gray doors, all spaced at regular intervals from one another. Zinka led them down the hall to their left. As they walked, Flissa saw each door had a gold nameplate with the resident's name on it.

"Here we are," Zinka said when she got to her own. "Dorm sweet dorm."

She put her hand on the doorknob, and Flissa again noticed Zinka's ragged fingernails. They didn't look like she'd been biting them, more like she'd been clawing her way through a brick building. Zinka's knuckles were red and raw also. Flissa had no idea what Zinka did to deal with stress, but if those were the results, Flissa fervently hoped she'd never be the one to stress her out.

"I'm trusting you," Zinka whispered, her hand still on the doorknob, "with something that could get me in a lot of trouble. Maybe expelled. So can you keep a secret?"

Flissa didn't hesitate. "Yes. Of course."

Zinka turned to Loriah.

"Sure I can," Loriah said. "I can't promise I *will*, but—"

"Comrades," Flissa reminded her. "Sisters-in-arms."

Loriah considered, then finally nodded. "Yeah, okay. I'll keep the secret."

"Good," Zinka said. "Come in, but do it like I do, and shut the door behind you. Quickly."

Zinka opened the door just enough for her to slide in, then Loriah followed suit. Flissa was the last to enter. She slid through as tightly as possible, letting the door edge scrape the front of her body on the way in.

The room was small but cozy. The walls were blue, much like the outside of the dorm. There was a desk and chair against the right wall, a closet and dresser on the left. At the far end of the room was a loft bed—a wooden platform that held a wide mattress. Beneath the loft was a couch just big enough for two people, plus a cloth beanbag pouf and a small wood square that could work as another seat or a coffee table. A fluffy white throw rug sat on the wood floor in front of the couch. There was some dirt on the rug, and on the floor too—it looked like Zinka had tracked it in on her shoes and hadn't had the chance to sweep it up. Still, compared to the disaster zone of Sara's side of their room at home, the place was pristine. And even though it was a fraction of the size of their room in the palace, there was something sweet and comfy about it, and Flissa felt immediately at home.

"I love it," she said. Then she turned to Loriah. "Are they all the same?"

Loriah nodded. "Almost. They change up the colors. My walls are tan and my rug is orange. But where's the secret?"

Zinka had climbed up the wooden ladder to her loft. Now she came back down using only one hand to brace herself. Her other arm had something tucked into it—something wrapped up in a blanket.

"So it's a rule at the academy that you can't keep non-magical animals as pets," she said. "They say it's weird for the Magical Animals. Even though none of them live on dorm, just to have *pet* animals around on campus . . . it gets complicated. But my first day here—weeks before classes even, right after the dorms were built and they moved us all in—I found this little sweetheart curled up on my bed."

She turned around. Wrapped in the blanket was an adorable orange tabby cat.

"Awwww!" Flissa cooed.

Zinka unwrapped the cat and set it on the couch. It immediately reached out its front paws and stretched, then hopped off the couch and curled around Zinka's ankles, purring so loudly Flissa could hear it across the room.

"She's so sweet!" Flissa said. Then she gasped as she realized, "You sculpted this cat in Magic Lab yesterday!"

Zinka nodded. "I named her Teddy, like a teddy bear. Because she's so cuddly. And from minute one. There's no way she wasn't someone's pet before. Probably got abandoned during the Battle for Unification."

Teddy was gorgeous. She was sleek with short orange fur, and symmetrical stripes of slightly darker orange all through her coat. She moved gracefully, like a dancer, her whiskers standing out long from her face.

Zinka scooped Teddy back into her arms. "Wanna pet her?"

"Yes!" Flissa said immediately. She moved to Zinka and took the cat in her arms, then laughed because it seemed like Teddy wanted to look at her as much as she wanted to look at Teddy. The cat rested her front paws on Flissa's chest and looked her right in the eyes.

"Those eyes," Flissa said. She frowned. "I don't think I've ever seen eyes like that on a cat."

"I have," Loriah said. Her voice was soft and grim. Flissa hadn't even realized Loriah had moved closer to her until she heard it. "And you're wrong, Flissa. You have too."

Flissa looked more closely at Teddy's eyes. The irises were yellow, but a bright flaming yellow. *Had* she seen a cat with eyes like that?

Then her limbs went weak, and she dropped Teddy to the floor.

155

"Yup, you got it," Loriah said softly.

"Flissa!" Zinka cried. "What are you doing?"

Flissa was woozy and her head spun. She glanced down and saw the cat was fine, just contorted into a knot to wash herself. "I'm sorry, Teddy," she said breathlessly.

The only cat Flissa had ever seen with eyes like that wasn't a cat at all. She was a brutal lioness named Raya—one of the few Magical Animals powerful enough to cast spells. When she lived in the Twists, Loriah had been forced into Raya's gang and compelled to do unspeakable things for her. That was how Loriah and Flissa met—met *again*, years after they'd seen each other in Kaloon. Raya and her gang took Flissa, Sara, Galric, Nitpick, and Primka prisoner. They'd barely escaped with their lives.

"What?" Zinka asked. "You're both acting really weird. You don't like cats?"

"Not that cat," Loriah said.

"Oh, come on," Zinka said. She scooped up Teddy and held the cat in front of her face. She moved the cat's paw as she spoke in a high-pitched voice. "I *love* you, Loriah. I'm the sweetest little love pig of a cuddle kitty and I make everything better."

"Okay, that was seriously creepy." Loriah took a giant step back. "Even if I did like the cat, I wouldn't now."

Zinka turned the cat to Flissa and did the same high voice. "You don't think I'm creepy, do you, Princess Flissa? You love all your subjects, even the cute and fuzzy ones."

Flissa looked closely at Teddy. She stared into those yellow eyes . . . but she didn't see anything special—none of that weird sense of something *more* she got when she looked into Nitpick's eyes, or the eyes of another Magical

156

Animal. Teddy was a cat. A tabby cat, with tabby stripes and that little dark orange tabby M over her eyes. And yes, her eyes had the same coloring as Raya's, but so what? Plenty of humans had the same-colored eyes, and it didn't mean they were automatically related.

Most importantly, Raya was in the Twists, and the Twists and everything in them had been—if not destroyed, then as good as destroyed because they were cut off from Kaloon forever. And even if somehow, in some way, Raya did get out of the Twists . . . she was a *lion*, and Teddy was a *cat*, and no magic that she knew of could turn one into the other.

Teddy meowed and rolled over in Zinka's arms so Zinka was holding her like a baby.

"Awwww, see?" Zinka said. "She wants you to rub her belly."

Cradling Teddy with one arm, Zinka rubbed the cat's belly with the other. The cat purred and closed her eyes like she might fall asleep.

Flissa laughed at herself for being so superstitious. The cat was ridiculously adorable, and anyone could see how sweet she was. It was cruel *not* to play with her and rub her belly.

"I'm so sorry, Teddy. Am I ignoring you?" She dangled her braid over the cat, who batted it at it, making Flissa and Zinka both giggle.

"No," Loriah said sharply. "Stop. Flissa, what are you doing?"

"I know what you're thinking, Loriah, but Teddy's a cat," Flissa said. "Just a cat."

"Not *just* a cat," Zinka said. Then her voice jumped two octaves. "The cutest-wutest-woogiest-wittle kitty cat!

157

Oh yes you are! Oh yes you are!" She took the end of Flissa's braid and waved it in Teddy's face. Teddy attempted a fierce face that was so sweet, Flissa and Zinka dissolved into giggles.

"Cut it out!" Loriah snapped. "You want to mess with that thing, Zinka, you go ahead, but, Flissa, I'm not kidding, I'll pull you away from it if I have to."

Zinka looked horrified. She flopped down on her couch and covered Teddy's ears with her hands. "What is wrong with you? Are you allergic to cats or something?"

"Not to cats, to evil," Loriah said. "I'm out of here. And, Fliss, if you're smart, you should follow me."

She stalked out of the room, slamming the door behind her.

Zinka picked up Teddy and held the cat up to her face. "That girl is mean-mean-mean," she said in baby talk. "We can be sisters on the field, but everywhere else she's the *worst.*"

"She's not," Flissa said. "I'm sorry, you have to understand—"

Loriah threw open the door and stormed back in, slamming it behind her. She'd been gone less than a minute, but already her eyes were wild and her ponytail stuck out in all directions. "Okay, I tried. I did. But I can't live in this dorm if that cat's here too. I'm turning you in."

"What?!" Zinka set Teddy down and jumped to her feet.

Flissa couldn't believe it. "Loriah, what do you mean you tried? It's been five seconds."

"Yeah. I tried for five seconds. I can't do it."

Zinka stormed across the room to get in Loriah's face. "You promised you wouldn't!"

"No. No, I didn't. *You* said 'promise.' I said 'I'll keep the secret.' It's different."

"You can't do this!" Zinka hissed. "They'll take her away!"

"Exactly! That's what I'm going for. Dig up the Forever Flames under the castle and toss her in!"

"Loriah!" Flissa said.

Teddy blinked up from the couch and gave a plaintive meow.

"Oh, nice," Zinka said. "She heard you. You made her upset."

"Really?" Loriah snapped. "Then she's not just a cat, is she, or she wouldn't understand what I said!"

Zinka leaned over Loriah, her eyes flaming with fury. "I swear to you, Loriah. If you tell one person about Teddy, or harm one piece of fur on her body, I'll magic *you* into the Forever Flames."

"I'd make you turn that curse on yourself before you even knew I was doing it," Loriah said.

"Whoa!" Flissa said. She threw herself between them and put a hand on each of their shoulders before they could hurt each other. "Too far. This has gone way too far."

Flissa felt Zinka and Loriah both leaning against her hands, eager to tear each other apart.

"Listen to me, both of you," she said. "Zinka, you have to understand where Loriah's coming from. Teddy reminds her of someone from the Twists. Someone very, very bad, who hurt her a lot. Hurt both of us, but especially Loriah. Hurt her *badly*."

Zinka's weight came off Flissa's hand a little, and Flissa watched her eyes. Something clicked in there, and though

Flissa didn't know for sure, she thought Zinka probably had a list of people who hurt her badly in the Twists too. She didn't take her fiery gaze off Loriah, but she nodded.

"Loriah," Flissa said. "I know exactly what you're thinking. I saw it too. I saw her eyes. But I'm telling you, Teddy can remind us of Raya—"

Loriah stiffened. "Don't say her name."

"Okay. I'm sorry. I won't." Flissa started over. "Teddy can remind us of . . . *her*, but that doesn't mean she *is* her. That's not how magic works. She's in the Twists. She's gone, and she can't hurt you. Turning Zinka in won't make anything better."

"It'll make me sleep better," Loriah said, her eyes fixed on Zinka's.

"It won't," Flissa said. "Because Teddy isn't her. Okay? She's not."

Loriah finally leaned back, taking her weight off Flissa's hand. Now when she turned to Flissa her eyes were tired and scared. "What if she is?"

"She's not," Flissa said gently, "but I'll tell you what. You don't have to see the cat ever again. I'll come see Teddy, though, and I'll pay close attention to her. You know if I believed Teddy was *her* I wouldn't hesitate, right? I'd do what had to be done."

Flissa heard Zinka start to object. She didn't want to take her eyes off Loriah, but she pressed hard against Zinka's shoulder so she wouldn't say anything. Thankfully Zinka obeyed.

Loriah thought about it, then she nodded. "Yeah. I know." She took a deep breath, then ran a hand over her face. "Okay, I'm out. Not saying anything. Yet. But keep that thing away from me, okay? Seriously. Far away."

"Why would I possibly torture my cat by letting it near you?" Zinka asked.

"Zinka," Flissa objected, but Loriah wasn't even paying attention anymore. She walked out of the room and slammed the door behind her.

"Thanks," Zinka said once she was gone. "But I don't care if we are teammates. I swear if she even comes near my room, I'll destroy her."

* * *

After another half hour of talking Zinka down and playing with Teddy—who was really amazingly adorable—Flissa sent a bubblegram to the carriage depot, then headed for the main entrance to the school. As she walked, she sent another bubblegram to her parents, just so they'd know she was almost on her way home.

It was well past dark now, and Flissa marveled at the brightening bugs blinking like twinkle lights around the topiary garden. She walked through the main building and came out the front. "Good night, Gilward," she said to the statue as she passed, then she strode down the walkway and into the waiting carriage.

Carriage rides usually lulled Flissa, especially after dark. There was something so soothing about a rocking carriage and the sound of hoofbeats. But tonight she kept shifting in her seat and jouncing her knee up and down. Her day had been wonderful and scary and bizarre and incredible . . . but none of it would seem real until she'd shared it with Sara. She couldn't wait to sit cross-legged on her bed and tell her sister every single detail. She was sure

Sara would have stories too, and Flissa was just as eager for them. This was two days in a row they'd had separate adventures to tell each other—adventures the other one didn't have to memorize and pretend she'd lived herself!

Flissa barely waited for the carriage to come to a full stop at the palace before she leaped out and ran inside. Her parents were waiting for her in the ballroom, so she stopped there to have some food, tell them about the school day, and get their congratulations on making the hoodle team. She was happy to spend time with them, but she *really* wanted to talk to Sara, who they said was already upstairs. Flissa claimed exhaustion as soon as it wouldn't be brutally impolite to do so, then flew up to her and Sara's bedroom, flush-faced and eager to spill her news.

Instead she found Sara in her nightgown, curls sticking out in all directions, wild-eyed and pacing back and forth.

"Sara?" she asked worriedly.

Sara snapped to attention. "Finally! You're home!" She caught Flissa by her shoulders and stared into her eyes. "Zinka's working with Amala, and they want to get rid of all the Genpos!"

Chapter 12
Sara

Sara supposed she should have given Flissa the information in a better, maybe calmer and less-super-crazed way, but she'd been dealing with it for hours now, and by the time Flissa walked in she was ready to explode.

"Wait . . . what?" Flissa asked. "You're not making any sense. Slow down."

Flissa stepped back from the shoulder-clench, then took Sara's hand and led her to Flissa's bed, where they both sat down. When they were facing each other, cross-legged, Flissa asked gently, "What happened?"

Sara took her through the whole thing: finishing detention, getting lost, hearing the voices, then the disturbing scene she'd witnessed in Amala's office. Flissa listened closely, her face intent and solemn.

"And that's everything?" she asked when Sara finished. "You didn't hear anything else?"

"Amala said it was almost time to 'wake the sleepers' and go, so I ran away as fast as I could. I got lucky and found the moving staircase before anyone came out and saw me."

Flissa nodded. "I understand. And did you tell Mother and Father?"

Sara's eyes widened. "No! I didn't tell anyone—you're the only one. Amala's a *Shadow*, Flissa. If she thinks I know about her plan, she'll do the same thing to me that she wants to do to the Genpos!"

Flissa bit her lip. "It's so strange . . . I know Mother and Father and the whole General Council spent days interviewing Amala before they made her head of school. They were all positive she'd changed."

"That's how good Amala is," Sara said. "She fooled them all."

"Maybe . . . but I saw Zinka right afterward. *Right* afterward. She came to hoodle tryouts the second she finished. I made the team, by the way—me and Loriah and Zinka. We're actually really good on the field together. Some Genpos made the team too, and Zinka was great with them. I won't lie, she was acting a little stressed out, but no more than she was at Magic Lab, before the Amala meeting. And after the hoodle tryouts we spent the whole evening together. There was some drama between her and Loriah, but if anything, *Loriah* was the one who was in a bad place. Zinka seemed like herself. She wasn't acting at all like she'd just been inducted into a massive plot to overthrow the Genpos. She didn't even talk about her meeting with Amala."

"Because I bet Amala told them not to," Sara said. "She probably told them 'act natural and don't let anybody know.'"

"Maybe . . . but are they all that good at acting? It's a big secret to carry around."

"We did it," Sara said. "We acted and carried around a big secret for twelve years. Mitzi acted and carried around a big secret for even longer. *Katya*—"

"Understood. People can handle big secrets and act however they need to act. You're right."

Flissa tucked the end of her braid in her mouth and got off the bed to pace. Sara was glad to see it; it meant she was thinking hard, and Sara could use her sister's full concentration on this. She was feeling lost without it.

"Okay," Flissa said. "Let's try this. It is one hundred percent possible that Amala lied to our parents, lied to the General Council, has been lying to *everyone*, and is now secretly grooming students to get rid of the Genpos. This is one explanation for what you saw."

"It's the *only* explanation for what I saw."

"Maybe," Flissa said. "But let's just look for others. I'm not saying you're wrong, I just want to see."

"Sure." Sara folded her arms over her chest. She didn't like this game, but if Flissa needed to do it in order to see the truth, fine.

"Okay," Flissa said again. "First, if she really wanted to go after Genpos, why bring them to the meeting in the first place?"

"Easy," Sara said. "So it wouldn't be obvious. She had to pick troublemakers from every group so it looked like she wasn't anti-Genpo. She knew she could knock out the Genpos so they wouldn't hear anything bad."

"But your detention was an hour, right?" Flissa asked. "You didn't hear the beginning of the meeting, you heard the end. Maybe there were things in the beginning that helped the end part make sense."

"Like what?" Sara asked. "Anything she said in the beginning was probably fake—just stuff she wanted the Genpos to remember before she magicked them out and had her real meeting."

Flissa took her braid out of her mouth and worked it through her hands as she paced. "Tell me again what Amala said. As close to word for word as you can."

Sara closed her eyes so she could put herself back there. She tried to remember the exact words. "She said, 'What you have to understand is that Mages are naturally superior to Genpos. Look how helpless they are; they're no match for you at all' . . . then she went through all the ways she could hurt them, like turning them into trees or taking them over or sending them away . . . then she said Anastasia, Zinka, and Skeed could have that power too. She said she chose them for a reason, she's counting on them, and she wanted them to spread the word to the right people and animals. Then it was 'If we work together, we can change everything. We can make the world we want.'"

Sara opened her eyes. Flissa stopped pacing and bit her lip. "'If we work together, we can change everything. We can make the world we want,'" she echoed.

She was still for a long time, looking out at nothing and playing with her braid. Then her eyes widened. "What about this?" She sat back on her bed, crossed her legs, and leaned closer to Sara. "It sounds like 'We can make the world we want,' is one without Genpos, right?"

"Because it *is*," Sara said. This game was getting frustrating. "That's the world she wants."

"*If* she was lying to everyone," Flissa said. "What if she wasn't? What if the world she *really* wants—the world she

166

wants *them* to want—is the same world *we* want, where everyone gets along?"

"Okaaaay," Sara said dubiously. "It's not, but sure, play it out."

"Wait-wait-wait," Flissa said. She rose up on her knees and walked on them to the wall by her bed, which was a massive, floor-to-ceiling bookcase. After Kaloonification, Flissa had spent an entire week reorganizing the books, placing the old, outdated ones filled with lies about Mages on the harder-to-reach shelves by the ceiling and under the bed—worth keeping for historical perspective of the Dark Times, but not worth having close at hand—and shelving lots of new books written in the immediate aftermath of the Battle for Kaloonification. She searched the shelves, then grabbed one of these newer books and started flipping through it.

Now Sara was getting annoyed. "I know what I saw, Flissa," she said. "You don't have to look for the answer in a book. You can get it from me, right here."

"This isn't just any book," Flissa said. "It's the reason Mother and Father believed Amala had changed. It's why they and the General Council were interested in her for head of school. This is a reprint, but Amala wrote the original centuries ago, right before the Dark Magic Uprising where Grosselor framed Maldevon." She smacked her finger down on a page. "Listen to this: *In a way, I was right all along. Mages are superior to Genpos. That's not a value judgment, it's simply an empirical fact. We have superior powers. My mistake was thinking that meant we're owed more than them, when in fact the opposite is true. As exceptionally endowed beings, it's our duty to use our skills*

167

to protect those without the same abilities. We Mages must be like parents of small children, sheltering and helping those who can't do the things we can. Genpos might chafe at this comparison and believe I'm saying they're inferior. To the contrary, I believe Mages and Genpos are equal in many ways. Yet it is an incontrovertible fact that Mages have more power and thus the responsibility to use it to help those without the same advantages.'"

Flissa looked up at Sara, her eyes dancing. "You see?"

"That Amala has a big head even when she's not projecting it over the lunch area? Yeah, I do."

"No!" Flissa said. "I think you saw Amala doing exactly what she said she was going to do right here. She's not grooming Zinka, Skeed, and Anastasia to get rid of the Genpos, she's grooming them to step up and *take care of* the Genpos!"

Sara shook her head. "Uh-uh. Doesn't make sense. Why have the Genpos there at all? Why put them to sleep and talk about all the terrible things she can do to them?"

"Didn't you hear what I read? She knows Genpos will think her philosophy sounds insulting—"

"It does sound insulting."

"But she doesn't mean it to be. True or false: as Mages, we have superior powers to our parents?"

Sara grimaced and opened her mouth to say of course that wasn't the case . . . but the truth was they did. It didn't mean she and Flissa loved or respected their parents any less, or that they wouldn't listen, but the reality was they had magic, so they could do things their parents could never dream of doing.

Flissa smiled. "See? And my guess is the part of the

meeting you didn't see was Amala talking to all of them about working together, but then she had a special message for the Mages, and she knew the Genpos wouldn't hear it the right way. You know Jentrie. She would have a fit and break everything in the office if she heard Amala say Genpos were like children for Mages to foster. But if you know where Amala's coming from, it's a lovely message about everyone taking care of one another . . . just tailor-made to appeal to Mages."

Sara considered it, then she shook her head. "No. You weren't there. You didn't see her. You didn't *hear* her."

"I don't have to hear her," Flissa said. "It's the only thing that makes sense. If Amala truly wanted to banish all Genpos from Kaloon, why wait until now? She had the perfect chance. We were in chaos when the Shadows rose up. She didn't have to come to our side. She could have rallied the Shadows to join Grosselor and the Keepers and other like-minded Mages to take Kaloon for themselves. Instead she went to our parents, the king and queen, two *Genpos*, and offered her services and loyalty. I'm right about this, Sara. I know I am."

"*Or* you're blinded because you have a bright and shiny new friend," Sara said.

Flissa frowned. "A what?"

Sara put on a high-pitched voice and tossed her head from side to side like she had a long braid. "*We're so good on the hoodle field together! We spent the whole evening together! I'm Flissa and I have a brand-new friend named Zinka!*"

Flissa's face darkened, and Sara inwardly congratulated herself for popping Flissa's happy little bubble.

Maldevon Academy wasn't all fun and happiness and looking on the bright side, and it was about time Flissa saw that too.

"Why are you acting this way?" Flissa asked. "Yes, I made a friend. I made a few; I'm on the hoodle team now, I have a whole group of new friends. You make friends all the time—all of Flissara's friends were *your* friends. You should be happy for me."

"Oh, I'm totally happy for you," Sara said. "I'm totally psyched that you're so thirsty for friends you can't even see that one's evil and working with Amala to take down the Genpos."

Flissa reared back as if Sara were radioactive. "'Thirsty for friends'?" Then her eyes widened and her jaw dropped. "You're jealous!"

"What?!" Sara said. "No. Jealous of what?"

"You're jealous that we're at a brand-new place, we're our own people, and *I'm* the one who already made new friends."

"That's . . ." Sara had no good comeback for that, so she just shook her head. "You're wrong. You're totally wrong."

"I'm not! You *are* jealous. And I have never, *ever* been jealous of you. Ever. All our lives, even though you were so much better at so many things. You could always talk to people and make friends and be sure of yourself . . . and I wasn't jealous at all! I admired it. I respected it. And yes, I maybe wanted some of that too, but I wasn't *jealous* of it, I was happy for you! And if you woke up tomorrow and you were incredible on horseback or a master jouster, I wouldn't be jealous of that either. I'd be excited for you."

Sara didn't know what to say. She'd *wanted* to make

Flissa feel bad, but now it was out of control and everything Flissa was saying was true. Sara felt small and petty and awful. She wanted to take it all back and start over, but she didn't know how. "Flissa . . ." she started, but she had no idea how to follow that up.

"I had a great day today," Flissa said. "A strange day, for sure, but mostly a fantastic day. And you know what I was thinking the whole carriage ride home? That I couldn't *truly* enjoy it, that it wouldn't actually be real until I shared it with you." Flissa's voice broke, and she pursed her lips as she blinked tears from her eyes. "Because that's how we work. That's how I *thought* we worked."

Sara's heart ached. She regretted every second of the conversation.

"It *is* how we work," she said. She moved closer to Flissa, but Flissa shook her head. She wouldn't even look Sara in the eye.

"Please get off my bed."

Ouch. "Flissa, wait—"

"Get off my bed," Flissa said more forcefully. "Please."

Sara did. "There, okay? I'm off the bed. Now—"

A massive blast of cream-colored mist appeared in front of Sara's eyes. When it faded, a cream-colored, floor-to-ceiling wall separated Flissa's side of the room from Sara's.

"Oh, come on!" Sara said. She banged her fist on the door. It was hard and solid. "Ow! Okay, that's pretty awesome magic, but take it down! I get the point!" She banged again, but this time she didn't use her knuckles. "Flissa!"

Flissa didn't respond. Sara wasn't even sure her sister could hear her from the other side of the wall. Sara knew she could have said she was sorry, but she was only sorry

171

for *some* of what happened. She was incredibly sorry for hurting Flissa's feelings, but she wasn't sorry for accusing Amala. The Shadow was up to something, and she was using the Ambassadors of Kaloonification to make it happen. And if Flissa wouldn't help Sara figure out what was going on, she'd find someone else who would.

In the meantime, she'd go to bed. She hated to think about Flissa falling asleep mad at her, but her sister would be calmer in the morning, and Sara was sure she could make everything better then.

* * *

The next day, Sara woke to Primka screeching into her ear. "Wake up, wake up, wake up!"

Sara groaned, then remembered last night's fight and her eyes snapped open . . . but all she saw across the room was Flissa's perfectly made bed. The cream-colored wall was gone, but so was her sister.

"She left early," Primka said, correctly guessing Sara's thoughts, "which means you have to leave early too."

"What?" Sara asked. She let her head flop back on the bed. "That's not true. We're not the same person anymore. We don't have to do the same things at the same time."

"You didn't do the same things at the same time when you *were* the same person! That would have defeated the purpose, wouldn't it? Now wake up!"

Sara sat up and looked at the clock on the wall. It was still early. If she got up and dressed now, she'd still have lots of time before class. "Whyyyyyy?" she whined.

"Because your sister was studying this morning at breakfast, and she left her Literature book behind. It's not like her. Something's clearly on her mind. Probably she's excited about the hoodle team and it all went to her head," Primka said.

Sara sat up straight. The hoodle team *could* be on Flissa's mind, or Flissa could be upset because of their fight. Maybe so upset that she was ready to talk to Sara and give her a chance to make up. "I'll take the book to her," she said.

Primka rolled her tiny eyes. "Yes, that was the point. That's why I'm waking you up, so you can get to school and take the book to Flissa well before classes start. Now get dressed and ready and I'll give you everything you need."

"Everything I need?" Sara asked as she rolled out of bed. "Don't I just need her book?"

"More to it than that," Primka said, "but I don't want to tell you till you're all ready to go so I know you'll remember everything. Now get ready and meet me downstairs right away!"

Primka zipped off through one of her holes in the ceiling, and Sara rushed to get dressed and ready. One of the great things about her short hair was how easy it was to style, so she was washed, groomed, and in a soft turquoise dress in no time. She threw her satchel over her shoulder and ran downstairs, where Primka met her and fluttered along as she walked to the front door. In her feet Primka held a canvas bag ten times her size—one she'd never have the strength to carry if she weren't magic.

"Take this," Primka said. "Inside is Flissa's book, some egg tarts for breakfast, and a signed note from your mother. You'll need to show that to the Dorm Fairy so they let you in."

"The Dorm Fairy?" Sara asked. It sounded made up, like the Wishmas Owl.

"Yes," Primka said. "Flissa told your mother she was meeting Zinka at her dorm room this morning. So you need to go to the girls' dorm, show the Dorm Fairy the note, then go up to the third floor and turn left. Zinka's name is on her door."

Sara was impressed. "Do you just know *everything*? How do you know so much about the girls' dorms?"

"Your mother sent a bubblegram to the school to get the information," Primka said, shooing Sara out the front door and toward a waiting carriage. "Now go. Your sister needs you."

Your sister needs you.

Sara thought about that during the long carriage ride to school. Did her sister need her? She'd always thought so. Flissa had always relied on Sara to help her make choices, and brave new situations, and meet new people . . . but now it seemed like Flissa was fine doing all that herself. Sara hadn't seen Flissa pull out her coin once since school started, even though she had a million new choices to make every day.

Maybe Flissa didn't need her. But maybe if Sara got the chance to apologize, she could make Flissa *want* her again.

When the carriage arrived at school, Sara jumped out so quickly she forgot Primka's canvas bag. She had to run after the carriage driver, shouting and getting pelted by pebbles kicked up from the wheels, so he'd stop and she could clamber back in and grab it. Then she ran all the way to the main building and hurled herself against the door before she remembered it stayed shut in the mornings so everyone could gather in the courtyard. Already exhausted, she considered sitting right there on the steps to wait for Flissa, but then she wouldn't have the chance to talk to her. She needed to find her sister with as much time before class as possible so she could try to make things right, so she took a deep breath and started the long run around the main building, then across the fields to the dorms.

Sara's legs ached by the time she faced the three houses beyond the back fields. She had no idea which house was the boys' dorm, which the girls', and which the orphanage, but there were a bunch of girls sitting on the porch of the house in the middle and that seemed like a good sign. Sara didn't know any of the girls, but she called out a breathless hello as she tromped up the porch steps, then put her head down so she could watch her feet, and ran full speed up the staircase until her head bonked into a solid wall.

"OW!"

Sara reeled back, one hand on the banister, one on the top of her head. She looked in front of her and saw absolutely nothing, but her skull pounded. When she saw a pink streak of light she thought she was hallucinating, until the light coalesced into a fairy flitting in front of her. The pink fairy looked irritated, like Sara had interrupted her morning. She had her hands on her hips and tapped her foot impatiently in midair.

"Hi, um . . . I think I hit my head on something, but I don't see . . ."

Sara reached her hand out to the emptiness in front of her . . . and her fingers tapped something hard.

The fairy raised an eyebrow. Sara suddenly understood.

"Got it. Magic wall," she said. Then she remembered what Primka had told her. "Right, the permission slip." She rummaged in Primka's canvas bag, then pulled out the parchment her mother had written out and signed, asking the Dorm Fairy to allow her upstairs by order of the queen. The fairy didn't take the parchment—it was bigger than her entire body—but she read it over while Sara held it up. She fixed Sara with a long stare before she nodded and flew away.

"That's it?" Sara asked. "Am I okay to go?"

The fairy was already gone. Sara edged her way up the stairs, hands outstretched . . . but when she reached the first landing without hitting anything, she poured on the speed. Keeping her skirts clenched in one fist and her other hand on the banister, she raced up and up and up, only tripping twice.

"Third floor . . ." she panted. "Why does she have to live on the third floor?"

Finally, she got to the top of the stairs and staggered out to the left. She leaned against a wall to catch her breath and took in her surroundings: a long hallway with identical windows lining one side, and identical doors lining the other.

A *really* long hallway. It would take her forever to inspect the nameplate on every door until she found Zinka's. No way would she have time to get Flissa her book and talk to her before school started. She should have ignored Primka and stayed asleep.

Sara lowered her head and tried to take deep breaths, then she heard a familiar voice. "Her room's this way," it said. "Six down from mine. But you should just go yourself. I don't have anything to say to her." Then a far more familiar voice answered, "You do. You're teammates. You're going to see each other all the time. You have to work this out, and I'm sure she feels better about everything now than she did last night."

That voice was Flissa's. Sara flung herself off the wall and hurtled down the hall in her direction. Flissa was walking with Zinka, and they both looked at Sara like she was something slimy about to splatter on them.

"*Sara?!*" Flissa asked, sounding heart-piercingly horrified. "What are you doing here?"

"How did you even get up here?" Zinka asked.

"That's a good question," Flissa asked, folding her arms. "From Zinka. You know, my *friend*, Zinka."

Zinka furrowed her brow and looked at Flissa like she'd lost her mind. "She knows who I am, Flissa."

Flissa didn't bother to explain the slight, she just raised an eyebrow to Sara.

"I brought your Literature book," Sara said, pulling it out of the canvas bag. "Mom wrote me a permission slip so the fairies would let me up to find you. Do you think we could talk for a second? Outside maybe?"

Sara glanced at Zinka. She really didn't want to do this in front of her.

"I can't right now," Flissa said. "Zinka and I have to talk to Loriah."

Flissa continued down the hall, right past Sara. Zinka kept pace with her. All Sara could do was follow them and plead her case. "Flissa, come on! I *ran*! A lot! Me! I got pebbles spewed at me by a carriage and I bammed into an invisible wall! It still hurts—I probably have a giant bump on my head." She gingerly touched the top of her head, then winced and quickly drew her fingers away. "Yes! I totally have a giant bump on my head."

It was humiliating to chase after her sister, begging for attention. Other girls in the hall were staring. But Sara didn't care. She was here, they had time before class, Flissa was clearly still upset . . . they had to talk it out.

"You can't come in here," Flissa said when she had her hand on Loriah's doorknob. "You weren't invited."

Sara reeled back at the iciness in Flissa's voice, but she pulled herself tall again. "I'll wait out here, then," she said. "And if there's still time before class, we can talk."

Flissa folded her arms and locked eyes with her. The *go away* message was loud and clear, but Sara wouldn't budge.

"For real, you're just gonna stand there staring at each other?" Zinka said. She leaned past Flissa, turned Loriah's knob, and pushed the door open.

"Whoa," Zinka said, then she grabbed Flissa's arm so hard Sara saw Zinka's red-scratched knuckles go white. At the same time, Sara and Flissa both looked into Loriah's open room.

Loriah was on her back, seizing in midair. Her eyes were rolled back in her head and her mouth foamed as her whole body twitched violently, as if she'd been struck by lightning.

Sara barely had time to register what was happening before Flissa screamed down the hall, "Somebody call for help! Loriah was cursed!"

"On it!" Zinka said. She pulled out her vial of message milk while Flissa raced into Loriah's room. Sara followed her.

"Help me turn her on her side!" Flissa shouted. "We have to keep her airway clear!"

Sara didn't doubt her for a second. Ever since their time in the Twists, Flissa had read everything she could about curses, and would throw out the most gruesome bits of information at the worst times, like just before Sara was about to bite into a drippy tomato-and-mutton sandwich.

Sara and Flissa gently placed their hands on Loriah's thrashing and jerking body and tipped her to the side. She was still convulsing, but at least she was in a better position.

"What if she falls?" Sara asked. "She's floating now, but what if the curse fades or changes or something and she falls? We should put something under her."

"Yes, that's good," Flissa said. "Grab the pillows from her bed. Hurry!"

Sara was glad she'd come up with something helpful. She scrambled up the ladder to Loriah's loft bed and found four pillows, which she threw to Flissa before climbing back down. She'd only made it halfway when she heard a loud *THUMP*.

Loriah had plummeted to the floor.

Sara scrambled down the ladder and joined Flissa, who knelt at Loriah's side. It looked like the pillows had helped;

Loriah had dropped down on top of them, but her eyes were squeezed shut and she looked drained.

"OW."

Loriah said it like a statement, not an emotional reaction to her pain. If anything, she sounded annoyed. Sara thought it was a good sign.

"Loriah?" Flissa asked, and Sara was impressed by how calm she made herself sound. She knew that, inside, Flissa's heart was thundering as loud as her own.

"Let me through!"

Amala's voice sliced through the room, and Flissa and Sara got up and moved aside so the Shadow could see Loriah. Two people Sara didn't know followed Amala in. Doctors, maybe? Other Shadows?

"Thank you, Princesses," Amala said. "We'll take it from here, but I'll have some questions. Please wait outside the room with Dame Yentley."

Dame Yentley's name made Sara purse her lips to hold in an inappropriate smile. She waited until she and Flissa had walked past Amala and the others, then she whispered, "Waiting with Dame Yentley would be delicious."

Flissa gave the littlest snort before she regained control of herself and softly added, "Yummy."

She darted her eyes to Sara's, and they exchanged a smile. It made Sara feel like everything that happened last night didn't matter. They were back to themselves again.

"Oh, darling Princesses!" Dame Yentley cried when they emerged into the hall. She wrapped them both in an awkward hug—especially awkward since she only came up to their shoulders and made them feel like giants. "It is *always* delectable to see you, but I'm sorry the circumstances are so unappetizing."

Sara caught Flissa's eyes over the top of Dame Yentley's head; they danced with suppressed giggles, and Flissa raised an eyebrow that begged Sara not to laugh, because then she'd do the same and there was no good way to explain why the situation would give them the giggles. Sara bit her cheeks, and when Dame Yentley let them go, she saw that the hall was empty. Only Zinka was out here with them, a giant oak to Dame Yentley's acorn.

"She okay?" Zinka asked, her brow furrowed as she looked at Flissa. Flissa immediately grew serious again, and Sara felt a flare of resentment, as if Zinka had physically stepped between them.

"I think so," Flissa said. "I'm not sure."

"Oh, come on! No. I'm fine!" Loriah's voice rang out from her room.

"It's a precaution," Amala said. "We want to make sure you're okay. You were cursed."

"Yeah. And I grew up in the Twists. You think that was the first time?" Loriah shot back. Then Amala must have done something, because two seconds later Loriah huffed and said, "Fine, I'm going, but not in that. I'm walking."

Loriah strode out of the room, looking every inch her normal self. She rolled her eyes at the girls. "They magicked up a stretcher and wanted me to get on it. Like that was gonna happen. They're making me go to the infirmary, though. Back for hoodle practice, for sure. Oh, hey, Sara."

She kept moving down the stairs, and the two men who'd come in with Amala had to scramble after her.

"She won't be at hoodle practice today," Amala said as

she emerged from Loriah's room. She looked serious, but her mouth turned up at the edges, like she was secretly impressed by the way Loriah had handled the situation. "Thank you, Dame Yentley. You may go."

"Oh, that's all right. I don't mind staying," Dame Yentley said as she patted the bun on her head. "I'm sure the princesses could use a friendly face after their trauma."

She reached up to pat both Flissa and Sara on the shoulder. Amala gave her a tight smile. "I apologize. I didn't realize I needed to be clearer. Instead of 'may,' I should have said 'You *must* go.'"

Dame Yentley blushed bright red. "Oh . . . yes . . . well . . . that's actually better then . . . I'm in the middle of an absolutely scrumptious lesson plan, and I'm eager to get back to it. Bye now, Your Highnesses!"

She waddled off, and Sara knew she should wait for Amala to speak, but she had a million questions and she couldn't keep them all in.

"What happened?" she asked. "Was there a magical signature? Do you know who did it? Is she okay?"

Amala raised an eyebrow. Sara had more questions, but she let her voice fade away.

"She seems fine," Amala said, "but we're going to keep her at the infirmary for a bit to make sure. There was no magical signature, but I believe that's because the curse wore off before I arrived. You didn't find her on the floor, is that correct?"

"No," Flissa said. She told Amala everything, from the moment they opened Loriah's door to the moment Amala walked in. Amala listened, nodding. Sara thought the Shadow might congratulate them on working so quickly to call her, turn Loriah to the side, and get the pillows under her, but she simply moved on to her next thought.

"I see," she said. "So we'll need to suss out who did this another way. Did anyone have a reason to curse Loriah? Some kind of grudge or argument? Even something insignificant. Anything."

Sara saw Flissa and Zinka share the briefest look before Zinka said, "Nope," at the same time Flissa said, "No, not at all."

Sara frowned. She was sure she remembered Flissa saying last night that Zinka and Loriah had some kind of drama. "But—" she began, then Flissa glared at her so harshly, Sara thought cream-colored mist might come out of her eyes and curse her on the spot. The look was almost as awful as if she had.

"Yes, Sara?" Amala asked. "Did you want to say something?"

"No," Sara said. "Sorry—I was thinking of something else."

"I see," Amala said. "First block has already started, but I'll send bubblegrams to make sure you don't get detention. If you want to visit Loriah later, I'll be keeping her at the infirmary for the day. You may go."

Flissa and Zinka exchanged a relieved look, and for the first time Sara noticed the dark circles under Zinka's eyes.

What were they keeping secret? Did *Zinka* curse Loriah? And if she did, why was Flissa protecting her? And why wasn't Amala picking up on all the things Sara saw?

Unless she *was* picking up on them but specifically ignoring them. Maybe because of whatever Amala was plotting with her Ambassadors of Kaloonification.

Sara's skin crawled as she thought of Loriah floating on her back. With the exception of the thrashing, it wasn't that different from the way Nikkolas and Jentrie looked when Amala had them suspended in the air, was it?

Sara took deep breaths and kept her eyes to the floor as she followed Flissa and Zinka to the stairs, but then Amala called out, "Sara, please stay a moment."

Flissa and Zinka wheeled to look at her, and Flissa's eyes flashed with that look again—as if Sara were guilty of some kind of horrible betrayal. Sara barely registered it; she was too worried about Amala. How strong was her Shadow magic? Did she know what Sara was thinking? Is that why she called her back?

"See you at Magic Lab," she croaked to her sister and Zinka. They both stared another moment, and Zinka looked so earth-shatteringly tired that Sara almost asked her what was wrong . . . but the moment passed. Zinka nodded and turned away, while Flissa said, "Yes. See you," and shot her a last meaningful look before following her friend downstairs.

Sara watched them go as if they were the last lifeboat leaving a sinking ship.

"I know you saw us," Amala said softly when they were gone.

Sara desperately didn't want to turn around, but she did. She half expected Amala to have morphed into a sallow-eyed venom-dripping beast, but the Shadow looked beautiful as always and completely relaxed and calm. She leaned casually against the wall, and it was so unlike her usual formal pose that somehow Sara found it even more intimidating, like she'd dropped her veneer specifically because Sara had already seen past it to the demon inside.

"Saw . . . what?" Sara squeaked.

"Oh, come now," Amala said. "Let' s not play games. I didn't want to say anything in front of the Ambassadors; I want them to feel comfortable in my meetings and not worried about prying eyes. But I heard you when you moved out of the hall, and I know you were watching and listening."

Sara was as terrified as she'd been when she saw Rouen in the Twists, before she knew he was on her side. When she thought he was an emissary from the Keepers of the Light, come to destroy her.

"No," Sara said. "I mean, *yes*, but I . . . I mean . . . I wasn't *spying* really, I just . . . it was an accident and—"

Amala smiled. "Sara, relax. I'm not upset. You were coming out of detention, you were looking for the bathroom, and you got lost."

"You—" Sara's voice caught in her throat. "You know all that? You can read minds?"

Amala's laugh was surprisingly full and rich. "No," she said. "I can ask questions, which is what I did. And I want to apologize for not coming to the palace and talking to you sooner, because I can imagine what you must have thought."

"You can?"

"Of course. Keeping Genpos in suspended animation while I regaled those with magic about their superiority? I'm sure you thought the Cleaner was back . . . that is, if you believed she'd ever left."

Amala raised an eyebrow.

Was she looking for an answer? Sara tried to stammer

something intelligent, but only got as far as, "Ahhhh . . . errrrr . . . ummmm."

"I am *not* against Genpos," Amala assured her. "Nor am I scheming with the magical students. I want Kaloonification to work—desperately—but I also recognize the reality that we're divided. And while we all have to take steps to make things better, it's a simple fact that those with magic—"

"Are more powerful than the Genpos," Sara said, remembering Flissa's words. "And because of that, we have a responsibility to help them. Like parents of small children."

Amala cocked her head, surprised.

"Flissa read me part of your book," Sara said. "When I told her what I saw."

"Really?" Amala's voice lilted with delight, and she clapped her hands, smiling wide. "That's wonderful. I had no idea anyone was still reading it. It's exciting, you know; you write a book, put it out there in the world . . . you really don't know if anyone will read it. But to have it on someone's bookshelf after all this time . . . Was it on her bookshelf?"

"Um . . . yes," Sara said, feeling very uncomfortable. "May I go now?"

"Of course, yes," Amala said, waving a hand in the air as if to brush away her own train of thought. "I just wanted to make sure you understood and didn't have the wrong idea. You *do* understand, yes?"

Sara didn't know *what* she understood, but Amala's eyes were suddenly cold marbles, and there was really only one possible answer to the question.

"Yes," she said. "I understand."

She hoped Amala wasn't lying when she said she couldn't read minds.

"Good. Off to class, then. I'll see you in Magic Lab."

Sara said goodbye and ran down the stairs, out the door, and down the patio stairs, her head swimming and so full that she barely registered it when someone called, "Hey!"

The familiar voice tapped into the edges of her thoughts, but it had to call out again before she saw Galric running across the fields toward her, Krystal at his side.

"Hey!" he said again as he bounded in front of her, panting from the effort. "What happened? Is Loriah okay?"

"I think so," Sara said. "How did you know?"

"Word spreads," Krystal said, grinning and bouncing on her toes so her hair flopped around.

Sara fixed her with a look. "Why are you here?"

She didn't mean it to sound rude. Not really. But Galric and Krystal both frowned, so Sara shook her head and tried to walk it back. "I mean, first block started, so . . ."

"I had Athletics with Lazando," Galric said. "He let me go. He kinda buys that whole hero thing, so . . ." He blushed and couldn't finish the sentence.

"He buys it 'cause you *are* a hero," Krystal said. Then she turned to Sara. "I had Chemistry, and my teacher got a bubblegram from Amala to come to the girls' dorm and take care of 'a situation,' so we all got the period free. Pretty cool, right? I mean . . . not cool that your friend got hurt, just cool that . . ." Krystal winced, clearly realizing she'd steered the conversation down a bad path. "Anyway, I saw Galric and tagged along. Is your friend okay?"

Like you actually care is what Sara was about to say,

but she stopped herself. She really needed to talk to someone, and it couldn't be Flissa since her sister was now lying to protect . . . Zinka? Amala? Who even knew? And while Sara would love to tell only Galric, there was no way she could keep everything in until after school, and there wasn't a chance she'd see him alone before that.

Sara looked over her shoulder to see if Amala was coming out of the dorm, then lowered her voice. "I need to tell you something, but I don't want to do it here. Topiary garden, okay? And not in a group." Sara knew she was being paranoid, but she could imagine Amala watching from the window and getting suspicious of the three of them sneaking off together. "Spread out and we'll meet there, okay?"

Both Galric and Krystal looked concerned, but they didn't question her. They turned and walked off in separate directions, and Sara walked with a purpose as if she were headed to Ethics class, yet once she was out of sight from the dorms, she curved around and took the long way to the topiary garden. Krystal was already there when she arrived.

"Hey," Sara said.

Krystal returned the greeting, then they just stood there, silent, like they both knew it didn't make sense for the two of them to be together without Galric. An eternity passed, then Krystal took one of her curls between her first and second fingers. She stretched it out, then let it boing back into place. "Sorry about what I said back there, about it being cool to get out of class," she said. "I really am sorry your friend got hurt."

Sara braced herself. Krystal hadn't said anything at all

upsetting, but Sara felt like any second now things would take a bad turn. "Thanks," she said warily.

"Yeah," Krystal said. She stretched out her curl again. "And, I, um . . . I'm sorry I wasn't so great to you before. Like, just, generally before. I've been hanging out with Galric and he's been telling me lot about you and . . . I dunno, I guess you're a lot cooler than I thought." She made a goofy face, like she smelled something strange. "That sounded weird. I just—"

"He told me stuff about you too," Sara said, remembering their conversation after the first day of school. "Good stuff," she added, when Krystal looked nervous.

They heard leaves rustle, and Galric tromped into the topiary garden. His face was flushed. "Sorry," he said. "Amala nearly walked right by me. I had to hide until she left, then I got here as fast as I could. What's up?"

Sara guessed it was good that Galric had taken so long; she felt a lot more comfortable including Krystal now. "You know how yesterday you both left detention before me?" she asked.

They nodded, so she launched in and told them everything: about Amala's session with the Ambassadors, about Loriah, and about how Amala tried to explain everything away. She almost left out the parts about Flissa because it seemed disloyal to say anything about her to Krystal, who didn't know her well. Yet in the end she included everything, because Galric and Krystal could only help if they knew the whole story. She told them that Flissa said almost the exact same thing as Amala about the Ambassadors session, but that Flissa had also lied to Amala about Zinka and Loriah having drama last night.

Krystal's eyes lit up as Sara spoke and she bounced on her toes. "Yes! It all makes sense. Amala's the Cleaner. She wants to get rid of Genpos, and she's using the Ambassadors to do it. I had a feeling. I asked Skeed about it last night. I asked him, 'What do you talk about in the meetings?' and he was all, 'We talk about unification and we talk about the ball,' but of course that's what he said. No way would he tell me the truth, 'cause I'm a Genpo. I *knew* it!"

"You specifically knew Amala was using the Ambassadors to go after Genpos?" Galric asked, incredulous.

"Not that *specifically*," Krystal admitted, "but of course that's what she wants. That's what she's *always* wanted."

Sara nodded. She even picked up on Krystal's energy and bounced a little too. "Exactly! You see it, right? But the stuff she and Flissa said—what do you think of that?"

Krystal shook her head. "I don't buy it. I buy that your sister believes it; I mean, I don't know her, but she's supposed to be super smart, right? But I think it's an excuse. Even back then lots of people didn't believe Amala had really changed. My grandmother had all these old diaries and I've read them—everyone thought she was just saying she changed to make Maldevon happy. They were actually surprised she didn't become a Keeper of the Light."

"Okay, but she *didn't* become a Keeper of the Light," Galric said.

"'Course not," Krystal said. "Maldevon was her husband; no way would Grosselor ever trust her. She went to the Twists, she became a Shadow, and now she's on the inside doing exactly what she always wanted: plotting against the Genpos." Then she spun to Sara. "So what do we do about it?"

Sara stood a little taller. She liked that Krystal was looking for her to lead the way. She just wished she had a good answer. "I don't know."

"Do we tell our parents?" Galric suggested.

Sara smiled; she always smiled when Galric called Rouen and Katya his parents. His suggestion made sense—their parents were among the most powerful people in Kaloon—but Sara wasn't sure it was the right call, since all four of them truly believed in Amala. They wouldn't take any accusations seriously unless there was something concrete to back them up.

"Not yet," Sara said. "I think we find out more information first. Krystal, keep talking to Skeed, see what you can find out. Galric, think you can talk to Nikkolas and Anastasia?"

"I don't even know them," Galric said.

Krystal smacked his arm and rolled her eyes. "You're a hero, remember? You can talk to anyone and they'll be psyched about it. Just flash 'em your battle scars."

Galric blushed. "I'm not flashing anybody anything. But sure, I'll try to talk to them."

"Great," Sara said. "I know Jentrie; I can talk to her. And I'll see if I can find out what Flissa and Zinka are hiding."

"You really think Zinka cursed Loriah and Flissa's protecting her?" Galric asked.

He sounded dubious, and Sara understood. She couldn't believe she was even thinking it, but Galric hadn't seen the way Flissa looked at her. The cold daggers in her eyes.

"I don't know," Sara said. "Maybe. Maybe it's just a hoodle thing that got out of hand. Maybe it doesn't have anything to do with Amala's Genpo plot. But it's something. And I want to find out what it is."

"We're with you," Krystal said.

She put out her hand—the one with the tattoo on the back. Sara smiled and placed her own hand on top of it, then Galric set his on top of theirs.

"It's on," Sara said.

Chapter 13
Flissa

"You genuinely don't remember anything?" Flissa asked.

It was lunchtime, and Loriah was in a bed in the infirmary, propped up with pillows and munching popcorn from a bowl in her lap. She played checkers while she ate; the infirmary staff had given her a magical board that made its own moves against hers. They liked sick kids to have something to do while they recovered. Loriah didn't feel even remotely sick, but if she got to hang out, snack, and play games instead of going to classes, she was happy to stay all day long.

"Nothing," Loriah said. "Same as I told Amala and everyone else who's been in and out of here asking me. I remember going to the orphanage and giving dandelions to those kids, then next thing I know I'm banging my head on the floor."

"On pillows," Flissa said. "Sara and I made sure you had pillows under you when you fell."

"Cement pillows?" Loriah asked. "'Cause falling on them *hurt.* HA!" she shouted as she jumped three of her invisible opponent's checkers. Then she took another handful of popcorn. "Where's Zinka? She's too cool to come see me?"

Flissa's throat closed a little at the sound of Zinka's name.

"She's with the hoodle team," Flissa said. "She knew they'd be worried, so she wanted to tell them all together. They'll be here soon."

"So they've got no idea who jacked me up, huh?" Loriah asked.

Flissa shook her head. "No magical signature. You recovered too fast. You're *sure* you don't remember anything from last night?"

Loriah turned to her, completely deadpan. "Flissa, I swear if you don't tell me whatever it is you think I should know, I will pour this bowl of popcorn on your head. And then I will pick the kernels off your head and eat them, because popcorn."

"Okay. Last night you went to Zinka's room and you saw . . ." Flissa looked around to make sure no one was looking, then she ducked close to Loriah and whispered, "She has a cat."

"A WHAT?!" Loriah boomed, and the nurses huddled at the other side of the room jumped. Flissa panicked. She shouldn't have said anything. Now Loriah was going to tell, and Zinka would lose Teddy and it would all be Flissa's fault and—

Loriah grinned. "Couldn't help it, you were all scared and quiet." She waved to the nurse and said, "Sorry, checkers thing." Imitating Flissa, she then leaned close and whispered back, "Why do I care if she has a cat?"

Flissa had no idea if she should even continue. There

could be a million reasons Loriah didn't remember the cat.

Or maybe she didn't remember because that was part of the curse. Maybe Zinka was so afraid Loriah would turn her in, she took drastic steps to make sure Loriah couldn't.

That would be horrible, and Flissa didn't want to think Zinka could do anything like that, but she also didn't have a better explanation. She'd wanted to ask Zinka, but when they left the girls' dorms, they'd run into one of the men who'd tried to take Loriah to the infirmary—Loriah had pointedly run off and taken *herself* so the men weren't needed—and he'd walked them to their first-block class. Then second block was Magic Lab, and she certainly wasn't going to say anything in front of Amala—or Sara, who kept giving her odd searching looks the whole block.

It was fine, though. Flissa didn't need to ask, because she didn't actually believe that Zinka would hurt Loriah—not on purpose, at least.

Besides, there *was* another explanation for what happened to Loriah . . . but it was so wild that Flissa chided herself for even thinking it. Still, it would make her crazy if she didn't at least mention it, and time was short—other people would be in to visit any minute now.

"The cat," Flissa whispered, "it wasn't just any cat. It had flaming yellow eyes. Just like . . . you know . . ."

All the mirth drained from Loriah's face. She knew.

"I freaked out," Loriah said.

"Yes! You remember!"

Loriah shook her head. "I just know I'd freak out. I hated those eyes. And these nurses keep making me think about them. 'Do you have nightmares?' they ask. 'Do you have a lot of nightmares?' 'How bad are they?' 'Tell us about them; go into *detail*.'" Loriah gave Flissa a dead-eyed look. "'Cause yeah, that's what I need—to think about all the stuff that keeps me up at night during the day, when I'm actually okay."

Loriah went back to her game. Flissa could tell she wanted to change the subject, but Flissa couldn't, not yet. "The way you reacted when you saw the cat," she said, "it wasn't just that it had *eyes* like . . . you know. It was that you acted like you thought she *was* . . . you know. And then you got cursed, so . . ."

Flissa let the silence hang, waiting for Loriah to finish her unspoken thought, or at least show she understood. Loriah didn't. She kept playing checkers, then finally asked, "So . . . what?"

Flissa blushed and squirmed in her chair. She didn't want to say it out loud. Then Loriah's eyes widened, and for a second she looked just as young and terrified as when Flissa first saw her surrounded by the Keepers of the Light.

"You think . . . *she* cursed me?"

"I . . . I don't know," Flissa stammered. "I mean, I don't. Not really. From everything I've studied, magic doesn't work like that. You can change things about how you look—like your hair or your clothes—or a curse could ravage your body, like what happened to my mother, or Gilward, or Mitzi . . . but you can't change the basic structure of who you are. I don't even know of a Shadow who can do that, never mind a Magical Animal. Most Magical Animals can't even do magic at all, but with the way you acted and then getting cursed right afterward, I just can't get it out of my head that maybe . . ."

196

Flissa saw the furrow appear in Loriah's forehead as she considered it. Then Loriah shook her head. "It's not her. There's no way she can turn herself into a cat. If she could, she'd have done it all the time, to sneak through tiny pipes or underground tunnels and spy on other Mages. Since she was too big, she had *me* do that stuff. Sometimes I'd get stuck, and she'd complain that we lost so much time getting me out, it'd be better to leave me to rot. I kinda always thought she might."

Flissa could imagine Loriah wedged tightly in a pitch-black underground tunnel, unable to see or move, waiting to see if Raya would rescue her, or if this was the time she'd remain helplessly buried alive. Just thinking about it made Flissa's heart thump, and she inhaled deeply, suddenly desperate for breath. She wanted to comfort Loriah, to reach out and squeeze her hand, but she knew by now that was the last thing Loriah wanted when she was thinking about her days in the Twists. Flissa just had to wait and know her friend would keep talking when she was ready.

"So no," Loriah finally said, "she can't turn into a cat. Maybe I freaked out, but no way it's her. Besides, I know what getting cursed by her feels like. If I felt it again, I'd remember it."

"Hail to our fallen comrade!" Zinka cried out as she stormed into the infirmary. The rest of the hoodle team were behind her, and they all swarmed Loriah's bed.

"Brought you biscuits from lunch," Dallie said, holding out a lumpy, napkin-wrapped bundle.

"Yes!" Loriah cried, snatching it out of her hand. "If anyone brought me honey, I will love you forever."

Rosalie lifted a wing to reveal a squat honey pot tucked underneath. "I closed the lid up tight," she said, "but sorry if there's any feathers in it."

"Don't even care," Loriah said, greedily opening the honey pot and dipping in a biscuit. "Just psyched to have it. I'd say I'd share with the rest of you, but I'd be lying; they're mine."

As everyone spoke at once, Zinka sidled up to Flissa. "Can we talk a sec?" she whispered.

Flissa nodded, and they slipped out together, tromping through the copse of trees behind the infirmary until they were well out of earshot of anyone near the building. Zinka had been all smiles inside, but now she looked desperately worried and Flissa could see the deep circles under her eyes were even darker.

"Did she say anything?" Zinka asked, her voice a whisper. "About Teddy?"

"She didn't even remember you have a cat," Flissa said. "I had to remind her."

"Why?" Zinka asked. "Why would you remind her?" She put her fist to her mouth, and Flissa wondered if that was why her knuckles were so red and raw, from pushing them against her teeth.

"It's okay," Flissa said. "She didn't really seem to care. She didn't say she'd turn you in."

Zinka nodded, but she didn't take her knuckles out of her mouth. She was obviously worried, and Flissa didn't want to make things worse, but now that Zinka was here in front of her and they were alone, she had to know the truth.

"Zinka . . . last night . . . you said if Loriah came

near your room, you'd destroy her. You didn't . . ."

Zinka whipped around and punched the tree behind her.

"I *knew* you'd ask that!" she snapped. She pushed her knuckles into her forehead, then wheeled to Flissa. "Is it because I'm from the Twists? You think I'm violent and that I'll curse anyone who makes me mad?"

Flissa's heart thudded. "No!" she said, though in her head she was already wondering how she'd protect herself if Zinka struck out at her. Would she be strong enough to repel a curse without Sara next to her?

Zinka's nostrils flared . . . then her eyes suddenly welled with tears. She leaned back against the tree and slid to the ground, burying her head in her hands.

"I'm sorry," she said, her voice thick. "I didn't mean that. I'm just tired. I don't sleep a lot. . . . Nightmares, you know? But Teddy helps; she keeps me calm when I remember stuff from. . . . And I was so afraid I'd have to give her up because of Loriah . . . but I didn't curse her. I swear I didn't. I won't lie—I might've, if she'd come to my room and tried to take Teddy. I wouldn't have done *that* to her, but I might've tried to shock her or set off a stink spell or something to keep her away. But I didn't see her after you left, and I didn't do anything to her."

Two seconds ago Flissa had been terrified of what Zinka might do, but now she saw her for what she really was: just a girl, a couple of years older than Flissa and Sara, who'd suffered through things the two of them could only imagine. Zinka wasn't dangerous; she was in agony. Her pain was so intense she couldn't sleep and she chewed at her nails and her knuckles, but she still fought to put

199

on a good show and make friends and build a life for herself.

Flissa sat down next to her against the tree trunk. "I believe you," she said. "I'm sorry I ever thought anything else."

"I guess it would be strange if you didn't," Zinka said. "But thanks."

She took a deep breath, rubbed the tears from her eyes, then jumped up and shook herself out before reaching out to Flissa. Zinka helped her up, and held out a scratched-up fist.

"Right fist, left fist, both fists, both hands," she said.

Flissa wasn't sure what she meant at first, but she followed Zinka's lead and fist-bumped their right then left fists, then both fists, then slapped both hands. Zinka smiled.

"Hoodle handshake," she said. "We came up with it on the way to the infirmary. Like it?"

Flissa beamed. "I do," she said.

* * *

Flissa spun the hoodlehoop on her hook and ran as fast as she could, dodging to avoid a block from Dallie.

"Yeah, Flissa!" Zinka roared from the sidelines. "You go!"

They were playing a three-on-three scrimmage, and while as a starter Zinka would normally be in the thick of it, she stayed on the sidelines since she'd had to miss the first part of practice for her Ambassador of Kaloonification meeting. Coach Rian had received a bubblegram from Amala at the beginning of practice telling her this would be an everyday thing, and while none of the other players spoke ostrich, Rosalie's feathers blushed bright red when she heard her mother's furious response. She kept her anger to herself, though; her reply bubblegram to Amala simply said, "Understood."

Zinka was a great player, and games were always better when she was on the field, but she was amazing on the sidelines too. She ran up and down almost as much as Coach Rian, constantly clapping and cheering them on.

"Yes, Trinni!" Zinka screamed as Trinni smacked the hoop off Flissa's hoodlehook and ran toward the opposite goal. "You take that hook! You got this!"

"That's right, you've got it!" came another voice . . . but this one made them put down their hooks and spin in disbelief.

"Loriah!" Odelia cried.

Within seconds, they'd dropped the game entirely and swarmed Loriah, each one of them jumping in for a hug and bombarding her with questions.

"When did they let you out?"

"Are you okay?"

"How do you feel?"

"Are you clear to play?"

The last question was from Coach Rian, all business.

"Got a note to prove it," Loriah said. She handed the coach a scroll. "Turns out I wasn't cursed."

"Seriously?" Zinka asked.

The question was for Loriah, but she was looking at Flissa.

Flissa didn't believe it either. She shook her head.

"That doesn't make sense," Flissa said. "We saw you.

You must have been cursed. That's the only way that would've happened."

"That'd be true if she were a Genpo," Coach Rian said as she re-rolled the scroll. "But she's a Mage. The scroll says the nurses did all kinds of tests, and they couldn't find any traces of a curse. They think it was self-imposed. The result of a nightmare."

"You cursed *yourself*?" Trinni asked in her too-loud voice.

"Oh yeah," Dallie said, nodding her bright blue head of curls. "Spell terrors. We talked about that first day, in my section of Magic Lab. It's not really a curse, though—more like you're acting out something in a dream. But like a really hard-core majorly bad dream." She raised three fingers on her right hand and met Loriah's eyes. "I feel you, sister."

Zinka and Trinni, the other Untwisteds on the team, nodded somberly. Hard-core majorly bad dreams were something they clearly all knew well.

Flissa knew she shouldn't be excited about the news that Loriah was plagued with dreams so terrible they'd made her hurt herself in her sleep . . . but she was. Even though her Magic Lab section hadn't talked about spell terrors the first day, the concept sounded familiar, and Flissa knew she must have read about them somewhere. She wished she'd remembered them sooner, because it made perfect sense. It wasn't that Zinka cursed her; and it wasn't that Raya had defied all laws of magic and become an evil rogue kitten. What happened was so much simpler than that: Loriah had seen eyes that looked just like Raya's, and they gave her a nightmare so horrible she'd had spell terrors. It should have been obvious.

Loriah blushed red enough to show off the skein of thin scars all over her face. Flissa was sure Loriah liked the support from the other Untwisteds, but she also knew Loriah hated anyone feeling sorry for her. She wasn't surprised when Loriah quickly changed the subject.

"So you read the note," she said to Coach Rian. "Can I play?"

Coach Rian ended the scrimmage and ran drills so all nine of them could participate. They played until dark, and by the time Flissa collapsed in a carriage to go home, her legs were noodles and her arms jelly. She'd bubble-grammed ahead to let her parents know she was leaving, so when she arrived, her mother and father were waiting in the ballroom, along with a feast from Filliam. Queen Latonya jumped up when Flissa staggered in and wrapped her in a big hug.

"My poor baby," she murmured into Flissa's hair. "You must have been so scared."

Her father was on his feet too and wrapped his arm around Flissa to lead her to the table. "Spell terrors," he said. "Amala gave us her full report. I'm glad that's all it was."

"We told Sara," her mother said. "She already ate and went up to do homework. I'm sure you'll want to talk to her about it."

Flissa had just shoveled a generous helping of stuffed pheasant and curried brussels sprouts onto her plate, but she froze with her fork halfway to her mouth.

She hadn't even thought about talking to Sara about it.

It's not that she didn't want to. She *would*, of course, and now that their mother said something, she was *dying* to talk to Sara because the spell terrors proved Zinka was innocent.

Still, this was the first time ever that something major had happened, and talking to Sara about it hadn't been her first thought. Or even her second. It was strange, and Flissa didn't know how to feel about it.

Since her parents already knew the biggest parts of Flissa's day, she filled them in on the rest of her classes and hoodle as she ate a second helping of dinner, then excused herself and ran upstairs to her and Sara's room. Knowing Sara was aware of the situation, she dove right in.

"Spell terrors!" Flissa said as she zoomed through the door. "That's all it was!"

Sara was standing by the window, where a bubblegram floated in and popped in front of her face. "I asked Skeed to tell me everything about the Ambassadors meeting today, but he didn't give a lot of detail," a female voice said. "He's definitely leaving stuff out. I know he'd never do anything to the Genpos he knows, but I don't think he gets that Amala won't let them pick and choose. I don't trust her. I don't trust Anastasia or Zinka either."

Flissa frowned. "Who was that?"

Sara didn't answer. She climbed onto her bed and settled herself on a pile of laundry, then crossed her legs and took out her own vial of message milk. "This message is for Krystal," Sara said.

"Krystal?" Flissa asked. "Galric's friend Krystal?"

Sara spoke into the message milk loop. "Thanks for the update. Good work with Skeed. End."

The bubble broke off the cone and floated out the window. Only then did Sara turn to Flissa. "What did you say?"

Flissa scrunched her face quizzically. "Why are you sending bubblegrams to Krystal?" she asked. "I thought you didn't like her."

"We're good now," Sara said, just as another bubblegram—this one the size of Sara's head—flew through the open window and popped in front of her.

"I can't actually believe it," Galric's voice said, "but the hero thing worked. Nikkolas thinks I'm his cool little brother. He made me have dinner at his house with his family, and they all wanted to touch my scar, which was weird, but he told me all about the Ambassadors meetings, except not about the parts where he was knocked out and floating 'cause he has no idea that's a thing, which, I mean, no surprise. Everything he's heard is all about the ball and working together and one Kaloon, but I guess we kinda knew he wouldn't have a lot to tell us. I'll try talking to Anastasia tomorrow. And I might have to go to a party next week. Nikkolas said it's his birthday and he wanted his 'little hero bro' there. I know, it's weird. Anyway, that's what I've got. I'll see you tomorrow."

Flissa was stunned. "What are you doing?"

"One sec," Sara said. She opened her message milk again and sent a bubblegram to Galric, thanking him for the update and saying she'd see him tomorrow, then she turned back to Flissa. "We're investigating."

"*Investigating?*" Flissa said. "Investigating what?"

"Amala's plans for the Ambassadors," Sara said. Then she tilted her head. "And speaking of Amala, how come you and Zinka lied to her today? You told me last night Loriah and Zinka had drama, but when Amala asked you if any-one was mad at Loriah, you didn't say anything."

"Because it didn't matter," Flissa said. "Zinka didn't curse her. No one cursed Loriah. It was spell terrors, Mother and Father said they told you."

"They did," Sara said. "And it's great Zinka *didn't* curse Loriah because now everything makes more sense. The Ambassadors and Amala are scheming to get rid of Genpos, not Mages."

Flissa gaped. "I *explained* to you why Amala put the Genpos to sleep during the meeting. I read you that part of the book!"

"You did," Sara agreed. "And Amala told me about it too."

"You talked to *Amala* about it?"

Flissa heard her voice jump up an octave, but she couldn't help it. Nothing Sara was saying made sense.

"She talked to *me* about it," Sara said. "After you and Zinka left the girls' dorm, she told me she knew what I'd seen, and she explained it to me." Her eyes darted to the window, where another bubblegram was floating in. "One second."

The bubblegram popped in front of Sara's face. "Your Highness!" a voice chirped, and Flissa immediately recognized it as Jentrie. "I was beyond thrilled to receive your bubblegram and would of course be honored to have lunch with you tomorrow. Maybe I can get your advice on the Kaloonification Ball; I'd love to make it as magnificent as the balls at the palace!"

Flissa opened her mouth to speak, but Sara held up a finger asking her to wait. Then she sent a chirpy bubblegram to Jentrie, saying she was thrilled too and that she looked forward to tomorrow. When the bubblegram was safely out the window, she turned back to Flissa.

"Sara, this is ridiculous!" Flissa exploded.

"No it's not. Galric, Krystal, and I don't think Amala's being honest, so we're doing something about it."

"But—"

Sara held up her finger again. "I know you'll say we're wrong, but that's why we're investigating. We're talking to all the Ambassadors to see what we can find out. If you want to help us and talk to Zinka, that'd be huge. She's the one we trust the least, for sure."

Flissa couldn't believe Sara was acting so matter-of-fact—as if this wasn't a huge deal, she wasn't completely ignoring everything Flissa had told her, and she wasn't insulting one of Flissa's friends.

"Why? Why do you trust her the least?"

Sara tilted her head to the side, considering. "Okay, we kinda don't trust Anastasia just as much, but she's less dangerous because she's a pig—boar—and her magic isn't as strong. But Zinka set off the stink spell, so we know she's not into Kaloonification, and she doesn't have a lot of close Genpo friends like Skeed."

"There are Genpos on the hoodle team!" Flissa said. "She loves Trinni and Odelia!"

"She was also the first one to shoot magic at the fake Keepers when they marched into the lunch area," Sara continued as if Flissa hadn't said anything. "And something's going on with her, have you noticed? She has these dark circles under her eyes, like she's keeping a horrible secret and it's not letting her sleep."

Flissa thought about Zinka and her poor battered

207

knuckles and ravaged fingernails. How she curled up by the tree, pouring her heart out while she fought not to cry.

"*Or*," she said icily, "it's like she spent her whole life in the Twists and saw and did horrible things, and *that's* why she can't sleep. And maybe also because people like the Princess of Kaloon think she's capable of anything just because she's an Untwisted."

"I'm fine with Untwisteds!" Sara shot back. "Just not Untwisteds who are scheming against Kaloon!"

"You're the only one scheming!" Flissa said. "You and Galric and Krystal. Amala and I both told you the truth about what's going on, and you won't believe us!"

"I won't believe *her*," Sara said coolly. "I believe *you* believe what you read in Amala's book, but I also believe you're mistaken."

Sara was so wrong, and at the same time so confident, Flissa felt like her head would burst into flames. She stomped to her own side of the room and poured all her fury into creating another solid cream-colored wall to separate herself from her sister.

It was the one charm she'd officially mastered.

* * *

Flissa thought she'd feel better about everything in the morning, but when she woke up, took down her magic, cream-colored wall, and saw her sister tangled up in her usual mix of bed linens and laundry, she only seethed. It felt wonderful to get out of the palace before Sara even woke up, and deliciously satisfying to run up to Loriah's room and unload about every single thing Sara was doing that made her crazy.

"Okay," Loriah said, completely unmoved by Flissa's diatribe.

"*Okay*'?!" Flissa echoed. "You had spell terrors from the stuff you went through in the Twists. You think it's 'okay' for Sara to come after Zinka because she doesn't like it that Zinka can't sleep?!"

Loriah made a face. "Unless you told the story wrong, that's not really what she said."

"Whatever, there was the other stuff too," Flissa admitted. "But still, doesn't it make you mad?"

"Nope," Loriah said. "If that's what Sara and Galric think, that's what they think. They can investigate whoever they want. Don't let it bother you so much."

But it did bother her, a lot, and while talking about it with Loriah was infuriating—how did she not see the problem?—just *being* with Loriah and the rest of her hoodle friends was wonderful, and it was definitely more fun than being with Sara. Flissa stretched the day out as long as possible so she wouldn't have to go home and see her twin. Of course she stayed for hoodle practice after school, but then Zinka rallied the team to stick around and have dinner in the girls' dorm kitchen, then a bunch of them stayed even later and sprawled out in the common room to do their homework together. Every assignment took a million times longer because they'd stop to tell stories or laugh about something.

It felt so easy just being herself with these eight other girls. Flissa was amazed because, aside from Loriah, they were all brand-new friends, but she already felt like she'd known them forever. It was as if instead of one sister, she now had a team of eight.

Still, none of her hoodle friends were Sara, and even though Flissa was angry with her, by the end of the day she could feel the rope from her heart to her twin's tugging them back together. She again raced through an evening snack and chat with their parents, then ran up to their room, bubbling over with stories she couldn't wait to tell.

She found Sara cross-legged on her bed, one of Flissa's old history books spread out in front of her, juggling bubblegrams from Galric and Krystal as she read. She didn't say hello when Flissa came in, she simply fixed her with a stare and asked, "Did you know that the year before Amala married Maldevon, she declared her village a Genpo-free zone, and magically harassed every Genpo who lived there until they left?"

It turned into a huge fight. It didn't end until Flissa re-erected the cream-colored wall and went to bed.

After that, Flissa forced herself to spend as much time away from the palace as possible. She even spent most of the weekend at Maldevon Academy; not only did she have hoodle practice both days, but Zinka had rallied the team to help the Ambassadors prepare for the Kaloonification Ball, which was now three weeks away. When they weren't practicing, Flissa and her friends joined Zinka, Jentrie, Skeed, and Anastasia on the Athletics field to make posters for the event. Amala was there to supervise, and she even opened up the main building so they could hang the posters all over the school.

"Sara and Galric would love this," Flissa told Loriah ruefully as Loriah magically added dancing sparkles to a poster. "All their investigation 'targets' in one place."

"Invite 'em to come," Loriah said, and Flissa reminded

herself that if she wanted someone to be snide and bitter with her, Loriah was the wrong person to ask.

Flissa didn't like avoiding Sara, but since fighting with her was far worse than keeping her distance, she went with the easier option. When the school week started, Flissa didn't even consider waiting for Sara for breakfast. She got up, washed and dressed in a flash, hugged her parents goodbye, then was out the door and on Balustrade's back early enough to surprise her friends on dorm with a basket of Filliam's egg tarts the second they woke up. Unlike Sara, Flissa's teammates were thrilled to see her, and in the bustle of their morning conversation Flissa could almost forget she was fighting with her sister.

It got even easier to forget when the school day started, and everyone saw the Kaloonification Ball posters. It made the event seem real, and suddenly it was all anyone could talk about. Flissa constantly heard people buzzing about it in the halls, and she was glad Zinka had made sure the hoodle team was involved. It made Flissa feel special, like she was on the inside of something big and important. That was especially true when the ball-posals started— that's what everyone called it when someone made a big deal out of asking someone else to the ball. They began with Nikkolas, who hijacked morning announcements by jumping onto the stairs of the main building along with four of his completion-year friends. They sang a cappella in front of the whole school, even though Nikkolas couldn't carry a tune to save his life, and at the end of the song Nikkolas got down on his knees, threw out his arms, and in a warbling tenor asked Zinka to go to the ball with him. The whole school applauded when she said yes.

"See?" Flissa whispered to Sara that day in Magic Lab. "Zinka's going to the ball with Nikkolas, a Genpo. She's not scheming against them."

"Maybe not," Sara said while magically twirling a lead ball high in the air. "Or maybe she just said yes to cover up her real plans."

Flissa didn't even bother arguing. She huffed and turned back to her own lead ball, which she couldn't budge from the floor.

After Nikkolas, the ball-posals came fast and furious—people and animals asking each other to the ball with songs, dance routines, bubblegrams that magically exploded into fireworks, brightening bugs spelling out the question in midair . . . Flissa had never experienced anything like it before. She'd been to all kinds of royal balls as Princess Flissara, but people didn't really ask one another to those. Everyone with a title just showed up with their families. Now everyone walked around school on pins and needles, either planning their own ball-posal, or eagerly awaiting the next one, and wondering if it would be for them.

Only Loriah seemed immune to the excitement, until that weekend, when the team had their first hoodle match against a team from the kingdom of Winterglen. When the whistle blew for halftime, Loriah tried to run off the field, but then a flute tooted, and her path was blocked by a single rose that sprouted up from the ground and grew as high as Loriah's chest. Flissa looked around to see who did the magic, and found a third-year with long red curls holding up a sign that read *Loriah, will you go to the ball with me?*

Flissa wheeled back to Loriah, who was smiling and nodding, her face so red it tinged her blond ponytail.

"Shut up," Loriah said when the rose had poofed away in another round of flute notes, and she stood with Flissa on the sidelines. She tried to sound stern, but she couldn't pull it off when she was still blushing and grinning.

"I'm just surprised," Flissa said. "I thought you didn't even talk to anyone except me, Galric, Sara, and the team."

"I *barely* talk to anyone else," Loriah said. "Marianna's in my Magic Lab class. She's tolerable."

Flissa smiled, and she wasn't surprised when Loriah played even harder the second half of the game, as if she knew someone was watching.

The team won easily, and afterward everyone streamed down from the stands, including her parents, Rouen, Katya, and Primka. Sara and Galric were with them, and seeing her sister there to support her at the game made Flissa's heart ache. She met Sara's eyes, and she could tell her twin felt the same way, but before she could say anything, their father picked Flissa up and spun her around, which he hadn't done in years.

"You are a hoodle genius!" he boomed, his mustache pointing giddily upward.

"I haven't gone to a hoodle game since before your father and I were married," her mother said. "It was fantastic!"

"Plus you won me a bet," her father said. "If you'd lost, I'd have owed the king of Winterglen ten bushels of plobquats. Now we get ten cases of their finest mulled quintberry cider."

"Shame on you for betting on the children's game," Katya said.

"And for not wagering more," Rouen added. "I'd have gotten us thirty cases. No way was this team going to lose."

While the adults argued about the merits of betting on a school hoodle match, Flissa stepped aside to talk to Sara and Galric. "I'm really glad you came," she told her sister.

"Wouldn't have missed it," Sara said.

"And Katya would have killed us if we'd tried," Galric added. "Wouldn't have missed it anyway, but . . . just saying."

"The ball-posal in the middle was pretty great, right?" Flissa said.

"Sure," Sara said. "If you forget that the whole Kaloonification Ball is a major lie Amala only created to cover up her true evil motives, then yeah, it was pretty great."

Flissa felt her face get hot. "Can't you let that go for one second? We just won our first game. It's a big deal."

"And someone trying to destroy the kingdom *isn't* a big deal?"

"Hey," Galric said, "remember that hoop you scored right at the end of the first half? That blocker was coming right at you, but then you did that gotcha zigzag. . . ."

He shifted his body left and right to imitate Flissa, but she wasn't paying attention. She was too annoyed with Sara, who was still staring at her with a smug look on her face, like she knew something Flissa was just too naïve to understand.

Flissa couldn't deal. She turned back to their parents, but then she saw Zinka walking down the field. She had her head down, and her knuckles were pressed against her teeth. Flissa was only a little surprised she didn't look happier; the hoodle team had elected her captain and she took the job very seriously. Flissa knew that even after a win she'd be playing the game back in her head, looking for things they could have done better.

"Zinka!" Flissa called. "Come here—I want you to meet my family."

Zinka wasn't far away, but she kept walking and didn't even look in Flissa's direction. Maybe she didn't hear her. Flissa tried again. "Zinka!"

Zinka wheeled to Flissa, her face a dark grimace. "Not now, okay?" she snapped, then continued stalking away.

"Gee, that's weird," Sara said, her voice making it clear that it wasn't weird at all. "I wonder why someone would avoid meeting the king and queen and members of the General Council."

"Just stop, okay?" Flissa said. She jumped into her parents' conversation to hug them all goodbye and tell them she'd meet them at home later, then ran to the girls' dorm to find Zinka. She hadn't wanted to give Sara the satisfaction of saying so, but it *was* weird that Zinka wouldn't want to meet Flissa's family, and Flissa was afraid something was really wrong. She knew Zinka had her plate full with hoodle, her classes, and working so hard to help plan the Kaloonification Ball. All the Ambassadors had thrown themselves into the planning, but Zinka seemed more involved than any of them—she was constantly pulling together ideas for the decorations, the music, the menu . . . it was a lot, and Flissa could see the pressure taking its toll on her. Most of the time she was herself, but sometimes she'd snap like she just did on the field, and Flissa knew Zinka was extra-stressed because she'd started wearing bandages over her ragged fingernails, and the circles under her eyes had only gotten darker.

Flissa ran up to the third floor and into Zinka's room. "Zinka?"

The room looked empty. Flissa was about to climb the ladder to see if Zinka was up in the loft bed, but then she heard a high-pitched squeak coming from the closet.

"Zinka?"

Flissa edged to the door and pulled it open. Zinka was huddled on the floor, Teddy curled in her lap. Tears rolled down her face as she stared at her ruined fingernails. Without the bandages, they looked even worse than Flissa had realized. They were shredded, split down the middle, and weeping blood. Zinka didn't try to hide them; she looked up at Flissa helplessly. "I can't get them to stop bleeding," she sobbed. "No matter what I do, they won't stop."

Chapter 14
Sara

"I am the worst sister in the world," Sara said. She and Galric were in a carriage on the way back to the palace. They'd stayed on campus after the game to meet up with Krystal so they could compare the latest notes from their investigation.

Grand sum of what they'd learned? Nothing. They'd spent the last week and a half talking to almost all the Ambassadors, and each of them had only the most glowing things to say about both Amala and their Kaloonification meetings. The Ambassadors also raved about Zinka. They all said she was the most amazing person in the world, who could juggle a million things and succeed at all of them. Even Jentrie, whom Sara had expected to spill all kinds of dirt, totally admired Zinka and said getting to know her had made her think differently about the Untwisteds.

Sara should have been happy. It seemed like everything she'd been worried about was a false alarm. Kaloon wasn't in danger. Amala wasn't scheming against the kingdom. The ball was just a ball, and from what Jentrie, Anastasia,

Nikkolas, and Skeed told them about it, it was going to be an incredible night.

Sara wasn't happy, though; she was miserable.

"You're not the worst sister in the world," Galric said. "I bet somewhere there's a person who did something really horrible to their sister. Like . . . I don't know. What's something really bad a person could do to her sister?"

"Attack one of her best friends and bring her down every time she's happy by talking about a conspiracy that doesn't exist?" Sara suggested.

Galric nodded. "Nice. I see what you did there. That's what *you* did to Flissa. But no. Guaranteed there's way worse."

Sara sighed. She let her head slump against the window and watched the kingdom stream by.

"Maybe Flissa was right," Sara said, keeping her gaze out the window. "Maybe I was only stuck on Zinka scheming with Amala because I was jealous."

Sara wouldn't look at Galric, but she could hear the confused scrunch of his brow when he spoke. "Why would you be jealous?"

"Because," Sara said. "She's . . . I don't know . . . popular. She's got a whole group of new friends, she's on the hoodle team, she's totally involved in planning the ball, plus you know she has to have the best grades in the school. She doesn't even flip her coin anymore—did you notice? Which is good, I know, but it's like she's a whole new person. She's just . . . winning. At life."

Now she did turn to Galric. The scrunch was there, just like she'd known it would be. "Okay," he said, "but that makes it sound like you're . . . *losing* at life. Which you're not."

"Aren't I?" Sara asked. "I haven't made one new friend since we got to school. And I know you're about to say Krystal, but we're only friends through you. And I'm only friends with her friends because of her *and* you. And I'm only friends with Jentrie because we knew each other before Kaloonification, and I went out of my way to talk to her to get dirt on Amala and Zinka."

"You literally just listed an entire group of new friends," Galric said.

"Well, sure, but—"

Galric raised an eyebrow, and Sara realized he was right. She hadn't felt truly alone since those first couple of days. Ever since then she'd always been with people. Sara and Skeed had made their peace once Skeed had embraced his role as Ambassador, so she always ate lunch with that crowd; and she'd actually enjoyed going over to Jentrie's house when they met up after school. Even she and Krystal turned out to have a lot in common. They were both artists, and Krystal had invited Sara to her house so they could make bowls on her pottery wheel.

Plus she'd always had Galric.

Sara buried her face in her hands. "I am the worst sister in the world, *and* I'm an idiot."

"Stop," Galric said. He shifted benches so he sat next to her and gently pulled her hands off her face. "You're not. And maybe it's not so much that you're jealous of Flissa. Maybe you just miss her."

The words hit home. She knew Galric was right. She didn't hate it that Flissa had other friends, she just missed the two of them together. They used to share *everything*, and now they didn't. She had thought living without all the rules of Princess Flissara would be heaven; instead it felt like she was missing a limb.

By the time they got back to the palace, Sara was determined to make things up to Flissa. She had dinner with her parents and talked about the hoodle game, then ran upstairs and spun in circles, scanning the room for something nice she could do for her twin.

"I'll clean!" she said out loud.

Flissa loved a clean room; her half was totally pristine. There was a clear dividing line down the center of the floor between carpet and trash heap. Sara set to work, determined to mirror Flissa's own tidiness with her own.

Five minutes later, she realized cleaning was exhausting. She shoved as much of her stuff as possible under her bed, in her drawers, and in her closet. The effect wasn't perfect, but it would do. She sprawled onto her not-entirely-disgusting bed and whipped out her charcoals and sketch pad. She wanted to make Flissa a portrait— something showing her in action on the hoodle field.

Sara lost track of time when she drew, so she had no idea how late it was when their door opened and Flissa came in. She looked exhausted, but Sara knew she'd perk up when she realized Sara had cleaned, and she'd go nuts when she saw the portrait.

"Flissa!"

Sara jumped out of bed but got tangled on the one remaining pile of laundry mixed in with her covers and tumbled to the floor.

"I can't, Sara," Flissa said wearily. "Not tonight."

She waved her hand and the cream-colored wall appeared between them, locking Flissa away.

"No!" Sara yelled, banging on the wall. "You don't understand! It's not what you think! Flissa, I *cleaned!*"

It didn't help. Sara knew it wouldn't; she'd already discovered the magic wall was soundproof. She wished she could just turn back everything and start the school year over again. She couldn't, but she'd do her best to start everything over in the morning. Tomorrow was a weekend day, but if Flissa was still upset she'd wake up early and head to campus, so Sara promised herself she'd wake up even earlier. And just in case she overslept, she tacked her charcoal drawing of Flissa to the door. Even if Flissa woke up super early and tried to slip out, she'd see the picture and know Sara wanted to apologize. Only then did she crawl under the covers and close her eyes.

The next thing she knew, tiny needles were digging into her cheek.

"Ow . . ." she muttered. "Cut it out . . . Flissa!"

"MEOW!"

Sara sat straight up in bed. The needles on her cheek weren't from Flissa at all. It was Nitpick. He'd been kneading Sara's cheek with his little paws, and when Sara bolted upright, she'd sent him tumbling into her comforter. He popped his head up and mewled again.

"Nitpick, I'm so sorry!"

She picked up the kitten and cuddled him, then looked around the room. The cream-colored wall was gone, but so was Flissa.

"Blast! I overslept!"

She looked at the door. Her charcoal drawing was no longer there. For a second she thrilled, imagining Flissa taking it down and keeping it with her . . . but then she saw Flissa had placed it on Sara's own desk.

She flopped back down, holding the kitten above her face. "She is *so* mad at me, Nitpick. What do I do?"

Nitpick didn't answer exactly, but he meowed and struggled in Sara's hands until she put him down, then he jumped off the bed and ran to and from the door, back and forth, meowing with every lap.

"You want me to follow you?" Sara asked.

Nitpick meowed louder.

Sara blinked the sleepy cobwebs from her head. Nitpick usually only came to her room when Galric was in the palace. And if the kitten wanted her to follow him . . .

"Is it Galric? Is he okay?"

Another meow from Nitpick, and this time he ran to the door and scratched at it.

Sara's heart thudded. Nitpick was never this insistent. Something must be wrong.

"Okay, I'm coming. One second."

She didn't even bother to wash up or fix her hair. She threw a robe over her nightgown, yanked on her slippers, and followed Nitpick through the palace. The kitten led her down the stairs, through the halls, then ran to the front door.

"Really?" Sara asked. "We're going outside?"

Nitpick's meow was so loud this time it was almost a roar.

"Okay, I got it, we're going outside!"

They pushed through the door and Nitpick zoomed ahead. It was impossible to go fast enough to follow him in her slippers, so she kicked them off and carried them in her hand. She slipped twice, and the morning dew left ugly wet splotches on her robe, but she kept running. When she finally caught up with Nitpick, he had settled on a spot of grass not far from the stables, and was twisted like a pretzel licking himself clean.

"Really?" Sara asked. "It's bathtime?"

Nitpick untwisted himself and stretched long and leisurely. Then he padded away a few steps, and Sara saw a glint of something on the grass. She picked it up.

It was a small silver square of metal, no bigger than her hand. The words etched into it wavered, like they were cut by an unpracticed hand, but they were clear enough to read.

The Exact Spot.

Sara's blood rushed in her ears.

"Galric?"

"I made a plaque," he said.

His voice came from behind her. She spun around and he was right there—almost too close. He flushed and she thought he might have felt the same way, but it would have been more awkward to move back.

Sara met his eyes; for a second she couldn't breathe.

"I know you had one commissioned and all," he said, "but I didn't know how long that would take, so I figured I'd just give it a try."

"It's good," Sara said. She looked away from Galric and down at the plaque, hoping her blood wouldn't whoosh so loudly in her ears. "Better than the one I commissioned, for sure."

"I doubt it," Galric said. He ran his hand through his hair, then took a deep breath. "Um . . . so the ball . . ."

Shivers danced down Sara's arms, and she met his eyes again. "Yeah?"

"It's happening, and . . . I mean, of course it's happening, but I, um . . . I kinda wondered if maybe you wanted to go with me. Together. I mean, you know, of course we'd *go* together, we'll both be coming from the palace, but what I'm saying is . . ."

Sara felt warm all over; she thought maybe the sun had come out from behind a cloud, but she wasn't sure. "I'd love to go with you."

"That's great," Galric said. "Really great."

They smiled at each other for a really long time—long enough that Sara thought maybe it should feel weird . . . but it didn't feel weird. Then she wondered—was that weird?

"Princess Sara!" Primka's voice echoed over the field. Galric and Sara jumped away from each other so quickly that Sara dropped her slippers, and Galric stumbled and plopped down on his rear end.

"Ugh," he groaned. "Dew on the grass. Wet butt. Very bad."

Primka soared between them and fluttered around their heads. "What is wrong with the two of you? It's a weekend morning, your mother's looking for you and your sister, and Flissa's run off to the academy while you're running around the fields in your robe and bare feet! And you on the ground," she added to Galric. "What do you think Katya would say if I told her the state you're in?"

Sara blushed. Katya was much more perceptive than Primka; she could only imagine what Katya would say.

"Sorry," Sara said. "I'll go back and see what Mom wants."

"Not looking like that you won't!" Primka said. "Your robe's smeared with grass stains. Back to your room and make yourself presentable. And, Galric . . . you're not my responsibility. Do what you want, but best to get cleaned up before Katya and Rouen see you."

"I'll do that, Primka," Galric said. He snuck a look at Sara and smiled. "Thanks."

"See you later, Galric," Sara said, returning the smile. "And thanks, Nitpick."

"Thanks, *Nitpick?*" Primka crowed as she followed Sara back to the castle. "The kitten did nothing. How about thanks, *Primka*, for coming to get you so your mother didn't have to send bubblegrams all over creation?"

Sara didn't listen to Primka. She squeezed Galric's plaque in her hand and grinned all the way back to the castle, then washed up and got changed before she went down to her mom's study.

"Flissa!" Sara cried.

Her sister was already there, sitting on the couch opposite their mom, who sat at her desk. The queen must have sent Flissa a bubblegram to call her back from her friends at school well before Primka went looking for Sara.

Sara was so full of things she wanted to tell Flissa, she forgot they were fighting. Then Flissa shot her an icy look, and Sara's voice dried up in her throat. She didn't want to make Flissa any angrier than she already was, so she sat at the far end of the couch, giving Flissa as much space as possible.

"Really?" their mom said. "Okay, then."

She got off her chair and plopped down on the rug in front of them, fluffing out her skirts so she could sit cross-legged.

"So," she said. "Want to tell me why the two of you aren't talking?"

"We're talking," they both said at the same time.

Normally that would make them lock eyes and giggle. The fact that it didn't made Sara want to cry.

"You say that, but I haven't seen you spending any time together. Not since school started. Flissa, you leave early and come home late; and Sara, you never stay up to wait for your sister with us."

"She doesn't have to wait for me," Flissa said. "We have the same room. She sees me there."

Sara wasn't sure if Flissa was sticking up for her, or just making an excuse to end the conversation. She tried to read the answer in Flissa's face, but all she saw was that her sister was agitated. She kept playing with her braid, and she shifted in her seat like she couldn't find a comfortable place to settle her body. It wasn't like her.

"Yeah," Sara said. "It's like Flissa said. We're good."

Their mom's long curls were like their dad's mustache. You could tell a lot about her emotional state by the state of her hair. Right now her curls drooped.

"I see . . . and how do you think your grades have been?"

Sara didn't have to think; she knew her grades were okay at best. She'd spent much more time on ferreting out Amala's secret anti-Genpo motives than on homework, and her classes had been the last thing on her mind.

"I think I'm doing well in Magic Lab," Sara offered.

"You are," their mom said. "You're doing excellently in Magic Lab. Flissa?"

Sara waited for Flissa to crow about her top-of-the-school marks, but instead she bit her lip. "I think I'm doing well in . . . Athletics?"

Their mom smiled. "Yes, you have perfect marks in Athletics. But Amala reached out to let me know that outside of those two classes, you both seem to be having trouble concentrating."

Sara was stunned. Flissa wasn't doing well in her classes?

"I know what you're going to say," Flissa quickly said. "You're going to tell me I'm doing too much, and I have to give up hoodle. But please, I promise you—"

Their mother's eyes rounded with sympathy as she held out a hand to stop her. "Flissa, honey, I'm not going to tell you to give up anything. The two of you have been through so much this last year. More than you ever should have had to bear." She leaned forward and put a hand on each of their knees. "I don't care about the grades. Your father doesn't either. I just want to know if they're a symptom of something bigger. So much is new for you right now; I want you to know you can come to me if you need to talk about anything. And I hope you can go to each other."

Sara felt tears well up. That's exactly what she wanted too, but it seemed entirely out of her control.

Their mom got up and kissed them both on the top of their heads. "Lecture over. You can go. Unless you want to stay and talk?"

She looked at them hopefully, but Sara didn't know what else she could say.

"Actually, I have a question," Flissa said. "Can I go to a sleepover tonight on dorm?"

Their mom frowned. "Tonight? But you have school tomorrow. And I was hoping maybe the two of you would spend the day together . . . ?"

"I know," Flissa said. "But it's for the team, to celebrate our hoodle win. I know we should have done it last night, but we didn't plan it, so . . . would it be okay? It would really mean a lot to us. A *lot*."

Flissa glanced desperately at Sara, and Sara saw the sweat on her sister's upper lip. She didn't know what the sleepover was all about, or why it mattered so much, but she could tell that for whatever reason, it was vitally important.

"I think she should go," Sara said. "I couldn't really hang out today anyway. I have a study group coming over. Trying to get those grades up."

Sara smiled, and her mom gave her a look that proved she didn't believe her at all, but after narrowing her eyes and studying Flissa's face, she nodded.

"Okay," she said. "You can go. But don't stay up late. I'll know if you're dragging tomorrow."

"Thank you," Flissa said. She threw her arms around her mom for a hug, then shocked Sara by hugging her too.

"Thanks," she whispered in Sara's ear.

Sara hugged her back. She squeezed her eyes shut and tried to fill the hug with everything she wanted to say.

"Got your back," she whispered.

They moved apart and Flissa gave her a smile, then she ran out of the room. Sara said goodbye to their mom and meandered toward the ballroom to scope out breakfast. On the way, she ducked into a corner by a window and pulled out her message milk vial.

"This message is for Krystal," she said.

The wand glowed blue. It was ready.

"Krystal, can you come to the palace? Let me know. End."

The bubble broke off the wand and floated away. Sara thought a second, then she pulled out the wand again and sent the same message to Jentrie.

She hadn't told the truth about the study group, but she *did* want to have a couple of friends over.

She had to pick a dress for the ball.

Chapter 15
Flissa

"**N**o!" Flissa said. "You're not allowed to do anything."

Zinka threw herself back on the common room couch and laughed. "Fine!" She clapped her hands together. "Hoodle team, create a party!"

The sleepover was Flissa's idea. When she found Zinka crying in the closet yesterday, Flissa had knelt down and hugged her, then taken her to the bathroom to wash off her battered fingernails and wrap them in bandages. Zinka had thanked her and asked for a minute alone, which Flissa had happily given her. She'd waited in Zinka's room with Teddy, who'd crawled right into Flissa's lap, and by the time Zinka strode back in, she was back to her confident, breezy self and acted as if nothing had happened.

Flissa didn't call her on it. If that's what she needed to do to feel better, Flissa understood. But she also knew Zinka had reached her breaking point. She needed time off from everything, and she needed to know that people loved her and cared about her. She'd bubblegrammed the whole team, and while she didn't tell them exactly what she'd seen, she let them know their captain needed them badly, and together they tried to decide what to do. Flissa honestly wasn't sure how the sleepover had popped into her head, but once she tossed it out there, everyone seized on it. Dallie got permission from the Dorm Fairies to use the common room overnight, and everyone who lived at home started wheedling for permission to sleep away on a school night. Amazingly, everyone got the okay, probably because all their parents were still filled with pride after the team's big win.

Now the whole team was crammed into the common room, pushing furniture around and decorating. Only Zinka was forbidden from lifting a finger. They all demanded she relax for once while everyone else did all the work.

"Truth time," Dallie said as she pointed at the couch and tried to move it with magic. Flissa heard a gong— Dallie's magical signature—but the couch didn't move at all.

"Here, let me get off," Zinka said.

"Nope!" Beverly-Ann said. "We've got it."

She physically picked up one end of the couch, and Dallie took the other, giving Zinka a ride across the room.

"Truth time," Dallie said again, huffing now as she set down the couch. "Who here has never been to a sleepover?"

Flissa, Dallie, and Zinka all raised their hands. Dallie narrowed her eyes at Loriah. "Hunkering down in a cave with other prisoners doesn't count," she said. "If it did, my hand would be down too."

"I know what a sleepover is," Loriah said. "I wasn't born in the Twists, remember? Hand stays down."

"You've never been to a sleepover, Flissa?" Nichelle

asked as she pointed upward. Teal sparks danced, and when they faded the ceiling was covered in multicolored twinkling star-shapes. Nichelle was short—not a lot taller than Beverly-Ann the chimp, but she had power on a hoodle field, and Flissa had seen her steamroll girls twice her size.

"Never," Flissa said as she pulled a blue shaggy rug into the middle of the room. "Sara and I were invited—*Princess Flissara* was invited—but my parents thought an entire night away from each other was too dangerous and we might slip up."

"Did you ever?" Rosalie said. She walked into the room from the kitchen, her wings filled with bowls of snacks. "I mean, did you ever come close to slipping up?"

Flissa had to think about it. "I don't think so." She looked at Odelia and Nichelle, who had always lived in Kaloon. "Did either of you ever suspect?"

Nichelle laughed. "That our princess was secretly twin Mages? Never in a million years. You hid it well."

Flissa thought she might have heard a hint of bitterness in Nichelle's voice, but she wasn't sure.

"We hid the twin part," Flissa said. "The Mage part we didn't even know."

"I like that," Odelia said. She was a Genpo from Kaloon, but she lived on dorm because her parents died in the Battle for Kaloonification and she had no other familiy. "Then maybe there's still hope for me." She threw out her arms as if she were casting a charm. "Booya!"

Every Mage in the room cracked up. "No one in the history of *ever* has said 'booya' when they did magic," Zinka said when she caught her breath.

Zinka seemed happy—genuinely happy. And Flissa was glad they'd managed to pull the party together. The room was in shape now, with most of the furniture pushed to the edges, and nine puffy sleeping bags on top of the shaggy rug, one opened out into a large nest for Rosalie. There were so many scattered pillows, it looked like a giant had dumped his bag of marshmallows all over the floor. The one piece of furniture left in the center of the room was a table crammed with pitchers of plobquat-mango smoothies and bowls of sweet and savory treats . . . which they ran back to the kitchen when they realized it was still only late afternoon and they had hours before they'd be even remotely sleepy.

"Am I allowed to make a suggestion?" Zinka asked. "Or is that against the rules of total relaxation?"

"One suggestion," Flissa said, knowing she'd suggest they all go out and play hoodle, which she did. They played until the brightening bugs came out, then they threw down their hoodlehooks and jumped around, catching as many as they could in their bare hands. They giggled as they ran back into the dorm with their treasures, then released them in the common room, where they flashed on and off amidst Nichelle's magical stars. The multicolored stars tinted the brightening bugs' glow, so the girls were bathed in colored strobes. Flissa held out her arms and let the circles of color dance over her skin.

The Dorm Fairies had long since stopped serving dinner, so the girls went into the kitchen and raided the refrigerator for leftovers, then grabbed the snacks and smoothies they'd stashed earlier and brought them back into the common room.

"A toast," Zinka said when she'd poured out smoothies for all of them. "To the greatest friends ever. Thanks for this."

They all clinked glasses, then drank their smoothies and munched on the snacks. They talked about everything—their lives before Maldevon Academy, things that happened at the school, but most of all the Kaloonification Ball. Loriah, Zinka, Trinni, and Rosalie all had dates, and Dallie demanded the rest of them admit who they'd like to go with, if they could go with anyone. Flissa blushed when it was her turn.

"Honestly," she said, "and I know this is going to sound like I'm making it up . . . I just want to go with all of you."

"Awwww," everyone chorused. Then they threw pillows at her because they swore she was lying. Still, they promised they'd all hang out as a group. Dates were welcome to join, but the team came first. Then they talked about what they'd wear, and Zinka told them the latest on the food and the music . . . but music reminded Odelia of Nikkolas's ball-posal and his horrible singing, and that got them into the best and worst ball-posals they'd seen, and they talked and laughed until their voices were hoarse and they were all exhausted.

Beverly-Ann opened the window to release the brightening bugs, then they crawled into their sleeping bags. Even though Flissa could barely keep her eyes open, she stayed up while everyone talked some more, until their voices faded as her friends dropped off to sleep one by one.

Before long, Flissa and Zinka were the last two awake. Their sleeping bags were right next to one another, and

Flissa could barely see her friend in the dim glow from Nichelle's magical stars. Still, she could swear the dark circles under Zinka's eyes were gone.

"You good?" Flissa whispered.

"So good," Zinka whispered back. "Thanks for this. And thanks for not bringing up . . . the thing. I'm sorry you had to see it."

"Don't be sorry. Honestly, I'm amazed it hasn't happened to more of us." She thought about Sara and her crazed obsession with Amala plotting against the Genpos. Her mom had said they'd been through a lot in the last year, and she wasn't wrong. Was that Sara's way of falling apart under the pressure? "Actually, I think it *is* happening to a lot of us, just in different ways."

"Yeah," Zinka said. She closed her eyes, and soon she was fast asleep. Flissa forced herself to stay awake—she wanted to make sure none of her friends woke up with horrible nightmares—but her body betrayed her and soon her eyes closed and she fell into darkness.

At one point Flissa heard a noise and opened her eyes. Zinka was standing up, trying to gingerly step over Loriah and move toward the door. Flissa reached out and touched her leg. Zinka jumped, and a half second later she crouched in front of Flissa's face.

"You scared me," she whispered. "I almost fell on top of Loriah."

"Sorry. Where are you going? Are you okay?"

"Bathroom," Zinka whispered. "And then I might check on Teddy. I feel bad that she's all alone. She likes to cuddle at night."

Flissa considered telling her to bring the kitten down

with her. It would be nice to have Teddy in their sleeping bags. But there was no way. The cat was still very much against school rules, and she definitely didn't want to risk Loriah getting spell terrors again. "Give her a kiss from me," she whispered.

"Will do," Zinka whispered back.

Flissa watched her as she cautiously picked her way over Loriah and Nichelle to get to the door. She wanted to wait for Zinka and make sure everything was okay, but after a while it seemed like she probably just went ahead and crawled into her own bed with her cat. Flissa couldn't blame her; she might have done the same thing. She let herself drift back to sleep.

The next time she woke up, it was to the sound of screams.

Flissa bolted upright in her sleeping bag. She saw Dallie in the middle of the room, eyes wide, hands over her face. She was looking down at Trinni and Odelia . . . both of whom had gone ramrod straight in their sleeping bags, eyes wide, mouths open in silent screams. Loriah was bent over them, the back of her hand in front of Trinni's mouth.

"What happened?" Flissa cried. She looked around the room and saw Beverly-Ann, Rosalie, and Nichelle were also awake, all of them still in their sleeping bags and looking as shocked as Flissa felt.

"I . . . I don't know," Rosalie said.

"They're breathing." Loriah moved her hand away from Trinni's mouth, then jumped back like she'd been bitten. When she spoke again, her voice was filled with dread. "Look . . . they're awake."

Flissa scrambled on her knees until she was next to her stricken friends. Both Odelia's and Trinni's eyes darted back and forth in terror, like they were trying desperately to escape their statue-stiff bodies.

"What happened?" Flissa asked them. "Can you move?"

No response. Just those darting eyes.

"Where's Zinka?" Nichelle asked, anxious. "She's not here."

"She woke up in the middle of the night," Flissa said. "I saw her. She—"

More screams came from upstairs.

"We should check that out," Loriah said.

"We don't have permission," Nichelle said, gesturing to Rosalie and Beverly-Ann. "We won't get past the wall. We'll stay with Trinni and Odelia; you go."

Flissa, Loriah, and Dallie tromped over the sleeping bags, burst out of the common room door, and raced up to the second floor.

The hall was littered with bodies. Some were dressed, others were in nightclothes or bathrobes, their baskets of toiletries spilled out next to them.

Every one of them had the same stiff-limbed rigor, mouths open, eyes dancing in a wild, desperate frenzy.

"They're *in there*," one girl wailed as she looked down at a stiff body. "They're in there, but they can't move!"

Flissa heard more screams coming from the third floor, but she didn't have to go up to know what she'd find.

"I have to go home," she told Loriah. "I don't want to send a bubblegram. I have to tell my parents and the General Council."

"Do it," Loriah said. "Go."

Flissa raced toward the stairs, then Loriah bounded after her and caught her arm. She leaned close and spoke softly enough that only Flissa could hear. "When you talk to your parents, you should tell them—did you notice?"

"Notice what?"

"They're all Genpos."

Chapter 16
Sara

Sara woke up grinning.

She hadn't been sure how the combination of Jentrie and Krystal would work out. They'd both spent their whole lives in Kaloon, but Krystal was a village girl who dressed like an Untwisted, while Jentrie was a noble who wore ball gowns to muck the stables.

That was of course a figure of speech; Jentrie would never muck the stables.

But whatever Amala had been telling the Ambassadors seemed to be working on Jentrie, because she really bonded with Krystal, especially when Sara told them about Galric's ball-posal and they grabbed each other's hands and squealed.

They'd spent hours going through Sara's dresses, and they were both impressed that every time they suggested a different color, or a different trim, or a slight change in the cut, Sara could wave her hands and let her scarlet-mist magic do the trick.

They thought they'd settled on the perfect dress, but Sara wanted to try it on one more time to be sure.

Then her stomach rumbled. Breakfast first. She pulled

on a light frock and opened the door to the Residence . . . then heard screams and shouts.

Her heart thumped—what was going on?

She raced to the railing and looked down.

It was chaos. The floor below was dotted with stiff bodies, people splayed out with every muscle tense and taut. Others flitted around them, jumping from one to another, feeling their necks and wrists for a pulse.

Sara didn't understand. Her skin prickled, then she turned toward the stairs and froze.

Rouen and Katya were walking her way, her mother's body stiff between them. Immediately Sara remembered Mitzi's curse, how it had withered her mother's skin and made it cling to her bones.

"It'll be okay, Sara," Katya said, "I promise. But you'll be better off if you don't look."

Sara was sure she was right, but she looked anyway. Tears instantly sprang to her eyes and her voice cracked.

"Mom?"

Unlike before, Queen Latonya hadn't aged eighty years in a blink. She looked like herself . . . but somehow trapped in her own body. She was brutally stiff, but her eyes darted around, as if fervently searching for help.

"What happened to her?" Sara asked.

"Katya, Rouen, you have to keep it moving, please," Primka said. "Filliam's right behind you."

That's when Sara looked up and saw Rouen and Katya weren't alone. Just behind them, Filliam and one of the royal guards held King Edwin's equally stiff body between them. "Hurry!" Primka urged them. "And be careful with him, for goodness' sake, he's our king!"

Sara fell into step next to Katya. "What happened? What's wrong with them? Are they okay?"

"Hush, child," Katya said gently. "We still don't know, but it seems like a curse on the palace. Right now only Genpos are affected, but I don't know how long that'll be the case. Galric already left to visit a friend, thank the universe."

Galric. For a second she imagined him frozen like her parents. The thought made her shudder and she pushed it out of her mind. She was glad he wasn't home.

Primka left the king to flutter around Sara's head. "You should go to your room," she said. "Stay put until we know what's going on."

"No," Sara said. She looked down at the unresponsive bodies of her parents. "I'm staying with them. They need me."

"They need you to be safe," Rouen said.

"I agree," Katya said. "Do what Primka said. In your room."

They were in the Residence now, in the long hall that branched off to her own room, then continued down to her parents' suite. Primka fluttered against Sara's chest, backing her toward her own door.

"Stay *here*. Trust that they're in good hands. I'll come get you when we know the palace is safe," Primka said. Then, under her breath she muttered, "Thank goodness your sister isn't home."

Primka slammed the door shut, showing the unusual strength she had for a tiny songbird. Sara made herself slowly count to twenty. Then she eased open her door.

Primka wasn't there, and her parents' door was closed.

241

She wanted to slip inside their room and check on them, but Primka, Katya, and Rouen would only shoo her out again. Instead she quickly slipped down the hall and out of the Residence.

She had to get to Flissa. She couldn't tell her about this in a bubblegram.

She ran through the palace. She tried to block out the bodies, and the people screaming and racing around to help. She focused on her sister and beelined to the front door. She didn't stop moving until she'd climbed into a carriage and leaned forward to tell the driver, "Maldevon Academy, please. And fast."

Unfortunately *fast* didn't seem to be in the driver's vocabulary. His horse took his own sweet time, meandering along the roads that might one day, several eternities from now, get them to Maldevon Academy.

Sara jounced her knee up and down. She shifted from one carriage bench to the other. She looked out the window and tried to count every blade of grass they passed. Then, when she was about to explode and scream at the driver that she was the Princess of Kaloon and he had best do as she said and speed it up—a thing she'd never normally do—she saw something out of the corner of her eye. Something small and black, running next to the carriage.

Sara leaned out to get a better look. "Nitpick?"

Nitpick meowed. Loudly.

Alarm bells clanged in Sara's head. She threw herself forward and frantically yelled, "Princess of Kaloon! Stop carriage! Now!"

It wasn't exactly the message she'd intended to deliver,

but it did the trick. The driver pulled his horse to a stop, and Sara jumped out of the carriage so fast she tumbled onto her side and rolled into a puddle of mud.

"Ugh!" she spluttered. She crawled her way out of the sludge and came face-to-face with Nitpick. He meowed.

"Show me," Sara said. "Show me where he is."

Nitpick quickly raced off. Sara scrambled to her feet and followed the kitten to the top of an orange-and-green grassy hill.

Galric was at the bottom, his body rigid amidst a thicket of thorny brambles. Nitpick ran down the hill, hopped onto his chest, and let out another plaintive meow.

"I see him," Sara said, her heart racing. "I'm coming."

Sara forced herself to take her time. She wouldn't do Galric any good if she tumbled down and broke a leg. She edged to her left until she was far away from the brambles at the bottom of the hill, then she lay down carefully on the grass, extending her arms and legs long.

Here we go.

She pushed off and rolled. The path she'd picked wasn't quite as smooth as she'd thought. She bounced into the air at one point and smacked down so hard she was afraid she'd cracked a rib, but once she reached the bottom and staggered to her feet she was fine. She lurched to Galric, praying to the universe that he was okay.

His tunic and pants were torn, but none of his limbs were bent in strange directions. She didn't think anything was broken.

Then she looked down at his face and yelped out loud. He was scratched all over, but the worst part was his eyes. They were open but darting around in a wild, helpless frenzy.

"Galric?!" she cried. "Galric, can you hear me? Can you say anything?"

He couldn't; she knew that before she asked. He looked the same way her parents had looked. Whatever curse took the palace, it had reached far enough to take Galric too.

He was alive, though, that was the only thing that mattered.

Sara took his hand and squeezed it. "Don't be scared, okay? I'm here. Nitpick too. We're gonna make sure you're okay."

Katya. It was the only thought in her head. Katya could help him; Katya would make him better.

"Help me!" she screamed up the hill. "Driver! Help me! I need help!"

It took a lifetime, but eventually Sara saw the driver stroll toward the top of the hill. He was whistling a jaunty tune, and Sara wanted to hurl something at him, but his song cut short when he looked down and saw Sara and Galric.

"Oh no . . . I'm coming, Princess!"

The driver scurried down the hill, and thankfully he was much more sure-footed than Sara. When he reached the bottom, he gently took Sara's arm and tried to help her up, but she whisked it away. "Not me—*him!*"

"Right," the driver said. "Sorry."

He picked up Galric and held him by the waist, but Galric didn't bend at all. He remained stiff and straight in the driver's grasp.

"Let me get him up, and I'll come for you next," the driver said, but Sara had no intention of waiting. She struggled up the hill, trying to step directly into the driver's footsteps so she'd have a clear path. Sara knew Nitpick could have scrambled up in an instant, but he stayed by her side until they crested the hill and she stumbled back to the carriage.

"Thanks, Nitpick," Sara said. "You're a good friend."

The kitten meowed, then leaped into the carriage and watched carefully as Sara and the driver eased Galric inside as best they could . . . which wasn't well at all. Since Galric's body couldn't bend, the best Sara and the driver could do was lean him so his body slanted diagonally across the carriage, his head pressed against the ceiling and his feet on the floor of the opposite side. Sara climbed in and contorted herself so she could slip her hand between his head and the carriage wall; that way he wouldn't get hurt as they jounced along the road.

"Back to the palace, please," Sara told the driver. "As fast as you possibly can."

This time he obeyed, and before long they were back at the palace gates. It was much easier slipping Galric out of the carriage than it was to force him in, and soon he was back in the driver's arms, still stiff and straight as a board. With Sara and Nitpick at his side, the driver walked down the main entry hall, but his eyes boggled when he saw all the bodies. "What in the . . . ?"

Sara didn't have time to explain. "KATYA!" she screamed. "KATYA!!!"

Katya must have heard the terror in her voice; Sara had never seen her ex-nursemaid run so quickly. When Katya reached the balcony and saw Galric standing stiff in the carriage driver's arms, she paled, teetered on her feet, and clutched her heart. "Sweet merciful heavens."

That was it; that was all the time she gave herself for sentiment. She raced down the stairs and ran to the driver. "Give me the boy," she said, though she didn't wait for the driver to listen. She took Galric out of his arms and strode down the hall to the parlor, Sara and Nitpick right behind. Sara had to jog to keep up. Once inside, Katya laid Galric down on a sofa and let her hands hover over his body. For several tense moments the only sound in the room was Galric's shallow breathing. Then Katya closed her eyes and pressed her lips together in a sad but grateful smile.

"He'll be fine," she said. "It's the same curse that got the others. I've tried, but I can't tease out the magical signature."

Then she stared at Sara. She narrowed her eyes and tilted her head as if she'd never seen her before.

"Katya?" Sara asked. "Are you okay?"

"We've been getting reports from Amala," Katya said, and for a minute Sara's breath caught in her throat because she was sure it was about what she'd overheard. "She says your magic is strong for someone your age. Exceptionally strong."

Sara couldn't help but glow under the compliment, but it seemed like an odd time to be talking about her classes. "Okay . . ."

"I want you to come with me," Katya said. She took Sara's hand and pulled her to the door.

"Wait!" Sara said. "What about Galric? I don't want to just leave him here."

"I'll send Rouen down to sit with him. This is important. Don't drag your feet."

Sara wasn't sure she had a choice. Katya was moving

full speed ahead; if Sara did drag her feet, Katya might accidentally pull her arm out of its socket.

"Stay with him, Nitpick!" Sara called to the cat, though she knew she didn't need to tell him. He was already sitting on Galric's chest, staring expectantly into his dancing eyes.

Katya pulled Sara through the hall and back up the stairs, then into the Residence and to her parents' room. She threw open the door. The guard and Filliam were gone; only Rouen and Primka were in the room with Sara's parents. Katya locked eyes with her husband.

"The parlor. Galric."

It was all she needed to say. Rouen sucked in his breath but said nothing. He strode out, pausing only for a second to grip Katya's hand on his way out. Primka, however, couldn't contain herself.

"*Galric?!* How was he cursed? He wasn't even in the castle!" Then she gasped as she realized, "It spread *wider* than the castle! Oh, may the universe help us all."

"I'm hoping Sara will be the one to help us all," Katya said.

"I don't understand," Sara said. "What am I supposed to do?"

"If a single curse hit all these Genpos, it was cast by a very powerful Mage. That Mage's signature is in there; it's inside them. We just have to tease it out, and I can't do it myself."

Sara waited to hear the rest of Katya's plan, but all she did was stare at Sara, her beady blue eyes boring down from deep in her cushiony face.

"Wait, you think . . . you think *I* can get it out? You're

stronger than any Mage I've ever met outside Amala. I'm, like, a thousand-million times weaker than you. If you can't do it, how can I?"

"It's possible you can't," Katya said. "But you *are* strong. And more important, you're family. I doubt you could get the signature out of anyone else, but you might get it out of your parents."

Now Primka was staring at her too. Sara didn't like it. There was no way she could do this if Katya couldn't, and she didn't want them counting on her. "But Galric's *your* family, and you couldn't get the signature out of him."

Katya took Sara firmly by the shoulders and placed her next to her mother's side of the bed. "You're blood," she said, "and you're their child. It's different. Now try."

Sara looked down at her mother's locked-open mouth and her jangling eyes. She was too terrified; she had to look away. "I don't even know what to do!"

"Place your hands on her," Katya said. "Close your eyes, and let your magic reach out for the magic inside her. *Feel* for the signature."

Trembling, Sara reached out for her mother, but she stopped as she remembered Gilward, when he tried to pull Mitzi's signature from her mom. She saw the green mist coming out of his ears and mouth; she saw his eyes turn to swirls of green.

Sara felt like a coward for asking, but she had to know. "Will it hurt? Like Gilward?"

Katya squeezed her into a pillowy hug. "Oh, child, no," she said. "No, I would never let you do this if it put you in any danger. Gilward was trying to remove another Mage's curse; that's very different. You're not healing; you're diagnosing. You're showing us what's inside your mother, and that's *all*. Whatever you find, no matter how strong it is, it can't hurt you. Understood?"

Katya held Sara at arm's length and looked at her. Sara nodded. She *would* die for her family if she had to, but she was glad she wouldn't have to do it today. She thought about what she'd seen Katya do downstairs with Galric. She'd held her hands over his body, but she'd told Sara to touch her mother, so she rested a hand on either side of the queen's unblinking face.

It felt cold.

"That's good," Katya said. "Now close your eyes, and just reach out with your magic. You don't want to do anything to the curse, you just want to see it."

Sara nodded again, then closed her eyes. She took deep breaths and sank every bit of her energy into her hands. She imagined her fingers had long red-mist tentacles that snaked out of her body and streamed through her mother's. The tentacles weren't bothering anything, just gently feeling around. Sara could sense those long strings of magic swimming through her mother's body. Scanning. Searching. Sara felt herself slipping away, like she wasn't in her own body at all. She was one of the tentacles. She was inside her mother, looking around. She wasn't anxious or rushed, simply curious, floating and looking . . . though she saw only blackness. Blackness, tinged with the scarlet of her own streaming mist.

Then there was something up ahead. A blue light. She eased closer.

Breaking through the blackness was a jagged web of lights.

No, not lights. *Lightning.* Bright blue lightning.

It crackled and sizzled. There was a chiming sound too—a single note—but it was hard to hear under the sputtering lightning bolts. From somewhere far away she thought she also heard someone calling her name—very angrily, in fact—but she was only vaguely interested. She wanted to see the lightning. Sara floated closer, and soon it took over her entire field of vision, shard after shard of lightning, so bright it burned her eyes, but she couldn't look away because she wasn't in her body. She was in the *lightning* now, surrounded on all sides. She heard the chime ding again, but it was the lightning that mesmerized her, and all she wanted to do was reach out and touch it and . . .

"SARA!"

Hands grabbed her shoulders and yanked her backward. Sara felt an unbearable, searing pain in her forehead, but it disappeared as fast as it came.

She blinked. She was back in her parents' room, her back pressed against Katya. She didn't remember letting go of her mother, but she was several feet away from the bed. Primka hovered just above her, looking worried.

"What happened?"

Primka fanned her face with a wing, deeply relieved. "Oh, thank the universe," she said.

Katya spun her around and eagerly searched her eyes. "Sara? You're okay?"

"I'm fine," she said. "My head hurt . . . but it doesn't anymore. What happened?"

Katya smiled and her eyes shone. "You did it. You gave us a scare and you nearly got swallowed by that curse, but you did it! We saw the magical signature. It flashed by your hand. Only for a second, but we saw it!"

"You did?" Sara asked. Then she tingled all over as she realized. "The blue lightning. That was it, wasn't it? The magical signature was blue lightning!"

"Indeed it was," Katya said, beaming. "And you are a Mage to be reckoned with!"

Sara frowned, remembering something more. "I heard something too," she said. "When I saw the lightning. A chime. Just one note . . ." Sara shivered because she suddenly knew where she'd heard that note before. "Did you hear it?"

"We didn't hear anything," Primka said. "Just that little flash of blue lightning, that's it."

"But we're on the outside," Katya said. "You would have picked up much more than us. Do you think there was another magical signature?"

Sara did. She'd heard *Zinka's* magical signature. That one clear chime. But now that she was away from that strange, magical realm, she wasn't sure if it was real. If Katya and Primka only saw the lightning, maybe that was all there was. Maybe the chime was just in Sara's head— her old suspicions making her imagine things that weren't there.

"I don't think so," Sara said. "The blue lightning. That's what I'm sure of. It was everywhere."

Katya slung an arm around her. "You did good, Sara. I'm proud of you."

"Is someone bragging on my girl?" the king's voice murmured groggily. "'Cause if so, count me in."

"Dad?" Sara whipped around. Both her parents were

251

blinking hard, scrunching and stretching their faces as if the muscles were brand-new.

"Dad! Mom!" Sara cried. "You're back!"

She threw herself on their bed like she had when she and Flissa were little and wrapped one arm around each of them. "You were cursed!" she said. "Lots of people were cursed! Then I . . ." Sara gasped and reeled back. She stared at her hands as if they were glowing precious gems. "I cured you!"

The bedroom door opened, and Rouen entered, his craggy face lit up with a smile. "Our boy's awake and he's fine. The curse is wearing off."

Sara's mouth opened wider. She was stunned by her power. "I cured *everyone*!"

Katya laughed and put a hand on her shoulder. "Easy, now. The strongest Mage in the universe can't remove a curse from more than one person at a time. You *diagnosed* the curse, and you did it just before it wore off."

Sara couldn't help but be a little disappointed. "You sure I didn't cure it?"

Primka swatted her with a wing and *tsk*ed. "*Someone's* getting big for her britches."

Katya laughed. "You didn't cure anything, but I'll tell you this: If not for you, the curse would've been gone before we ever got the magical signature. Be happy about that."

"I'm happy about it," her dad said proudly. "We saw and heard everything."

"That's true," her mom agreed. "It was a terrible curse. I was awake and aware, but I couldn't move; I was trapped inside my own body."

"It hit every Genpo in the palace," Katya said, then with

a meaningful glance to Rouen she added, "and at least one outside the palace too."

Sara knew she was talking about Galric, and she tried not to sound overly anxious as she asked Rouen, "Is Galric still in the parlor?"

"He is," Rouen said. "Nitpick's with him, but I'm sure he'd welcome your company."

"Go," Sara's dad said. He gave her a hug and spoke to Rouen over her shoulder. "We need a full debriefing, then we should assemble the General Council."

"Agreed," her mom said. She wrapped her arms around Sara and squeezed. "We're very proud of you."

"Love you both," Sara said as she squeezed her back, then climbed off the bed. She managed to walk calmly out of the room . . . then flew through the hall and down the stairs. The palace buzzed even louder than before, and Sara saw all the Genpos back on their feet, most of them walking gingerly, or stumbling with their arms around someone else's shoulders. Sara didn't stop running until she made it into the parlor.

Galric was still on the couch. He was sitting up now, stretching his arms and working his mouth while Nitpick purred and rubbed up against him.

"Hey!" Sara said. Her heart was beating faster, which she chalked up to the run.

He smiled. "Hey."

"You okay?"

"Kinda," he said. He tilted his neck from side to side, and Sara heard it crack. "I sorta feel like someone grabbed my ankles, spun me around their head, then threw me across a jousting field. Into a really thick tree trunk."

"Pretty close," Sara said. "You fell down a hill and crashed into a thornbush."

"And you rescued me," he said.

"I did."

They smiled at each other for a little too long, then she twirled the diamond stud in her ear. "I mean, it's not like it's the first time, though. I totally rescued you in the Twists a bunch too."

"Really?" he said. "'Cause I'm pretty sure it was Flissa who did most of the rescuing. I kinda remember you almost getting devoured by a plant."

"A big, giant, person-eating plant that happened to look like a really comfy chair!"

"Sara?!" Flissa thundered into the room and grabbed Sara's shoulders. Her eyes were wild. "Sara—I have to talk to Mother and Father. It's terrible. The girls' dorm . . . the Genpos were cursed! It has to be a curse. They all went stiff and collapsed. And their eyes . . ."

Galric rose to his feet. "It happened at school too?" He winced and put a hand on his stomach, then plopped back down. "Nope, still queasy."

"'Too'?" Flissa echoed. "It happened *here*?"

Sara nodded. "To all the Genpos. Galric and Mom and Dad—"

"Are they okay?" Flissa cut her off. "Where are they?"

"Up in their room with Rouen and Katya and Primka. They—"

"I have to go see them," Flissa said. She ran two steps toward the door, then turned back and reached out to Sara. "Come with me?"

Flissa looked scared, and in her head Sara whisked

254

back to the day their mom was cursed by Mitzi. She and Flissa had held hands as they walked down the Residence hall, terrified to see what the curse had done to her. Sara could assure Flissa that their mom was fine and seeing her wouldn't be a problem, but she didn't want to. Maybe it was selfish of her, but Flissa hadn't reached out to her in ages; it felt too good to stop her from doing it now.

Sara promised Galric she'd catch up with him later, then took Flissa's hand. Together, the sisters ran out of the room.

Chapter 17
Flissa

Flissa hadn't realized how much she'd actually missed her sister until they were hand in hand, flying up the stairs. Their clasped fingers felt like a lifeline and gave her the strength to face whatever she might find in her parents' room.

What she found was her mother, her father, Katya, and Rouen, fielding a slew of bubblegrams, with more flying in through the open window every moment. Her mother was just sending a bubblegram of her own when she saw the girls enter the room. She quickly dropped her message milk vial and ran to them.

"You're here!" she said as she hugged Flissa tight. "I'm so glad you're all right."

"I told you she'd be all right, Latonya," Flissa's father said gently. "She's a Mage. The curse hit the whole kingdom, but only the Genpos were affected." He put his arm around Flissa and lowered his head to hers. "I'm glad you're okay too."

"So it *did* hit the whole kingdom," Flissa said. "Not just here and the school?"

"We're getting reports from everywhere," Rouen said, "from both victims and witnesses." As if to make his point, a bubblegram floated in and popped in front of him, delivering another report. Rouen put up a finger to excuse himself as he gave it his full attention.

Katya, meanwhile, was unscrewing her message milk to send a bubblegram of her own. "From what we're hearing," she said as she tapped the excess milk off the wand, "the curse came all at once, and struck every single Genpo."

"*All* of them?" Sara asked. "In all of Kaloon?"

"That's what it sounds like," their mother said. "But it also sounds like it wore off around the same time as well. We sent Primka to find out, and we have other scouts making sure."

"Do we know who did it?" Flissa asked. "Was there a magical signature?"

Her parents smiled so wide Flissa thought their faces might crack, which seemed like an odd reaction to the question. "Was there?" she prodded.

"There was indeed," said Flissa's dad, his mustache tips pointing straight up, "and your sister is the Mage who found it."

"*You* did?" Flissa wheeled to Sara, who blushed and smiled.

"Katya told me what to do, but, um . . . yeah, I did it."

"Pfft," Katya huffed. "None of this 'Katya told me' nonsense. *You* did it. Blue lightning bolts, that's the signature. Right, Sara?"

"Right," Sara said, but she shifted uncomfortably and wouldn't look Katya in the eye. Flissa could tell there was more to the story that Sara wasn't saying.

"Blue lightning," Rouen reiterated. "Now we just need to find the Mage attached to it."

"Can one Mage be strong enough to attack the whole kingdom?" Flissa asked. "It sounds like it would take a bunch of Mages combining their power."

Next to her, Sara exploded in a coughing fit. Their mother came and patted her back until she got it under control.

"Sorry," she choked. "I'm okay."

"It could be a group of Mages," Katya admitted, "or it could be just one . . . but only if the Mage had help."

Flissa frowned. "Right, so . . . a bunch of Mages." But even as she said it, she remembered. "Or a blinzer stone!"

"Exactly," said Rouen. "Exactly what we've been thinking."

"A blinzer stone . . ." Sara said. "We talked about those the first day of Magic Lab, right?"

"Yes," Flissa said. "They're stones from the Twists that magnify magic."

"So one Mage *could* curse the whole kingdom on their own," Sara said, "as long as they had a blinzer stone."

Flissa was sure Sara was skirting around something, but she was just as sure that Sara didn't want to say it in this room.

"Of course as I understand it, the stones might not truly exist," their mother said. "But it's on our list of possibilities."

Rouen, Katya, and their father had all turned back to deal with bubblegrams, and another one was floating in and beelining for their mother. She spoke quickly to get her words out before it popped. "Sorry, girls, we need to deal with this. We'll let you know what we find out."

Flissa and Sara left the room. Flissa's head was spinning with ideas, and she was dying to unravel them with Sara, but they hadn't exactly been on the best of terms lately. Would Sara even want to talk to her?

She was relieved when Sara took her hand and pulled her into their room. She shut the door.

"We need to talk," she said. "About everything—like a million different things—but the first thing you have to know is I gave up on the Zinka-and-Amala-out-to-get-Genpos thing. I know you told me, and Amala told me, and everyone told me, but I didn't listen, 'cause you were right, and I was only hung up on it because I was totally jealous and I'm the worst sister in the world—"

"You're not," Flissa said, but Sara was talking so fast, Flissa wasn't sure she heard her speak.

"But we looked into it—me and Galric and Krystal— we looked *really hard*, but there wasn't anything—no evidence against Zinka or Amala. Nothing. Like, if anything, we found evidence that they're both amazing and really want Kaloonification to be a thing. I was gonna tell you all that the night of the game, but you put up the magic wall and I—"

"I'm sorry," Flissa said. She hadn't even realized Sara was trying to reach out and make things better that night. She'd been so sure she didn't want to hear what Sara had to say, she hadn't given her a chance.

Sara waved off her concerns. "It's fine, not the point, just saying all this to let you know—and you can ask Galric or Krystal, they'll tell you the same thing—we were *done*. Not suspecting them *at all*."

"I understand," Flissa said, "and I'm so sorry I didn't give you the chance to—"

Sara shook her head and sliced a hand through the air, stopping her short. "Not looking for an apology. Here's why I'm telling you all this. Yes, because I want you to know, but also . . ."

Sara looked around the room. She specifically gazed up at Primka's entry-holes as if making sure the songbird wouldn't soar in. Even after that check, she leaned closer to Flissa and lowered her voice to just above a whisper.

"When I was in there, when I doing the magic thing to search for the curse's magical signature, I *did* see blue lightning. Lots of it. It was big, bright, and really loud." Sara took a deep breath, as if girding herself for what came next. "But I also heard something. It was softer, a lot softer than the lightning, but I heard it. A single chime."

She locked eyes with Flissa, as if waiting for the meaning to sink in, but Flissa understood right away.

Zinka's magical signature was a single chime.

Sara must have seen it in her face that she knew, because she hurried to continue. "I didn't say anything to anyone. Even though I saw tons and tons of blue lightning, Katya said she only saw the littlest bit. And she didn't hear the chime at all. So I thought maybe it was in my head and I was still jealous or something, but, Flissa . . . I'm so sorry . . . I really, really believe I heard it."

Flissa let this sink in and mix with everything else she knew. Something about it made sense in a strange way, but she wasn't sure how to put the pieces together.

"Are you mad?" Sara asked. "Please don't be mad. I'm

not making things up, and I'm not looking for Zinka to be the bad guy, I—"

"Shhh," Flissa said. "I believe you, I just need a second." She paced the room, chewing on the end of her braid. She strode four lengths before she started talking. "I'm going to tell you everything I know," she said, "but don't jump to any conclusions right away. Promise?"

"Promise," Sara said.

"When the Genpos were cursed, Zinka wasn't with the rest of us at the sleepover. I saw her leave in the middle of the night, and when we all woke up to everyone screaming, she still wasn't back."

"Where was she?" Sara asked, and Flissa was glad she didn't sound accusatory; just curious.

"I think up in her room," Flissa said. "I don't know. That's where she said she was going when she left, and I didn't follow her to find out. I didn't see her before I left this morning either."

"Wow," Sara said. "Okay . . . but even if maybe she was . . . involved, blue lightning isn't her magical signature. And the blue lightning was a lot stronger."

Flissa's heart sped up. She had an answer for that, but she didn't like it. Part of her couldn't believe she didn't seize on it right away, but it was too horrible and too impossible.

Unless it wasn't.

"Blue lightning," Flissa said. "Think about it. Have we ever met someone whose magic signature is blue lightning?"

Sara thought about it, then frowned and shook her head. "No."

"But the blinzer stones amplify powers, right? So

maybe the blue lightning is actually the exact same magical signature we've seen before, but more powerful, so it's bigger. So you *saw* it as blue lightning, but it's really blue *sparks.*"

Flissa stopped pacing and met Sara's eyes. If she was expecting sudden comprehension, she didn't find it.

"Blue sparks?"

"*Blue sparks.* Sara, you know this. It hasn't been that long, and it was *not* forgettable. When a Magical Animal with all the powers of a Mage takes over your body, you remember it."

Now Flissa got the reaction she was looking for. Sara's eyes became moons and her mouth dropped open.

"Raya?! The lioness?!"

"Exactly," Flissa said.

Sara shook her head. "No. That's not possible. Raya's in the Twists, and the Twists are all locked up. It can't be her."

Flissa chomped harder on her braid. "There's a chance Raya's not in the Twists. There's a chance she's at Maldevon Academy. In Zinka's room."

Now Sara just looked at her like she'd lost her mind.

"Hold up," she said. "You're saying Zinka has a *lioness* in her room? Raya the Lioness. In her room."

"Not a lioness," Flissa said. "A cat. A small orange cat named Teddy. She's Zinka's pet. Or at least, Zinka thinks that she is. Zinka showed Loriah and me, but she told us we had to keep it a secret because non-magical animals aren't allowed at the school. She said the cat was a stray. They found each other when Zinka first moved into the dorms, and they've been together ever since. Zinka loves this cat, and she seems normal and even cuddly. . . ."

Flissa shuddered, thinking about the way she'd held Teddy in her arms. She'd even been tempted to bring her to the common room and keep her in her sleeping bag last night! She shook off her disgust, then continued. "But when Loriah saw the cat she panicked. She was convinced Teddy *was Raya.*"

Sara frowned. "Why? Why would she think a cat was Raya?"

"The eyes," Flissa said. "You know how Raya had those bright yellow eyes? Teddy's are exactly the same. *Exactly.* I was even spooked when Loriah pointed them out to me, but then I thought I was just being ridiculous because Magical Animals can't change their shape. Even powerful Mages can't do that. But Loriah didn't let it go. She was terrified, and you know Loriah. If she gets terrified, she doesn't normally show it. She was positive Teddy was Raya, and evil, and she told Zinka she was going to turn her in for having a cat. That was the drama that night—Zinka and Loriah got into a huge fight about it."

"Did Loriah turn Zinka in?" Sara asked.

Flissa shook her head. "She didn't get the chance. The next morning was when you, Zinka, and I found her floating in her room."

"The sleep terrors," Sara said. "Because she was so afraid from seeing Raya . . . or the small, cuddly cat she thought was Raya."

"Yes!" Flissa said. "That's what I thought too. But what if it *wasn't* sleep terrors? What if Raya actually cursed her? When Loriah woke up, she didn't even remember Zinka had a cat. I had to remind her."

"What did she say when you reminded her?" Sara asked.

Flissa shook her head. "She didn't care. Even when I said she'd thought the cat was Raya—she blew it off. But maybe that was part of the curse—that Loriah wouldn't remember it, so she wouldn't believe it was possible. Maybe she would if she saw Teddy again, but she hasn't, not since that night."

Sara reached up and twirled one of her earrings. "But if you think Teddy—*Raya*—cursed Loriah and it wasn't sleep terrors, how come we didn't see blue sparks then?"

"The curse wore off by the time anyone tried to get the signature out," Flissa said. "That meant there wasn't any evidence of a curse, but there were lots of reasons for Loriah to be having terrible nightmares. The sleep terrors made the most sense."

"And since you and Zinka lied about the fight," Sara said carefully, "Amala didn't have a reason to look at Zinka, and maybe find the cat."

Flissa opened her mouth to object, but she stopped herself.

"You're not wrong," she admitted. "I don't know if they would have found her, but maybe if Amala had gone right into Zinka's room and Teddy was surprised . . . We should have told the truth. I just didn't want Zinka to get in trouble. I knew she didn't curse Loriah, and I knew it would seem like she did."

"I get it. I'm just saying." Sara looked up at the ceiling, thinking. "Biggest question: How can Raya be Teddy? You said it before—even powerful Mages can't change their shape. How could Raya do it? And how would she have gotten out of the Twists?"

It was exactly the question that had thrown off Flissa, but the way Sara said it made her think about it in a new way. She whipped her head around so fast, her braid smacked her in the face. "That's it! What if how she got out of the Twists *is* how she became a cat?"

"Um . . . that'd be really amazing . . . if I had any idea what you were talking about."

"Okay, stay with me," Flissa said. "What if Raya escaped the Twists, but just barely? What if she was in the Brambled Gates right when all the Mages hit it with their blast? We know the magic that escaped was incredibly powerful and did all kinds of unexpected things. It made the ring tree, it blew orange grass and plobquats and other plants into Kaloon, it turned regular bushes into moving animal topiaries . . . what if it also changed her shape?"

Sara's eyes lit up. "So maybe, just like the plobquats and the grass and stuff, Raya was blasted out of the Twists . . . but all the mixed-up Mage magic in the explosion changed her. So she's not a lioness shape-shifted into a cat at all. She's an *ex*-lioness who's now in a cat's body!"

"Yes!" Flissa said. It would have sounded completely crazy if she'd come up with it on her own, but working through it with Sara, it made perfect sense. She couldn't believe she'd shut Sara out for so long. Nothing was as good as the two of them together.

"So Raya comes back, and she has the same personality and the same magic, but in a much smaller and less powerful body," Flissa said.

"And she's probably angry, right? I mean, she did well in the Twists. It was her kind of place. But once everyone decent was rescued, it was just a bunch of seriously bad

Mages. She wouldn't have had prisoners like Loriah, she'd have *been* one."

"That's why she'd have tried to escape," Flissa agreed, "and got caught in the big magic blast."

"I'm with you through all that," Sara said. Then she tapped a finger against her mouth. "But that brings us to the Zinka of it all. Why did Raya find Zinka and become her pet? How does that help her?"

Flissa twirled her braid around a finger. She really wasn't sure why Raya would want Zinka.

"I've got an idea," Sara said. "But you won't like it."

"That's okay, tell me."

"Maybe they worked together in the Twists," Sara suggested. "We never saw Zinka there, but maybe that's because she wasn't Raya's prisoner; maybe they were more like friends. So when Raya got to Kaloon, she found someone she knew would help her. That's why I found both their signatures in the curse; they were working together."

Flissa knew it was a good theory, but it didn't sit right with her. It just didn't track with the girl she knew. She realized it was possible Zinka had been lying to her, but if she was, she was the best actress in the universe. And Zinka had done things that wouldn't make sense if she was trying to blend in and secretly work with Raya. Like after the hoodle game, when Flissa found her in the closet, crying her eyes out because her fingers wouldn't stop bleeding.

Her fingers wouldn't stop bleeding.

"Sara!" Flissa cried, grabbing her sister by the arms. "Sara-Sara-Sara—I've got it!"

"What? What've you got?"

"Zinka's fingernails! They're horrible. They're cut to

bits. Her knuckles too, they're always raw and bleeding, and I thought it was because she was stressed and the worst nailbiter in the history of nailbiting, but what if she's not?"

Sara looked at her uncomprehendingly. "I don't know . . . what if she's not?"

Flissa shook her head. She needed to back up. "What would Raya have needed to put a curse on all of Kaloon?"

"A bunch of really strong Mages," Sara said. "Or a blinzer stone."

"Exactly," Flissa said. "And on our first day in Magic Lab, where did Amala say the blinzer stones might be in Kaloon?"

"First she said they might not be in Kaloon at all," Sara said, "but if they were . . ." Sara ran her tongue over her teeth, trying to remember. "If they were, I think she said they could have been blasted anywhere. Like in a tree, or . . ."

Her eyes got wide, and Flissa smiled as she put the pieces together.

"Or deep underground," Sara finished. Then she gasped. "You think Raya's getting Zinka to dig up blinzer stones! That's why her nails and knuckles are thrashed!" Then Sara frowned. "But they still could be in it together. Just now that Raya's tiny, Zinka's the one with the strength. Not that Raya would've dug anything up even as a lioness. She'd've made Loriah do that for her."

Flissa smiled wider. Sara had figured out Flissa's next point all on her own, and she hadn't even realized it yet. "Exactly what you said," Flissa said. "She wouldn't dig on her own, even as a lioness. She'd have magicked Loriah or someone else. She'd have taken over their body and made

267

them do it. *That's* why Zinka's nails and knuckles are a mess, and it has to be why she always has dark circles under her eyes. Raya's making her dig at night, so she doesn't get any sleep."

Flissa folded her arms, proud that they figured it out. She didn't understand why Sara still looked skeptical. "What?" she asked.

"I'm with you a hundred percent," Sara said, "but we still can't say for sure if Raya's taking over Zinka, or if Zinka's in on the plan."

"Maybe this will help," Flissa said.

She told Sara all about Zinka's breakdown in the closet. She knew Zinka would see it as a betrayal, but she had to show Sara the digging and the sleeplessness were tearing Zinka apart. It proved she was doing it all against her will. Besides, it's not like she was sharing Zinka's secret with just anyone. It was her sister. She and Sara might not have really been the same person anymore . . . but at the same time, they kind of were.

Flissa was sure that when she finished the story Sara would be convinced, but instead, she frowned again. "Yeah, she was crying, but you said the cat was in her lap. If she didn't want to do Raya's dirty work, why was she cuddling with her?"

"There's no way Zinka knows Teddy is Raya," Flissa says. "She *adores* that cat. We've been under Raya's power; we know how it feels. Zinka probably just gets that horrible feeling that her body isn't her own, then she walks off and spends the whole night digging for blinzer stones. She probably has no idea how it's happening or why."

Thinking about it made Flissa feel horrible. At least when Raya took *her* body over she knew the source. It had to be unimaginably terrifying to feel yourself manipulated by a force you couldn't even see or understand.

"I hear you," Sara said, "but if you're right, why wouldn't she tell somebody? She's close with Amala. She's close with *you*. She could say something. I mean, if someone's taking my body over, keeping me up all night, and making me dig until I bleed and I don't want to do it, I say something."

"You're not wrong," Flissa said. She sat down on her bed and started playing with her braid again. "I don't really have an answer for that. Maybe Raya's threatening her? You remember how hard it was to even turn our heads when Raya had us under her curse. She could stand right behind Zinka and talk to her, and Zinka would have no idea it was her cat. So maybe Raya's threatening her, and Zinka's too frightened to say a word. Maybe she's afraid that if she tries to speak up, this invisible thing that's already taking her over will do something even worse to her."

"Maybe," Sara said, "but I'm still not convinced they're not working together. Can we agree it's a possibility?"

In her heart Flissa knew it wasn't, but Sara didn't know Zinka the way she did. She was following the facts, and her conclusions were understandable. "Yes, as long as you agree it's also a possibility she's totally innocent and just being used."

"Deal," Sara said. "So now Raya—with Zinka's willing or unwilling help—cursed all the Genpos . . . but why? Why go after the Genpos?"

"No idea," Flissa admitted. "But if she wants to hurt them, she won't stop at a curse that just knocks them out for a while then fades away. She'll do something else."

"So what do we do?" Sara asked. "Do we tell Mom and Dad?"

"That a lioness from the Twists is now a tiny cat, which is something not even considered within the realm of possible magic, and that tiny cat is controlling or working with an Untwisted to dig up blinzer stones and curse Genpos?" Flissa asked. "I don't think they'll ever believe us. They'll think we caught Loriah's spell terrors."

"Then we need some kind of proof . . ." Sara said. "A blinzer stone! We sneak into Zinka's room, find where she's hiding them, and bring them to Mom and Dad and the Council."

"*Raya's* in Zinka's room," Flissa said. "She won't let us take the stones. She'll kill us first."

"She won't know we're looking for them," Sara said. "We won't let on. And we'll sneak them out."

"But if we find the stones, that's not proof Raya cast the curse; it's proof Zinka cast the curse."

"Not true," Sara said, "because Raya's magical signature was the one everyone saw me get out of Mom. We sneak out the stones, we show the Council, they surprise the cat, take her away, and see her magical signature . . . then boom!" Sara threw herself backward on her bed before popping her head back up. "Problem solved."

Flissa laughed. She wondered how much faster she'd have figured everything out if she and Sara had been talking this whole time. "I like it," she said. "There's still just one problem: Zinka won't let us go through her room.

Not if she's afraid of Raya. She won't want us to find the stones."

"She won't know we're doing it, because I have a cunning plan." She fixed Flissa with an impish grin. "How would you like to be the same princess again? Just for old times' sake."

Chapter 18
Sara

After they'd planned everything out, Flissa and Sara went back into their parents' room. The two of them, Katya, and Rouen were still busily wrangling bubblegrams, but they said they'd be heading out soon for an emergency meeting of the full General Council.

"That's okay," Sara said. "We were thinking we'd head to school."

Their mother looked surprised, then she smiled sympathetically. "I'm sorry, girls. I thought you realized—with everything that happened this morning, classes were canceled. I know the school hasn't sent out the official scrolls yet. They've been busy checking on all the Genpo students on dorm—"

"We weren't thinking it was a school day," Flissa said. "We wanted to go and show our support."

Sara nodded. "We know you're busy, but we thought someone from the royal family should be at Maldevon Academy to let them know we're standing with them, and we still support their mission."

Flissa had written that speech; the two of them had rehearsed it several times before they came into the room.

It had the desired effect. Their dad stopped listening to his bubblegram, and he and their mom gaped at their daughters, completely delighted and impressed.

"That's *precisely* what we should be doing," their dad said. "I can't believe we didn't think of it ourselves."

"And you want to do it together," their mom said, her voice a warm hug. "Yes. Go. Send a bubblegram when you'll be back. Thank you. And be safe."

"That's right," their dad said. "Any sign of trouble, don't be afraid to use your magic. In self-defense," he added when their mom looked at him askance, "only in self-defense."

Flissa and Sara left the room, holding in their giggles until they were out of earshot.

When they got outside, Flissa looked longingly toward the stables. "Can't we take Balustrade?" she asked.

Sara shook her head. "You know we need the carriage. That's part of the plan."

Flissa sighed and the two climbed into a carriage.

"Maldevon Academy, please," Sara said.

The carriage started off, and they'd only been on the road for a moment when two winged scrolls flew into the open windows. Sara and Flissa opened them at the same time, and Sara's eyes scanned quickly down the page.

Sara,

Due to the recent attack on Genpos, Maldevon Academy is hereby suspending operations until further notice. Dorms will remain open, but there

will be no classes or extracurriculars. In addition,
the Kaloonification Ball is postponed indefinitely.
Another scroll will arrive when and if these
circumstances change.

"'If' the circumstances change?" Flissa said. Clearly her scroll had said the same thing as Sara's. "They might close the school for good?"

Sara was much more concerned about another part of the scroll. "They're canceling the ball?"

"Well, yes," Flissa said. "If they're closing the whole school, of course they won't have a ball. It only—"

"No," Sara said. "Unacceptable. We have to fix this. We're having the ball. Next step of the plan, let's go."

Flissa tilted her head. "Why are you so concerned about the ball?"

Sara blushed. This wasn't the time to go into it. "Who doesn't like a good ball? Come on, next step."

Flissa raised an amused eyebrow, then pulled out her message milk. She unscrewed the top, tapped off the excess fluid, and spoke into the wand. "This message is for Zinka." The wand turned blue, and Flissa recorded her message. "Zinka, it's me, Flissa. I'm coming over; I want to check on everybody. Are you around? End."

The bubblegram broke off and flew out the window.

"She'll say she's around, right?" Sara asked. It was the only part of the plan that made her worry.

"She'll be on campus," Flissa said, "so she'll want to hang out."

"Unless she's busy covering up for a Genpo attack," Sara said.

"*Especially* if she's busy covering up for a Genpo attack," Flissa said. "If she worked with Raya on purpose, she'll want to make sure she acts as normal as possible. Which doesn't mean that if she wants to hang out it means she worked with Raya on purpose."

"Got it," Sara said. She was sure Flissa was right, but she was still fidgety, and she knew she would be until Zinka sent her response.

"So, the ball," Flissa said, giving her a knowing smile. "Sounds like you really wanted to go."

Sara smiled. She couldn't help it. "I was looking forward to it."

"I see," Flissa said. She looked out the window and didn't say anything for a while. Then, as if it was just something random she'd pulled out of thin air, she asked, "Heard any good ball-posals lately?"

"All right!" Sara cried. "I'll tell you. Yes. Someone asked me to the ball."

She stopped there. She didn't know why it was so hard to just spit it out to Flissa. Probably because she wanted Flissa to approve and didn't want to know if she didn't.

"Someone, huh?" Flissa said.

Sara rolled her eyes. "Galric, okay? Galric asked me to the ball."

She meant to sound like it was no big deal, but she could feel the loopy grin on her face.

"That's perfect!" Flissa cried, and her words came out in a giddy rush. "When? What did he say? I want to know everything. Every word."

Sara loved how happy Flissa was. It made her feel all fluttery, and she wanted to tell her every single detail, but

275

then a large blue bubble flew in the window and popped in front of Flissa's face.

Immediately they both heard the sound of Zinka sobbing.

"Flissa, yes, please come see me . . ." More sobbing, then a big wet sniff. "I don't know what to do. Teddy's gone. She ran away . . ." Lots more sobbing. "I looked everywhere, I went out with her favorite snacks, I tried everything . . ." Uncontrollable sobbing that turned into hiccuping, then Zinka took deep, shuddery breaths. "I'm—sorry— I just— Please come— Bye."

Flissa and Sara looked at each other, wide-eyed.

"What do you think it means?" Flissa asked.

"What do *you* think it means?"

"I think maybe Raya got what she wanted out of Zinka, then ran away. I think maybe she'll find someone else to take over for whatever comes next," Flissa said.

"And leave her blinzer stones behind with Zinka?" Sara asked. "I don't think so."

"Maybe Raya took the blinzer stones with her," Flissa suggested. "She could have moved them with magic."

"Maybe," Sara said. "Or maybe Zinka's putting on a show to cover up what they did, just to throw everyone off before the next attack."

"Throw who off?" Flissa asked. "We're the only ones who suspect anything."

Sara had to admit that was an excellent point, but she still didn't believe Zinka was entirely in the clear.

"Let's stick with the plan," she said. "We'll see if the stones are in Zinka's room, then figure everything else out from there."

Flissa agreed, and they soon arrived at Maldevon Academy.

"Please just wait here," Sara called up to the driver. "We'll let you know when we're ready to go." Then she ducked back inside to run over everything with Flissa.

"Send me a bubblegram when you're about to go into the dorm," Sara said. "I'll wait a little while for you to get Zinka to the topiary gardens. There's no way she'll see me from there. Then I'll go in and check out the room. You're sure I can get past the Invisible Wall of Doom?"

"You can if you look like me," Flissa said. "I mean, of course you look like me, but—"

"Watch," Sara said. She closed her eyes, concentrated, and focused on exactly what she wanted to happen. When the image was perfectly sharp and clear in her head, she ran her hands in front of her body, wiggling her fingers down from the top of her head to the bottom of her feet. She could feel the scarlet mist coming out of her. She felt her silk dress change to slim-fitting jodhpurs with a blouse and jerkin. She felt her delicate shoes grow into heavy boots. Most of all, she felt the almost-forgotten heft of long hair as it wove into a braid that thunked down over one shoulder.

"Wow," Flissa said.

"So it worked?"

"I mean, you didn't change yourself from a lioness into a cat—"

"Because even the strongest Mage can only make cosmetic changes, not completely alter their species," Sara pointed out defensively.

Flissa smiled. "You did an amazing job. We look like

twins." She slipped out of the carriage, then leaned back into the window. "Bubblegram you in a bit."

She ran off, and Sara jounced her knee impatiently. She turned her head from side to side just to feel her braid flop around. She didn't miss all that weight, but it was definitely fun to play with. She had the end of her braid in one hand and was spinning it around like a lasso when a bubblegram floated in through the window and popped in front of her face.

"Just outside the dorm," Flissa's voice said, "about to head in."

Sara made herself slowly count to one hundred, while in her head she went over what Flissa had told her about blinzer stones. They could be any size, and since they were so rare, different sources said they were different colors. What every book Flissa read seemed to agree on was that blinzer stones were smooth, shiny gems and could always be identified because they would hum when a Mage touched them. Even one blinzer stone could amplify a Mage's magic significantly, but it seemed likely that Raya had used several to curse every Genpo in Kaloon, so who knew how many Sara might find?

By now Sara was sure Flissa and Zinka would be at the topiary garden. She waited just a little bit longer, in case Zinka was so upset about the cat it took more time to get her out of her room, then she left the carriage.

When Sara had come up with the plan to masquerade as her sister, she'd figured it would be easy—she'd done it a million times before. Yet now that she was out of the carriage, she realized that actually wasn't true. She'd been *Flissara* a million times before. That was someone different—a combination of Flissa and Sara that was somewhere in the middle of them both.

Now she had to be Flissa . . . and she was stunned that she wasn't sure exactly what to do.

She thought about it. Flissa was confident. At least physically she was. She was great at sports and she was all kinds of coordinated, so she would have a super-confident walk. That meant Sara would do the same. She stood as tall as she could and kept her head up as she strode toward the dorms.

She got nervous when she saw people walking around on the fields. Would Flissa nod and smile to them? That didn't sound like Flissa's style, but what if her style had changed? She was a popular girl now. Maybe that meant people expected her to smile.

Or maybe she was so popular that people expected her *not* to smile.

This was a lot harder than Sara had thought. She was grateful when she felt sweat on her upper lip—that she *knew* was pure Flissa, so she was doing something right. She made it to the girls' dorm porch and climbed up the steps. She kept her eyes forward, opting *not* to look at people and smile.

There. That was a choice. One down, a million more to go. She opened the door and slammed into a girl with bright blue curly hair and a silver ring through her eyebrow.

"Oh," Sara said. "Sorry."

"Flissa?" the girl asked. "I thought you and Zinka just went out."

Uh-oh.

"Oh. Um . . . yeah!" Sara said. "I just . . . I . . . had to come back and use the bathroom."

"Got it." The girl bounded down the porch stairs, and Sara let out her breath.

"Oh hey!"

It was the girl again. Sara winced, then turned and smiled. Then she wiped away the smile. Then she smiled again.

The girl scrunched up her face. This was going fabulously unwell.

"I'm guessing Zinka told you, but Odelia and Trinni are good. Trinni went home, but Odelia's upstairs if you want to see her."

The names meant nothing to Sara, but they had to be Genpos and friends of Flissa's. She tried to look both concerned and relieved. "Good. I'm glad they're okay."

The girl gave her another weird look, then she raised her hand in a goodbye and took off up the field.

Sara shook her head and went inside the dorm. Now she just had to hope the blue-haired girl didn't run into Zinka and the real Flissa in the next few minutes.

She loped up the steps, cringing a bit in anticipation of the magic wall, but she must have looked enough like Flissa to pass. She ran to the third floor, took a left down the hall, then stopped in front of the door with Zinka's nameplate. Flissa had said the doors weren't locked. Sara hoped it was true.

She tried the knob and it opened. Perfect. She slipped in and closed it behind her.

The floor was covered in dirt. Big chunks of it. Like as if someone had been tromping around digging for blinzer stones and dragged all the dirt back on her clothes and shoes.

She'd had a whole plan about how to act in front of the cat. She was going to say something out loud, like, *Good thing Zinka's letting me borrow her History book, or I'd be in huge trouble!* That would've shown the cat she was in there for something real and certainly not a blinzer stone.

Now that she was actually in the room, she was very glad that Raya had run off. Considering how horribly she'd done with the blue-haired girl, she knew Raya would have seen through her act in a heartbeat.

Of course, there was a chance Zinka was lying about the cat disappearing.

Sara quickly gave the room a quick once-over, peeking in the closet, under and behind the couch, and on the loft bed. No cat. No obvious blinzer stones either, but she hadn't imagined they'd be out in the open.

So . . . where would a girl and her evil ex-lioness friend put a bunch of blinzer stones?

Sara shuffled through everything on top of Zinka's desk. She unrolled scrolls, peeked in ink pots, and lifted piles of parchment. Nothing. She went through the desk drawers next, first just glancing through for any large stones, then shifting things around in case there were smaller ones hidden inside. Still nothing.

With the desk exhausted, Sara quickly went through every drawer in Zinka's dresser and moved or patted down all her clothes. No luck. She climbed onto the loft bed and felt under the mattress and inside the pillowcases; she patted down all the couch cushions; she peeled back the throw rug.

She didn't want to stay in the room much longer. She had no idea how long Flissa could keep Zinka distracted, plus it could be a hopeless search. What if Flissa's theory was right and Raya had magicked the stones away with her?

Still, this was their one chance to look around, and Sara didn't want to leave until she knew for sure she'd checked every possible spot.

The closet; if she searched the closet and the stones weren't there, she'd give up. She opened the closet door, then stood on a chair to check the shelf on top before sifting through every hanging piece of clothing, and putting her hands in every pocket.

No stones.

Sara didn't know whether to be relieved or disappointed. She didn't even know what it meant. Was Zinka innocent because the stones weren't there, or was moving the stones part of her and Raya's mutual plan?

She had no idea, but now wasn't the time to figure it out.

Sara walked to the door and was about to leave when she noticed four pairs of boots sitting in a line. They were set by the wall, where they'd be blocked by the door when it opened, which was why Sara hadn't noticed them on the way in.

Could Zinka have stashed a blinzer stone or two in one of the shoes?

Sara crouched down and picked up a black leather ankle boot. Not only was the sole coated in dirt that chunked off and crumbled all over Sara's clothes, but it reeked like spoiled egg tarts. "Ugh, what do you do in these?"

She did *not* want to reach inside. She held it up to her ear and shook it to see if anything moved.

Ka-THUMP.

Sara's skin prickled. Now she was dying to reach inside.

WHAP!

"OW!"

Sara fell over as the door to the room smacked her in the back. The boot fell out of her hand, and a perfectly smooth, shiny orange stone the size of her palm tumbled out of it.

Sara glanced up. Zinka stood in the doorway, towering over her, green eyes blazing. Her hands clenched into fists.

She looked like a warrior, ready for battle.

Zinka slammed the door shut behind her, and Sara lunged for the shiny orange stone. Her fingertips were on it and she could hear the stone hum.

"NO!" Zinka yelled.

Sara heard a single, clear chime, then an electric shock bit into her hand.

"Ow!"

She pulled her hand away, and Zinka scooped up the stone. She stared at Sara, and in the one second before she heard that clear chime again, Sara realized Zinka didn't look like a warrior at all. She looked terrified, and there were tears in her eyes as she closed her hand around the orange stone.

Then the chime rang out, and all Sara felt was pain.

Chapter 19
Flissa

Flissa ran full speed up the girls' dorm stairs, taking them two at a time.

She never should have agreed to the plan. It was a bad idea.

It was Flissa's fault it failed. She should have known she had too many friends on dorm. She should have known someone would see her and mess things up. And she *definitely* should have known that once Zinka lost Teddy, she'd be too distraught to stay out of her room for long. It took forever for her to even convince Zinka to go for a walk, so they were nowhere near the topiary garden when Dallie called out, "Zinka! Flissa!" and told them that she thought Flissa's twin was playing tricks on them, because she just saw someone who looked exactly like Flissa—but acted a lot weirder—outside the girls' dorms.

Zinka seemed to understand right away, and Flissa remembered the look she gave her—a horrible mix of anger, betrayal, and terror.

Then she broke out in a run.

Flissa ran after her. They'd raced before; Flissa thought

she could catch up to her. What surprised her was that Zinka turned around and flicked out her hand midstride. Flissa heard a clear chime, then her feet slid out from under her, as if she were running on ice. Every time she got up, she fell back down again, until Flissa realized Zinka had magicked the soles of her shoes. She threw them off, then kept racing after her, but she'd lost precious time.

Please be out of the room, Sara, she thought to herself. *Please be long, long gone.*

Flissa reached the top of the third-floor stairs and barreled down the hall. She saw some girls standing around outside Zinka's door, and she felt sick. They'd only be gathered there if they'd heard something strange. Flissa struggled to find more breath, more speed, but she didn't have anything left.

Then she heard the screams.

It was Sara. She'd know her sister's voice anywhere. And she sounded like she was in agony.

Miraculously Flissa moved faster.

Her lungs breaking apart, she threw open Zinka's door.

Zinka stood in the middle of the room, her hair splayed wildly around her head. She squeezed a smooth, shiny orange stone in one hand and sobbed as she stared down at Sara, screaming and writhing on the floor.

Flissa didn't stop to think. She looked at Sara and her blood boiled. She drew all her anger from deep inside herself, then threw her arms forward and flung it out at Zinka.

Cream-colored mist covered Zinka, and she zoomed backward as if shoved by a giant hand. She slammed against the wall so hard the blinzer stone clanked to the floor, and within seconds the mist around her had hardened into a cement that covered every inch of her, from her chest to her knees, and plastered her against the wall.

Flissa quickly picked up the blinzer stone and slipped it in her pocket. She didn't really want it anywhere near her, but she couldn't let it fall into anyone else's hands. Then she knelt down next to Sara. Whatever curse Zinka had put on her, it had shocked Sara's twinning charm away so she looked like herself again. She was curled into a ball, twitching and spasming as if someone were nudging her with a cattle prod.

"Sara?" Flissa said. "Are you okay? Sara, please be okay."

Sara didn't respond. Aside from the twitching, she didn't move.

Flissa spun around to Zinka, plastered to the wall. "What did you do to her?!"

Tears ran freely down Zinka's face. "I'm so sorry. I didn't want to. Sara had the stone. I couldn't let her take it. She said she'd hurt me, so much worse than before. . . ."

Flissa jumped to her feet and ran to Zinka. "*Who* would hurt you? Raya? I mean, Teddy?"

Zinka shook her head, confused. "*Teddy?* I don't understand . . . Teddy ran away. What does she have to do with anything?"

Flissa wanted to shake her, but she forced herself to take a deep breath and stay calm. "Forget I said Teddy. Who wants to hurt you? Is it the someone who made you dig up the stones? The someone who takes over your body and makes you stay up digging until your fingernails break and bleed?"

Zinka's tear-filled eyes widened in shock, like she couldn't believe Flissa actually understood. She gave the slightest hint of a nod, then Flissa saw the fear come back and she shook her head hard.

Flissa's heart broke for her. This was her friend, not a monster; she'd only cursed Sara because Raya terrorized her into it.

"Zinka," she said, "I'm begging you. If you're really innocent, tell the truth. To everyone. To Amala, to my parents, to the General Council . . . they'll believe you. I'll help you."

Zinka's eyes watered all over again, then Flissa saw the steel seep into her face. Her jaw set, her tears dried, and she seemed to stand taller, even while plastered to the wall. "I'm not innocent," she said. "I knew Raya in the Twists. That's why she came to me."

Flissa backed away like she'd been stung. "What?"

"Move *away* from the door!"

Flissa heard Amala's voice, and a moment later the Shadow was in the room, tailed by the same two male teachers who'd come when Loriah was in trouble. They must have been Shadows as well. In one moment Amala took in the entire scene: Sara unconscious and twitching on the floor, Flissa in the middle of the room, Zinka plastered to the wall. She closed her eyes a moment as if it weighed on her terribly, then turned to Flissa.

"I'll need to talk to you," she said, "but I'm happy to do it at the palace so you can stay with your sister. She'll do better with Katya than she will at the infirmary." She turned to the men behind her. "Please take Flissa and Sara home. Stay with them until I get there. I'll bubblegram the king and queen to let them know."

One of the men stepped up to Flissa and gently took her arm. "One second, please," she said.

She pulled the blinzer stone out of her pocket. It hummed as it slipped into her palm. "Here," she said handing it to Amala. "This should be with you."

The stone hummed even louder in Amala's hand, and she let out a soft gasp. "Yes," she said, and slipped the stone into her robes. "Thank you."

Then Flissa went home with her sister.

* * *

The next few days were a strange haze that flowed in and out like a dream. She must have told the story of what happened a million times: to her parents, to Katya, to Rouen, to the entire Council, to Amala . . . then to all of them all over again in every combination and permutation. Plus she had to tell her friends.

Putting the story of Raya and Zinka together with Sara had been almost exciting. Reciting it on her own made her feel hollow and foolish for trying to accomplish anything without more help. The price was too steep. Katya thought Sara would be okay, but she wasn't sure how long it would take before she fully recovered. Maybe days, maybe weeks, maybe months. That was the problem with a blinzer stone. Even if Zinka had meant to curse Sara lightly—just lightly enough to keep her from coming after the stone—its powers would have magnified that curse in ways Zinka couldn't control.

In the meantime, Sara lay in her bed, eyes closed, as if she were sleeping. She still twitched every now and then, but she didn't respond to anyone's voice. Every time Flissa went to bed at night and saw her sister lying there across from her, she inwardly cursed herself for ever putting a wall between them and losing precious time together.

With Sara recovering, it seemed like there were always visitors in and out of their room. Galric came all the time and talked to Sara as if she were alert and understood. Sometimes Krystal came too, with Skeed or her other friends. Jentrie came by as often as she could. And of course Loriah was there all the time. Everything that had come out about Raya had made her nightmares worse. She suffered from real spell terrors now and felt much better when she slept at the palace.

Flissa's other friends also came by a lot; they wanted to show their support. At any given time there were several hoodle team members around, and even though they talked and laughed together, the team seemed like they were in the same daze as Flissa. Flissa understood; in a way, they were missing a sister too. They were missing Zinka.

A week into Sara's illness, Amala came to visit, and said she wanted to talk to Flissa privately. Flissa met her in the parlor, and they sat together on the couch.

"I feel like you deserve to know where things stand," Amala said. "I've spent the last week doing many interviews, many meetings, and all kinds of research, and I believe we understand now how everything happened."

"You do?" Flissa asked.

"Yes," Amala said. "For starters, Zinka and Raya did know each other in the Twists. I've spoken to your friend Loriah about this and she didn't know Zinka, but other Untwisteds saw them together. More than that, some overheard Zinka and Raya talking about blinzer stones, and the damage they'd do to Kaloon if they ever got hold of them."

"*Zinka* said that?" Flissa asked.

Amala simply gave a slight nod and continued. Honestly, everything else she told Flissa was just confirmation of things Flissa and Sara had discovered themselves. The Shadows had decided yes, the explosion from the Twists could indeed have released Raya into Kaloon and permanently changed her from a lioness to a cat without diminishing her power. They thought once that happened, Raya sought out Zinka, thinking she'd be an ally. They also believed Zinka dug up blinzer stones for Raya—or at least went digging to try to find them. And they'd changed their opinion on Loriah's spell terrors. They now thought she'd been cursed by Zinka or Raya.

"Raya did it," Flissa said. "I don't believe it was Zinka."

Amala continued the story of "Things Flissa Knew" with the sleepover and the Genpo curse, and then what happened to Sara. "Since that day," Amala said, "Zinka has been kept in a Shadow-designed detention cell, with magic-absorbing walls that ensure she can't get away."

Flissa listened to the whole story, then shook her head. "You left something out. You didn't say if Zinka worked with Raya because she wanted to, or because she was forced to."

That was the question that tortured Flissa. It was the one thing she needed to know. Had she been completely fooled by Zinka, or were her instincts about her right?

"I did leave it out," Amala said. "I had to, because Zinka's not telling us. That means one of two things: either she was willingly working with Raya all along, or she wasn't, but she's too frightened to tell us the truth."

"What about Raya disguising herself as Teddy?" Flissa said. "Zinka had no idea Teddy and Raya were the same. Why act like a hidden pet cat if Zinka *wanted* to work with her?"

"First of all, you're the only one who says Zinka didn't know the cat was Raya," Amala said. "It may be the case, but Zinka hasn't said it at all. If it *is* the case, it does seem likely that Raya didn't trust Zinka would work with her, and acted like a loving pet to learn about her. That way she'd know Zinka's soft spots—the best ways to threaten her to keep her in line. But unless and until Zinka speaks up for herself, we have to follow the evidence and keep her where she is."

Flissa shook her head. "It just doesn't feel right," she said.

"For what it's worth, I agree," Amala said. "I've been around a very long time, and I'm a very good judge of character. I spent a lot of time with Zinka, and I believe she was acting under duress. I can only hope she tells the truth, or that the truth makes itself clear."

Amala left after that, and Flissa crawled into bed with Sara. She did that sometimes; she didn't think her sister would mind.

A week or so later, Flissa was sitting on her bed playing a card game with Loriah and Galric. They'd dealt a hand for Sara too, and each took turns playing her move and telling her what they were doing.

"I'm discarding three," Galric called to her. "You good with that?" He waited as if she was answering, then said, "She thinks that's a really bad move. I'm discarding two."

"They got her!" Flissa's father announced, stepping into the room. "They found the cat!"

"What?" Flissa breathed.

"Where?" Galric asked.

"The scenthounds who grabbed her scent from Zinka's room tracked her to a tree near the edge of the kingdom. She was curled up in an abandoned raccoon nest," the king explained. "And there was a blinzer stone in the nest. She *did* have two stones to do the Genpo curse, and now we have them both in Shadow hands."

"What about Raya?" Loriah said. "Did she run?"

"She did *not*," Flissa's father said, and the tips of his mustache pointed straight up. "They grabbed her while she was sleeping; only then did they get the stone. Now she's locked up in the same detention center as Zinka, the blinzer stones are secured, and Maldevon Academy reopens its doors in the morning!"

Flissa's father cupped his hands over his mouth and made the sound of a roaring crowd. Flissa and Loriah exchanged a look. Sometimes Flissa thought her father was far too silly to be a king.

"How do we know those are her only two blinzer stones?" she asked.

"Well, it stands to reason she'd keep them near her," her father started, "plus the Shadows have been doing magical sweeps, and so far there are no signs of others. They'll keep searching, but the headline of the scroll is 'The Danger Has Passed.'"

The words were barely out of his mouth when they

292

all turned to look at Sara, still lying motionless on her bed.

"Her danger will pass too," their father said, placing a comforting hand on Flissa's shoulder. "She'll be better soon. Now you should wind up this card game early tonight. School tomorrow!"

"Wait," Loriah said. "Are you *sure* the cat's Raya, and not some other decoy cat?"

"When they grabbed her, she woke up and used her magical signature," he assured them. "Blue sparks—no blinzer stone to magnify it. And to make doubly sure, while I wouldn't dream of putting you through it, we had other Untwisteds who had met Raya come in and identify the sparks. Magical signatures are like fingerprints. It's her, and she's locked away."

He walked to Sara's bed and kissed her head, then came back and planted a kiss on Flissa's head as well before he walked out of the room.

Flissa looked at Loriah and Galric. None of them really knew how to react. Flissa thought they should be jumping up and down and hugging each other because Raya had been captured, but everything just felt strange and unsettled.

The next day, Flissa felt awful leaving Sara behind to go to school, and when Amala told everyone that the Kaloonification Ball was back on and would occur in two weeks, Flissa's heart sank. The ball had meant everything to Zinka, and Sara had been so excited to go. It felt wrong to even think of it going on without them.

At lunch she sat with the hoodle team, but none of them had an appetite. It was as if they could all feel the empty space where Zinka used to fit.

"I just don't get it," Rosalie said, listlessly batting at an apple with her wing. "All the things they're saying she did . . . none of it sounds like Zinka."

"'Cause it isn't," Dallie responded. "She wouldn't do any of it. It's bogus."

"Dallie," Trinni snapped. "She did *some* of it. She cursed Sara."

"Because she was scared and someone was making her do terrible things," Beverly-Ann said.

"Why would you say that?" Loriah said. "Flissa's right here."

"It's okay, I agree," Flissa said. "We all know Zinka. We know her better than anybody. She wouldn't hurt anyone. Not willingly."

Flissa knew in her heart it was true. Even though it destroyed her every time she thought about Zinka turning that stone on Sara, she remembered the tears running down Zinka's face and she knew—she was absolutely certain—that Zinka had only done it out of terror, and she hadn't meant to hurt Sara as badly as she did.

So how could she be okay with everything going back to normal when it didn't feel normal at all?

For three days she slogged through school and came home right after hoodle practice. The team never hung out for dinner and homework anymore; they were all still friends, but Zinka had always rallied them together. She was their glue. Flissa knew it would get better. They'd get used to it, and maybe another team member would step up and take Zinka's place at the center of the team, but right now it just felt strange.

That's what was on her mind when she tromped up to

Chapter 20
Sara

"How do I look?"

Sara wore a soft pink ball gown trimmed with lace and beads. The bodice clung to her body, tapered at her waist, then flared into a full skirt over crinolines. The sleeves sat just off her shoulders, and a tiara of tiny pink roses nestled in her hair.

"Is that the dress you picked out with Jentrie and Krystal?" Flissa asked.

Ever since Sara woke up from Zinka's curse, Flissa had been teasing her about going ball-dress hunting without her. Apparently Krystal and Jentrie told her the story while Sara was out cold.

"You really need to let it go," Sara said. "I would've loved your help; you weren't talking to me then."

"And that is to my eternal shame and regret," Flissa said.

She said it with such pain in her eyes, Sara hated to see it. She wished her sister wouldn't beat herself up. Then again, she supposed if she'd watched Flissa lie on a bed her room, dropped her satchel, and plopped down on her chair to take off her shoes.

"Aw, come on," said a voice from the other side of the room. "Aren't you even gonna say hi?"

Flissa's insides leaped.

"You're awake!"

Sara grinned. She was still lying flat on her bed and looked devastatingly weak, but she was awake and she was talking and she was smiling and—

"Miss me?" Sara asked.

"You have no idea!"

She bounded onto Sara's bed and squeezed her tight, then opened up a vial of message milk to call their parents.

Sara laughed. "They're right down the hall. Can't you just go get them?"

"Not a chance," Flissa said. "I'm staying right here with you."

barely moving for three weeks, she'd feel terrible about a lot of things too.

"Fliss, I love you," she said, taking her twin's hands. "And we both messed up in the beginning of the school year, remember? But I'm okay, and everything's good . . . and I really need you to tell me if this gown works on me."

"I love you too," Flissa said with a nod. "Twirl."

Sara did. Her skirt flared beautifully, like a pink cloud all around her.

"You look *beautiful*," Flissa said.

Sara beamed. "You do too. I think it's the first dress you've worn all year."

Flissa wore an A-line dress in a dramatic shade of deep purple. Her hair was loose and long, a single tendril from each side pulled back and pinned with a jeweled barrette. They stood side by side and grinned at one another in the mirror.

"It's the first ball we get to go to together," Sara said.

"Together with your *date*," Flissa said.

Sara felt her cheeks get hot and she couldn't stop smiling. "Stop! We're *all* going together. And yeah, Galric asked me and I'm going with him, but he's not my 'date.' That just sounds weird."

"Weird 'cause it's a date, or weird 'cause it's Galric?"

"Weird 'cause it's weird!" Sara said. Then she took Flissa's hand. "Come on. I bet they're all downstairs with Vincenzo ready to take a zillion portraits."

As Sara and Flissa walked out of the room, Sara thought about the last few weeks. A lot of it she didn't remember. She remembered finding the blinzer stone, and she definitely remembered the horrible pain when Zinka cursed her, but nothing after that until she woke up in bed.

"Stop right there!" Primka shouted as Flissa and Sara got to the top of the staircase. Sara stole a look at Flissa because it was exactly what she'd expected: Katya, Primka, and their mom and dad, all of them dressed up because they were going to the ball too; and all of them huddled together around Vincenzo and his easel, looking way too close to tears. The only ones not there were Galric and Rouen; Sara wondered if Rouen was helping Galric get ready.

"Get their picture, Vincenzo," their mother urged. "You're both so beautiful!"

"Thank you," they chorused, then they burst out laughing.

"No laughing!" Vincenzo wailed. "I need to paint you quickly so you won't be late! Pose!"

Sara struck a dramatic pose on the railing, while Flissa smiled demurely, her mouth closed in a prim, straight line.

"A little something in the middle, please?" Katya asked.

Sara rolled her eyes and leaned one hand casually on the railing, while Flissa flashed an actual smile.

"Perfect!" Vincenzo said. "Now don't move, or I'll scratch you."

Sara caught Flissa's eye again and they smiled without moving.

Apparently Katya had thought Sara might stay cursed for months, but three weeks was more than long enough. By the time she woke up she was like a baby zebra—wobbly in every joint as her body tried to remember what it was supposed to do. Her parents had suggested she stay home from school and get better, but she had wanted to go back as soon as possible. Amala adjusted her schedule so she'd have someone close to her—Flissa, Galric, Loriah, Krystal, or Jentrie—in each class so she could lean on them or get help if she needed it, but the truth was she didn't really need anything; she just liked being in classes with her friends.

"Another pose!" Vincenzo called. For a sloth, he worked very quickly.

"Spin around," Sara said.

Flissa did, and they stood back-to-back, arms folded.

"Yes! Very nice!" Vincenzo raved as he started another canvas.

One thing Sara had definitely remembered when she woke up from the curse was that the Kaloonification Ball had been canceled, so she was happy when Flissa had told her it was back on. It was *almost* the best news she'd missed—the fact that Raya had been captured was the best. Sara knew Flissa felt a little weird about the Kaloonification Ball since Zinka had put so much work into it, but Sara was sure once they were there she'd love it.

"One more!" Vincenzo called.

"These are beautiful, Vincenzo," Katya sniffed. "Just beautiful!"

Sara and Flissa put their arms around each other and posed once again.

It felt so good to be back to normal with her twin. Their new normal, anyway. They didn't share a life, and they didn't ignore each other either. They each had their own friends and their own things they loved to do, but at the end of the day they always came back to one another. It was perfect.

"Oh my universe, would you look at that!" cried Katya.

Sara looked and saw Rouen and Galric come in from the back hall. When Galric stepped into the light, her breath caught. She'd never seen him so dressed up. He wore black velvet pants and a jacket, and his hair was slicked back. Sara had never thought this word about Galric before, but he looked . . . kind of handsome.

"What do you think, Sara?" Katya crowed. "Did he dress up nice enough for ya?"

"*Stop!*" Sara and Galric said at the same time, but Katya was having way too much fun. She made sure Vincenzo was done with his painting, then she took Sara's arm and pulled her down to Galric.

"He has something for you," Katya said. "Give it to her."

Galric looked down at his hands as if he expected something to appear there, then Rouen leaned over and handed him a wrist corsage with a single large pink daisy. "It's a corsage," he said awkwardly. "Your mom said it was a good one to go with your dress."

"I did," agreed her mom excitedly. "And I sewed it to the wristband. And look, I made him a boutonniere to match."

Galric did, indeed, have a small pink flower in his lapel.

"Put it on her wrist," Sara's dad said.

"Yeah," Rouen said. "Vincenzo, get a picture of it."

So Galric and Sara had to stand perfectly still while he held the corsage halfway on her wrist. Luckily Vincenzo had them both looking down at the corsage while they posed, so their heads were close together and they could talk without moving.

"Our parents are the most embarrassing human beings on the planet," Galric said.

"Beyond," Sara agreed.

After that torture, Sara's mom had the whole group get together for one final portrait, and only then did they get to escape with Flissa to their carriage. The adults were taking their own carriage and following them.

"Oh. My. Universe. That was too much," Flissa said as they shut the carriage door behind them.

"I think they need a hobby," Galric said.

"I think *we* are their hobby," Sara said. "Oh, check this out—I've been practicing."

She concentrated, then leaned out the window and shot off a bubble of scarlet mist. It quickly morphed into a solid red paper lantern, lit from the inside as if from a candle, and floated into the air.

"That's so cool," Galric said. "Do another one."

"I'll do a different shape," Sara offered. "Give me one."

"A frog," Galric said.

"A *frog*?" Flissa echoed.

"I don't know, it was the first thing that came to my head!"

Sara spent the rest of the ride launching magic paper lanterns out the carriage window in all shapes and sizes, then they arrived at the school . . . and stepped out into a wonderland. The long main walkway was lit by floating red paper lanterns ten times the size of Sara's own, and the statue of Gilward glowed as if lit from the inside. The main event, however, was in the back fields. Magical twinkle lights sparkled in the trees, balloons full of brightening bugs floated above a dance floor that glowed and shifted from color to color, and fairies dressed in perfect tiny gowns flitted everywhere, leaving their colored contrails as they served appetizers and fancy fruit drinks. The music was thumping and loud; a buffet table bursting with delicious food sat just outside the topiary garden; and right in the middle was an intricate papier-mâché replica of Maldevon Academy itself.

"It's beautiful," Sara said.

"It is. It's exactly the way Zinka planned it," Flissa said. Then she quickly added, "Sorry," because the best way for them not to argue about Zinka was to try not to talk about her.

Sara squeezed her hand. "It's okay; she's your friend. And if this is what she planned, she did an incredible job."

Flissa smiled gratefully, then she and Sara raised their hands in the air and each sent a single wisp of their magical signature into the sky so their friends could find them. Krystal, Skeed, Loriah, and Loriah's date, Marianna, were the first to make it through the crowd. Krystal wore a flared skirt with a close-cropped spangled doublet and Skeed a bright purple doublet and kilt; while Loriah wore her usual leggings, boots, and comfortable shirt, though she'd added a brooch to the top for dramatic effect, and to match Marianna, who wore a sparkly silver dress. They hugged all around, then Krystal grabbed Sara's arm and shouted over the music.

"I have to take you to Jentrie!" she said. "She has to see the final effect of our work!"

Krystal pulled Sara through the crowd. It seemed like not just all of Maldevon Academy but all of Kaloon was there, and even though she looked over her shoulder to tell Galric where she was going, the crowd closed around him almost immediately.

"Jentrie!" Krystal called when they got to her. Jentrie was wearing an amethyst-colored gown with remarkable spinning properties; Sara saw them firsthand when Jentrie spun to face her.

"Your Highness, you are a *vision!*" Jentrie snapped to get the attention of her friends, all of whom also wore gem-colored gowns. "Tell me—she's a vision, right?"

All Jentrie's friends agreed that Sara was indeed a vision.

"Let's check out the buffet table," Sara said. "I'm starving."

Sara, Krystal, and Jentrie all maneuvered their way to the buffet table and filled their plates with little K-shaped puff pastries filled with all kinds of savories, then took bites of one another's choices. Sara had just taken a big chomp of a pheasant-puff when she felt a tap on her shoulder. She spun to see who it was.

"Galric!" she said through a mouthful of pheasant. Then she held up a finger—one second—chewed and swallowed, then tried again. "Galric! I thought I'd lost you."

"You did. But I found you again." He adjusted his jacket and shifted nervously from side to side. "So, um . . . I was wondering . . . do you think you'd maybe . . . want to dance?"

Sara smiled. "I'd love it. Wait—I don't have pheasant in my teeth, do I?"

She grinned big and Galric laughed. "No. You're perfect."

Even in the colored twinkle lights, Sara could see him blush.

"I mean, your teeth are . . ." He realized there was no good way out of it, so he just gave up and laughed again. "Let's dance."

He held out his elbow, and Sara rested her hand on it. Everything in her seemed to frizzle as he led her through the sea of gowns and suits and twinkle lights to the dance floor. She felt her heart skip as he settled his hands on her hips, and she reached up to put her hands on his shoulders. They swayed to the music and smiled, looking into each other's eyes.

Sara was very aware of his hands on her hips. In a good way. It was weird. She'd hugged him a million times before, and now they weren't even hugging, they were an arm's length apart, but it felt . . . jittery. She liked it.

"I don't think I said it yet, but you look really pretty," he said.

"You too," Sara said. "I mean, not *pretty*, but, you know . . . you look great."

"Thanks."

They swayed some more, and Sara felt him bend his arms in a bit, moving a little closer. She wondered if he could hear her heart speed up.

"I was really scared when you were sick," he said.

"You were?"

"Really scared," he said. "I wouldn't be okay if anything hap—"

Sara heard a crash so loud she screamed. She turned to see the entire buffet table collapse in a sea of blue sparks. *Blue sparks.*

Sara clung to Galric and her eyes searched for Flissa, but everything happened too quickly. Another flurry of blue sparks danced over the papier-mâché replica of Maldevon Academy, and it split open to reveal a pile of shiny polished stones, in every color of the rainbow.

Before anyone could even react, a blur of orange tore across the floor and pounced onto the pile of blinzer stones, which let out a loud hum.

Now that she'd stopped moving, the blur of orange was just an adorable cat . . . with bright yellow eyes that Sara would remember anywhere.

The cat opened her mouth to speak, and blue lightning crackled above her as her voice reverberated over the fields.

"Allow me to introduce myself," she said. "I'm Raya. But you can call me . . . your destruction."

Chapter 21
Flissa

Flissa was too far from the buffet table to see the crash. She heard it, then she saw the blue bolts of lightning in the sky and heard Raya's booming voice.

"No," she said. She pushed through the crowd, Loriah right behind her, until she could see the cat sitting on the ripped-open husk of the papier-mâché replica of the school, the stones bursting out of it like lava.

The pieces fell together in a rush. The replica had been Zinka's idea. She must have hidden the stones inside it when she was working on the ball. This was part of Raya's plan all along . . . but how? How did she break out of the Shadows' magic-absorbing cell?

"Raya," Loriah growled, her voice full of venom. Flissa saw her friend's fists balling at her sides.

"Don't!" Flissa snapped. "She's on a pile of blinzer stones! With that kind of power—"

Loriah didn't listen. She screamed and shoved her way across the dance floor. She leaped for Raya, but the cat just laughed and pointed a paw. Blue lightning crackled around Loriah as she soared backward through the air and landed like a rag doll in a clump of bushes.

"Get the cat!" someone cried.

"Get the stones!" someone else wailed.

And as the entire crowd surged forward, the sky came alive with endless bolts of blue lightning.

Flissa felt her body grow rigid. She couldn't turn her head. Voices screamed in terror all around her, and Flissa knew the same thing was happening to everyone.

Raya had taken over their bodies. *All* of their bodies. No one could move.

"Silence!" the cat roared as more lightning cracked in the sky. Her yellow eyes flashed, and she looked to her right. Flissa couldn't turn, but she darted her eyes in that direction. Amala was there, but even she stood perfectly still, only her long white hair and dress shifting in the breeze.

"As I'm sure you've realized, Shadow," Raya's voice boomed. "I'm standing on a pile of blinzer stones, dug up from all over Kaloon by my unwitting friend. Thank you, by the way. I appreciate your kindness in locking her away before she dared try to betray me."

Unwitting friend, Flissa thought. So she'd been right. Zinka was innocent. Raya was using and threatening her. Flissa burned with rage, but Raya's grip on her was too strong. She couldn't do anything with it.

Flissa darted her eyes around to find her family. Sara and Galric were on the dance floor, while her parents, Katya, and Rouen were farther back on the field. Flissa could see the four of them exchanging glances, wordlessly making a plan of attack.

Suddenly she wondered—were Katya and Rouen actually frozen? Was Amala? Or was their magic somehow strong enough to fight against Raya's, even when it was enhanced by the blinzer stones?

"I have twelve blinzer stones, to be exact," Raya continued to Amala, "each one magnifying my powers beyond measure. So I win."

"Win what?" Amala said. Flissa had no idea how she managed it, but her voice sounded as calm as if she and Raya were sitting back and sharing lemonades.

"Well, what I'd *really* like is my home the way it was, before you gutted the place. Certainly I'd like my body back," Raya said, "but since none of that's really possible even with twelve blinzer stones . . . I'll settle for chaos and destruction."

Blue lightning flashed over Flissa's father. Moving like a marionette, the king staggered quickly to Amala. Screaming in agony and fighting his every movement, he wrapped his hands around her neck and squeezed.

"I'm so sorry . . ." he croaked. "I'm trying to stop it . . ."

More lightning flashed. It was everywhere. One by one in quick succession Flissa saw everyone at the ball—Mages, Genpos, Magical Animals, parents, teachers—jerk to puppeteered life and attack one another, punching, kicking, and gouging.

Flissa couldn't believe it. "She wants us all to kill each other."

Even as the words left her mouth, her body jerked toward the dance floor. Her stomach dropped as she saw exactly where Raya was leading her.

She was heading right for Sara, but her sister was

308

already in trouble. Dallie had her in a headlock, and Sara was gasping for air.

"Dallie, stop!" Flissa screamed, but Dallie's body wasn't her own. Behind Dallie and Sara, Flissa saw Galric punch Skeed in the stomach. "Sorry!" he wailed. Then he smashed an uppercut to Skeed's chin and cried, "I'm so sorry!"

When Flissa reached Dallie, her hands reached out all on their own and peeled her away from Sara, then she kneed Dallie in the stomach.

"I am so sorry, Dallie!" she said, but she didn't see what happened next with Dallie because she spun like a top to see Sara doubled over and wheezing for breath. Then Raya's magic yanked Sara back upright. She saw Flissa and for a heartbreaking moment she looked thrilled.

Then Flissa drew her fist to strike.

"I'm so sorry, Sara. I'm so, so, sorry."

Sara stood stiff as a board, an open target.

"No!" Sara said. "We can fight it. We fought her before, we can do it again!"

Tears sprang into Flissa's eyes. "She didn't have twelve blinzer stones then."

Her fist tightened and cocked farther back.

Suddenly Sara smiled. Or at least she tried to smile. Her mouth turned up as far as the spell would let her, so it was more of a wide grimace. "Okay," she said. "Do it. But when you do, think about fighting *her*."

Sara looked at her meaningfully, and in a flash Flissa understood. She didn't know if it would work, but maybe it could. With her arm cocked back and ready to strike, Flissa focused all her strength on beating Raya and fighting against her magic. She closed her eyes—it would kill her if she watched herself hit Sara. Then, leaning into it with all her might, she punched.

Flissa heard the horrible *thwack* of flesh on flesh and cried out. She opened her eyes . . . and saw Sara had caught Flissa's fist in her own open palm. At the spot their hands connected, Flissa felt the heat of their combined power. They hadn't done magic together since that first day of Magic Lab, but Flissa knew the feeling. It warmed her and fed her and electrified her skin. Flissa saw the pink sheen of their combined magic spread over Sara's body until it radiated a rose-colored aura.

"You're glowing!" Sara said. "And we can move!"

It was true. Flissa felt the stiffness of Raya's control drain from her body. Despite the blinzer stones' power, they could still fight back. But they were only two people in a sea of others. They needed to do more.

"We have to get her off the stones," Flissa said. "But we need more power."

Flissa looked around. Skeed and Galric were the closest people to them; Galric was sprawled on the dance floor and Skeed had a foot in the air, about to stomp on Galric's back.

"Grab Skeed!" Flissa shouted. "Hurry!"

Sara screamed Skeed's name and grabbed his hand, and Flissa instantly felt the hum as his energy joined theirs, and their pink glow tinged purple. He shook his head like he was shaking off a daze, then turned to Flissa and Sara in stunned awe. "Thank you!"

"We need more if we want to stop her!" Flissa yelled to him. "Take Galric's hand!"

"But he's a Genpo," Skeed said. "He can't help."

"He can!" Flissa said. She had no idea how she knew this, she just felt it and knew she was right. "We need him. We need everyone!"

Skeed took Galric's hand and sure enough, Flissa felt a surge of power. She quickly grabbed Dallie with her free hand, instantly adding her energy to the mix. "More!" Flissa shouted. "Grab more people and animals!"

"Join the chain!" Sara screamed. "Don't let Raya win! If we all work together, we can fight back! Join the chain!"

It became a chant. "Join-the-chain! Join-the-chain!" Flissa held tightly to Sara and Dallie and watched as more and more latched on. Hooves clung to wings clung to hands clung to paws. People who never would have chosen to be in the same room latched on to one another, added their energy to the chain, and took control of their bodies. Flissa saw Rouen holding Rosalie's wing; Jentrie holding hands with Beverly-Ann; Dame Yentley holding tightly to a pony's forelock. Everyone grabbed on, and the glow around them morphed and changed with each additional burst of power until Flissa couldn't even tell what color it was; they were all just wrapped in a constantly morphing cloud of energy.

Then Krystal, at the far end of the chain, reached out and grabbed Amala's hand. Flissa's ears filled with a vibrating thrum. Wind buffeted her backward as the overwhelming scent of oranges filled her nose. The glowing bubble encasing them all grew brighter and brighter until finally Flissa had to close her eyes against it and . . .

She felt something explode in front of her and she fell back to the ground.

Her hand slipped from Dallie's, but she held firmly on to Sara's as if her life depended on it.

Then everything faded away.

* * *

When Flissa opened her eyes again, the broken papier-mâché replica of Maldevon Academy was there, but Raya was gone. Then she saw the cat in Amala's arms . . . inside a clear sphere. Amala held the sphere over her head. Though Raya ran around and hurled her body against the sides of the sphere, it didn't give way. "Raya won't be hurting any-one anymore," Amala said.

Some people cheered. Most, like Flissa herself, were in too much of a daze.

Flissa saw Rouen and Katya picking up the blinzer stones and putting them in a thick drawstring pouch. "What are you going to do with them?" Flissa asked.

"Keep 'em with the other two," Katya said, "hidden under lock and key until we can find the best way to destroy them."

Flissa nodded. She was glad the stones would be Rouen and Katya's responsibility. Even if they couldn't destroy the stones, they'd make sure they never fell into the wrong hands.

"We did it, Flissa," Sara said.

Flissa hadn't even realized she wasn't holding Sara's hand anymore. Her twin had fallen a few feet away, but the two got to their feet and hugged each other.

"Hey!"

It was Galric. He'd been close to them in the chain, but the blast that had knocked them all off their feet was so powerful, he now had to dodge around several other people to get to them.

"Hey," he said again once he was close. "I thought I lost you."

"You did," Sara said with a grin. "You found us again."

They shared a look that meant something Flissa didn't understand, but before she could say anything, their parents called out for them, and Flissa and Sara ran to throw themselves into their arms.

"I'm so proud of you," their mother said.

"As always," their father added with a smile.

"I'm proud of you too," Amala said, stepping up to join them. "You served your kingdom well."

Flissa and Sara beamed.

"I hate to ask for anything more from you," Amala continued, "but, Flissa, I'll shortly be making a trip to fetch an innocent friend of ours from her detention center. Would you like to come?"

She raised an eyebrow, and Flissa knew she meant Zinka. "Yes!" she said, then she asked her parents. "I mean, can I, please?"

"Of course," her mother said, and her father nodded. She turned to her sister.

"Sara?"

Whatever Raya had been threatening her with, Zinka was still the one who cursed Sara. Flissa didn't want her sister to think she was betraying her by remaining Zinka's friend. She searched Sara's eyes for how she really felt, but she looked like she meant it when she said, "It's fine. Just . . . if she asks, tell her I'm okay."

"I will," Flissa said. "And I know she'll ask."

Amala gave a satisfied nod, then she turned back to the crowd. The smell of oranges wafted through the air as she amplified her voice. "To the community of Maldevon Academy—this ball may not have gone as we expected, but I can think of no better testament to Kaloonification than what happened here today. We are one Kaloon, and together we are strong."

This time everyone cheered.

Chapter 22
Sara

"MAL-DE-VON! MAL-DE-VON!"

Sara stood in the stands with Galric, Krystal, and Skeed screaming at the top of their lungs as Flissa, Zinka, and Loriah stormed down the hoodle field in the last seconds of the game, leaping and tumbling as they feinted away from their opponents and passed the hoop to one another. It was the third game of the season, and if they landed this hoop they'd be undefeated.

It was a month after the Kaloonification Ball, and things had settled back to normal. No one had suffered any lasting damages from Raya's attacks, and those with minor injuries had long since healed. Classes were back in session, and while it wasn't as if everyone had already forgotten about it, there were bigger things going on—like the hoodle team's winning streak.

Still, some things had changed since the ball. They knew all the facts about what had happened now. Once Zinka knew for sure that Raya was both in custody and had already revealed that she was innocent, she'd told Amala everything. She said she *had* talked to Raya in the Twists about wreaking havoc on Kaloon with blinzer stones, but it was just talk. She also said she'd had no idea her beloved cat was actually Raya. She said whenever Raya wanted her to do something, Zinka would feel the magic take over her body, and though she'd hear Raya's voice, she assumed it was coming from the lioness, not Teddy. She'd refused to tell anyone what was happening because Raya convinced her no one would believe her, plus Raya said she'd torture and kill her if she did. Once Raya saw that Zinka had friends, she extended her threats to them too.

On the field, Flissa did a flip over a defender's back—the defender happened to be a large bull—then hurled the winning hoodlehoop into the air. It clanked down perfectly onto the goalpost as the clock ticked down the final second.

"WOOOOOO-HOOOOOOO!!!"

The crowd erupted, and Galric, Sara, Krystal, and Skeed joined the mad rush down to the field.

Once she was released, Zinka had also told Amala that the attack against Genpos was only a distraction. Raya forced Zinka to do the curse with her so she'd be implicated, but while everyone was rushing around trying to figure out what happened, Raya made Zinka hide the blinzer stones in the papier-mâché sculpture. Raya had always intended to attack at the ball, so she arranged her own capture just to make sure it went ahead as planned. She simply kept a tiny blinzer stone between her paw pads so she could escape.

That last bit of information hadn't come from Zinka; Amala found the stone when she was trapping Raya inside the sphere. That meant there were now fifteen blinzer stones total, all of which had been stashed away somewhere by Katya and Rouen, to be studied and, hopefully, destroyed.

When Sara reached Flissa on the field, she pushed through everyone else swarming for her sister's attention and threw her arms around her twin. "Superhero! You were amazing!!!"

Flissa beamed. "Thanks! Undefeated!"

Standing nearby, Zinka and Loriah also shouted, "Undefeated!" then all three of them did their secret fist-bump, hand-slap, hip-shake.

Zinka caught Sara's eye. "Hey, thanks for coming."

"Are you kidding? I wouldn't have missed it."

Flissa had been right. Zinka's first question when she got out *was* about Sara. Apparently cursing Sara was the worst part of the ordeal for Zinka, and she was so overwhelmed when she heard Sara was okay she cried. Sara didn't hold anything against her. They weren't exactly close, but they got along. That was fine, though; Zinka was Flissa's friend. Flissa wasn't exactly close with Krystal either; they got along. It's just how it worked.

Sara watched Flissa and the rest of the hoodle team get in line to high-five the opposing team, and Sara couldn't stop smiling. She was proud of her sister. She really was a superstar at Maldevon. She was a titan on the hoodle field, and she and Zinka had taken over what used to be the Ambassadors of Kaloonification and made it a planning committee for all kinds of events to bring everyone together outside of classes. They wanted one big event a month. Next month was a Field Day where everyone signed up for silly sports and played for prizes, and Amala had just given them permission to hold another big dance in the last month of school. Sara wanted to be the one to make the ball-posal this time, and she was already scheming ideas.

The hoodle team finished their high fives, then Sara saw Flissa and Zinka turn to Amala. The Shadow didn't come down to the field, but she watched every game and nodded to them from her spot in the stands. She had made some school policy changes since the ball too. Given all of Zinka's late-night excursions under Raya's control, she'd implemented a strict lights-out policy and made sure the Dorm Fairies kept everyone inside after hours. She also made sure there was an all-night patrol on campus, just in case.

Almost everyone else from the stands had peeled off, but Sara, Galric, Krystal, and Skeed stuck around. The others knew Sara wouldn't want to leave without talking to Flissa again. She waited until Flissa said goodbye to the last person waiting to talk to her, then jogged back her way.

"Seriously, great game," Sara said. "You were incredible."

"You think? It felt incredible. I'm really glad you saw it."

Flissa's name rang out across the field, and she and Sara both turned to look. The rest of the hoodle team was clumped together, making goofy faces at Flissa and yelling for her to get back to them so they could all go celebrate.

Flissa grinned. "I'm going to dinner with the team," she told Sara. "You?"

"We're headed to Skeed's," Sara said. "He built some kind of magic version of horseshoes in his backyard. There's moving obstacles involved, and I'm pretty sure he used the words 'giant inflatable penguin.' We're pretty psyched to check it out."

"Have fun. We'll catch up with each other later, though, right?"

"Always."

They shared a smile, then at the same time rushed in to hug one another tight. They broke away, then each sister darted off in the opposite direction to catch up with her friends.

They didn't look back.

Acknowledgments

First and foremost, thank you so much to everyone who read and supported *Twinchantment*. I've been blown away by the positive response to the book, and it's a privilege to bring you this next chapter in Flissa and Sara's adventures.

UnTwisted simply doesn't happen without the help of many amazing people. Kieran Viola, there just aren't enough words (and you know I like writing a lot of words) to explain how much I value your guidance and insight. I trust you, I love working with you, and holy cow this is our sixth book together and I hope there are many more. Readers, you should know Kieran isn't just an amazing editor, she's also an author, and you can find her at www.kieranscott.net.

Huge barrels of thanks also go to Jane Startz, manager extraordinaire. Jane, you are an unstoppable powerhouse, and I'm honored to have you in my corner. I love playing in every sandbox with you, and I'm excited for our continuing adventures.

At Disney Hyperion, many many thanks to Mary Mudd

and Vanessa Moody in editorial for your invaluable advice; designer Jamie Alloy; copy chief Guy Cunningham; managing editor Sara Liebling; production manager Jerry Gonzalez; and Jackie De Leo in sales. Also, big thanks to publicist Lyssa Hurvitz, and Danielle DiMartino, Holly Nagel, and Dina Sherman in marketing. Danielle and Holly, I can't thank you enough for including *Twinchantment* in the Barnes and Noble Kids' Book Hangout—it was a triumph, and you are amazing for arranging it. Speaking of the hangout, giant shout-out to everyone at Barnes & Noble Calabasas: Christine, Sara, Michelle, ROCKSTAR Kim, and of course Tiffany J. Mouse for letting me be a part of your fantastic event.

Sticking in the world of publicity, ENORMOUS thanks to Wendy Lefkon for making my Disney dreams come true and setting me up with the best Disneyland tour guide ever, Barbra Dunkley (if you're getting a tour guide there, request her by name). Thank you also to Kelly Hofmann at YAYOMG (www.yayomg.com) for giving me an Instagram takeover and a reason to take Disneyland by storm (as if I need a reason); and to Karri Lucas, the greatest producer around (www.duckonapondentertainment.com), for producing the day like a BOSS!

Dawn Ius (www.dawnius.com), you are my doctor on call. I love you and thank you, and I would not have my sanity without you.

Nancy Kanter, you have my ultimate admiration and respect. Thank you for supporting *Twinchantment*. I know it will thrive in your hands.

Maike Plenzke . . . wow. Readers, Maike did the cover illustrations for both *Twinchantment* and *UnTwisted* and her work makes me cry with joy. Check out her stuff on Instagram @maike_illu—you'll be blown away.

The biggest thanks as always go to my husband, Randy, my daughter, Maddie, and our dog, Jack. The three of you are my everything. And if any of you out there have been following my acknowledgments pages in other books, you know about Mom-Mom Sylvia, who is now ONE HUNDRED AND THREE YEARS OLD and still sharp as they come. Mom-Mom, I'm wildly lucky to have you in my life and I love you.

Finally, thank YOU for reading the book. I love hearing from readers, and you can find me at www.eliseallen.com (where you'll see a picture of Jack the dog), @EliseLAllen1 (Instagram), or @EliseLAllen (Twitter).

Xo,
E